I0610502

The Tower of Destiny
and Other Stories

also translated and introduced by Brian Stableford:

Anonymous: Sâr Dubnotal vs. Jack the Ripper; *Anthologies*: News from the Moon; The Germans on Venus; The Supreme Progress; The World Above the World; Nemoville; *Allorge*: The Great Cataclysm; *Asselineau*: The Double Life; *Bérard*: The Vampire Lord Ruthwen; *Bessière*: The Gardens of the Apocalypse; *Bleunard*: Ever Smaller; *Bodin*: The Novel of the Future; *Brown*: City of Glass; *Caroff*: The Terror of Madame Atomos; *Champsaur*: The Human Arrow; *Derennes*: The People of the Pole; *Driou*: The Adventures of a Parisian Aeronaut; *Dunan*: Baal; *Duvernois*: The Man Who Found Himself; *Eyraud*: Voyage to Venus; *Falk*: The Age of Lead; *Féval*: Anne of the Isles; The Black Coats ('Salem Street; The Invisible Weapon; The Parisian Jungle; The Companions of the Treasure; Heart of Steel; The Cadet Gang; The Sword-Swallower); John Devil; Knightshade; Revenants; Vampire City; The Vampire Countess; The Wandering Jew's Daughter; *Féval, fils*: Felifax, the Tiger-Man; *Haraucourt*: Illusions of Immortality; *Kahn*: The Tale of Gold and Silence; *La Hire*: The Nyctalope vs. Lucifer; The Nyctalope on Mars; Enter the Nyctalope; *Lamothe-Langon*: The Virgin Vampire; *de Lautrec*: The Vengeance of the Oval Portrait; *Le Faure & de Graffigny*: The Extraordinary Adventures of a Russian Scientist Across the Solar System; *Le Rouge*: The Vampires of Mars; The Dominion of the World (w/*Guitton*); *Lermina*: Panic in Paris; Mysteryville; The Secret of Zippelius; *Méry*: The Tower of Destiny; *Mettais*: The Year 5865; *Moselli*: Illa's End; *Nizet*: Captain Vampire; *de Parville*: An Inhabitant of the Planet Mars; *de Pawlowski*: Journey to the Land of the 4th Dimension; *Pellerin*: The World in 2000 Years; *Ponson du Terrail*: The Vampire and the Devil's Son; *de Régnier*: A Surfeit of Mirrors; *Renard*: The Blue Peril; Doctor Lerne; The Doctored Man; A Man Among the Microbes; The Master of Light; *Richepin*: The Wing; *Robida*: The Clock of the Centuries; The Adventures of Saturnin Farandoul; Chalet in the Sky; *Rosny Aîné*: The Givreuse Enigma; The Mysterious Force; The Navigators of Space; Vamireh; The World of the Variants; The Young Vampire; *Rouff*: Journey to the Inverted World; *Ryner*: The Superhumans; *Spitz:* The Eye of Purgatory; *Steiner*: Ortog; *Tiphaigne de la Roche*: Amilec; *Varlet*: The Xenobiotic Invasion; Timeslip Troopers (w/*Blandin*); The Martian Epic (w/*Joncquel*); *Vibert*: The Mysterious Fluid; *Villiers de l'Isle-Adam*: The Scaffold; The Vampire Soul; *Ward & Miller*: The Song of Montségur.

The Tower of Destiny
and Other Stories

by
Joseph Méry

translated, annotated and introduced by
Brian Stableford

A Black Coat Press Book

English adaptation and introduction Copyright © 2012 by Brian Stableford.
Cover illustration Copyright © 2012 by Mike Hoffman.

Visit our website at www.blackcoatpress.com

ISBN 978-1-61227-101-9. First Printing. July 2012. Published by Black Coat Press, an imprint of Hollywood Comics.com, LLC, P.O. Box 17270, Encino, CA 91416. All rights reserved.
Except for review purposes, no part of this book may be reproduced or transmitted in any form or by any means, electronic or mechanical, including photocopying, recording, or by any information storage and retrieval system, without permission in writing from the publisher. The stories and characters depicted in this novel are entirely fictional. Printed in the United States of America.

TABLE OF CONTENTS

Introduction

Joseph Méry (1798-1866) was a very popular and prolific writer in his heyday. In the first edition of Larousse's *Grand Dictionnaire*, the relevant volume of which was issued shortly after his death, his unusually-detailed entry extended over three large-sized pages, but it was reduced very considerably in the second edition and minimized thereafter, the portable Larousse of 1924 retaining only a note that he had written poetry in collaboration with Auguste Barthelémy and a comment that his novels were "full of verve."

All writers suffer such declines, of course, but Méry's was steeper than most. In all probability, the principal reason for that was that much of the early work he did was humorous, and much of the humor was political satire, which tends to date very rapidly. He continued to spice his work with wit even when he subsequently turned to melodrama, and sometimes seemed not to be taking his work very seriously, which appeared to have deterred some critics from taking it seriously. He was also a man with an unusually good memory, who could quote large sections of works he had read—especially those read in his youth—almost verbatim. Because the education of the day was focused on the Classics, much of what he could quote was Latin, and all of his work is casually peppered with Latin phrases, which some members of subsequent generations of readers must have found a trifle annoying; that made it difficult for publishers to keep reprinting his works after his death, and they vanished from the scene with a unusual rapidity.

To judge by the biographies that were written in his own day by people who knew him—including Eugène de Mirecourt and Gustave Claudin—Méry was very popular as a man as well as a writer, reckoned exceptionally good company by virtue of his wit and good will, but it is not obvious that his friends took his literary work entirely seriously either; Victor Hugo kick-started Méry's career in the theater, but the recommendation he gave him was that he could produce work rapidly, and was therefore a good man to fill a gap in a schedule at short notice. Méry was in on the birth of the French Romantic Movement, of which he was a fervent supporter, and the friends with whom he occasionally collaborated in that cause included Alexandre Dumas, Théophile Gautier and Gérard de Nerval, but he never acquired a reputation to match any of them, and always seems to have been regarded by the generals of the movement as a mere sergeant.

Méry was a native of Marseilles and very proud of being a southerner; the humorous epitaph he wrote for himself (which did not actually appear on his grave) ended with a punch-line that declared him quintessentially "Méry-dional." The Mirecourt and Claudin biographies do not say much about his youth, but the Larousse article (which is not entirely in agreement with the biographies, perhaps because Méry gave different accounts to different enquirers and was not entirely committed to accuracy) describes exactly the sort of background that one would expect of a turbulent Romantic. According to that account, he was initially intended by his family to enter holy orders, but contrived to get himself expelled from the seminary after being caught reading Voltaire. After completing the first phase of his education at the *lycée* instead, he was then sent to Aix to study law, but he contrived to get himself expelled again, this time for dueling.

Still at odds with his family, according to Larousse, Méry then went traveling, initially to Italy (the biographies claim that he did not visit Italy for the first time until much later, in 1832) but was forced to return home yet again when an affair with a cardinal's mistress resulted in attempts being made on his life. He subsequently decided to go and seek his fortune outside the bounds of Christendom in Constantinople, but was thrown out of that city after quarreling violently with the French ambassador.

Larousse, Mirecourt and Claudin all agree that Méry spent three months in jail in the early 1820s, but Larousse suggests that it was for writing a pamphlet attacking an Archbishop, while Mirecourt and Claudin make the clergyman a mere abbé and specify that he was the local inspector of schools, who incurred Méry's wrath by arguing the all school prizes ought to be given for strict religious observance, irrespective of the merit of any work submitted. At any rate, Méry fell thereafter into journalism, initially in association with Alphonse Rabbe, and moved to Paris when he was offered the editorship of a periodical called the *Nain jaune* [Yellow Dwarf]. It was that editorship that brought him into contact with Victor Hugo, and by the time the periodical folded—which, as usual, did not take long—Méry had been introduced into the world of *cénacles*, soon becoming friendly with Dumas, Gautier and other habitués of that milieu.

The closest relationship that Méry formed, however, was with a fellow Marseillais, Auguste Barthélemy, who was two years his senior. From 1825 onwards the two worked in close collaboration, mostly producing political satires in the form of mock-epic verse. *Les Sidiennes* [The Sidians] (1825) was the first, but their big break came when they decided to attack one of the Restoration's least popular ministers, Monsieur de Villèle, in the highly successful *La Villéliade* [The Villeliad] (1927), which went through fifteen printings in its first year. The two followed it up with further assaults of the same kind, including *La Corbièriéde* [The Corbièriad] (1827) and *La Bacriade, ou la Guerre d'Alger* [The Bacriad; or, The War in Algiers] (1827), and probably made a significant contribution to Villèle's eventual fall—which they must have regretted a little, as it robbed them of their main target. The two usually signed themselves "Barthélemy et Méry," as double acts usually do, and Méry never bothered to recover his Christian name, continuing to sign himself "Méry" throughout his career.

Not everything that Barthélemy and Méry did was satirical; by far their longest poem was an attempt at a genuine epic, *Napoléon en Egypte* (1828), which treated Napoléon as epics of old had treated such heroes as Odysseus, Aeneas and Alexander the Great. When two authors whose reputation for scathing sarcasm undertake an exercise like that, however, the reading public is bound to be a trifle hesitant about accepting it at face value, and although it had some success, it was treated with a certain critical circumspection. Barthélemy and Méry followed it up with two shorter "sequels," *Le Fils de l'Homme* [The Son of Man] (1829) and *Waterloo* (1829). According to the Wikipedia article on

Barthélemy, he was jailed and fined because the second item was considered to have overstepping the mark by addressing itself explicitly the emperor's son (about whose potential as a figurehead of opposition the tottering Bourbon monarchy was understandably sensitive), but if that was the case, it is difficult to understand why Méry was not imprisoned too, unless Barthélemy's policy of representing himself as the senior writer backfired on him. At any rate, both writers initially welcomed the July Revolution of 1930—Mirecourt and Claudin both claim that Méry helped to man the barricades—celebrating it in a flamboyant account of *L'Insurrection* (1830).

Disillusion with Louis-Philippe's new government soon set in, however, and between March 1831 and April 1832 Barthélemy and Méry produced a weekly periodical, *Le Nemesis*, in which they published verse satires attacking the new government in what was by now their typical fashion. The Wikipedia article on Barthélemy claims that when the periodical folded, rumors circulated that he had been bought off by the government, but it seems more likely that *Le Nemesis* had simply run its course, and that Barthélemy's subsequent silence merely indicates that his contribution to the collaboration had always been a minor one, in spite of his apparent seniority.

According to Mirecourt and Claudin, it was at this point in his career that Méry decided that he needed a break and went traveling, having received an invitation to reside in Italy for a while as a guest of one of that country's royal families. He appears to have been absent from Paris for a considerable time, but he probably returned with a stack of manuscripts, because he resumed his career with a sudden profusion of publications in

1836, when he became a regular contributor to the *Revue de Paris* and various other periodicals, becoming an enthusiastic *feuilletonist* as well as an active journalist. Their mutual association with the *Revue de Paris* cemented Méry's friendship with Honoré de Balzac, although they had presumably met before in Émile de Girardin's *salon*, at which Méry was a regular. In this new phase of his career, Méry wrote short stories, plays and articles in similar profusion, and although much of his fiction was melodramatic rather than satirical, his wit kept coming into play. Much of his work of the period was a trifle slapdash, presumably being hurriedly written to sharp deadlines, but it was unusually far-ranging and never dull.

Méry was very interested in chess, co-founding the first periodical devoted to the game, *Le Palamède*, in 1836 and writing numerous poems, articles and stories about the game. According to Claudin he was also an inveterate gambler, but if Claudin's anecdotal accounts of his strategy are accurate, his grasp of probability theory was evidently slight—which might help to explain why he had to write so much. Claudin reports in this context that Méry was intensely superstitious, to the point that he would never used the page number 13 in his manuscripts, and tried (unsuccessfully) to persuade his publishers to skip directly from page 12 to page 14 in his printed works.

Méry's first novel, following a number of novellas, was *Un Amour dans l'avenir* [A Love-Affair in the Future] (1840 in book form, following a feuilleton version in the *Revue de Paris*), whose title is slightly misleading, as the story is not futuristic. He continued to produce novels on a regular basis thereafter, but increasingly attempted to concentrate his most strenuous efforts on what the fashions of the day would have reckoned the most respectable aspect of his endeavor: his work for the theater. Most of the plays that reached print were comedies, both in prose and verse, but he probably put a higher value on his librettos, partly because they carried the most prestige and partly because he was a great opera lover himself. It is probable that he thought that the high point of his career eventually arrived when he got the opportunity to work with his favorite composer, Rossini, for whom he wrote the libretto for *Semiramis* (1860).

Like every writer in Paris, Méry found his career troubled by the economic disturbances surrounding the 1848 revolution and the 1851 coup d'état, but the theater proved more resilient than periodical or book publication, and he never stopped work; it was in that period that he produced two plays in collaboration with Gérard de Nerval. Nor did he suffer the same fate as some of the leading lights of the Romantic Movement, who had been strident advocates of Republicanism and had even accepted positions in the post-Revolutionary government, with the result that some—most famously Hugo and Dumas—were sent into exile after Louis Napoléon's coup. Although he had written for such radical newspapers as *Le Corsaire* during the late 1930s, Méry had not been politically active in the 1840s, and he still had to his credit the fact that he had co-written *Napoléon en Egypte* and its two sequels, thus retaining impeccable Bonapartist credentials. *Napoléon en Egypte* was, in fact, exactly the kind of hero-myth that Napoléon III was anxious to promote, so there was no chance of Méry being declared *persona non grata* after 1851, and the emperor eventually granted him a pension, although he can hardly have needed it unless his gambling losses were colossal.

Indeed, Méry made his second major comeback in the print medium when the economic situation of the Second Empire stabilized and improved in 1853, and the publishing industry got fully into gear again. Not only did he produce new work steadily but he began issuing books in profusion that reprinted much of his earlier prose work, including a good deal of work done for periodicals that had not previously been reprinted in book form. He produced half a dozen books a year throughout the mid-1850s, while this backlog lasted, and continued to produce new work in some profusion until he died—he published four books in 1866, the year of his death, and left enough material unpublished or unreprinted to fill a further handful of volumes thereafter.

The prose works that were most successful in Méry's own day, both critically and commercially, included a trilogy consisting of *Héva* (1844), *La Floride* [The French used Floride—Florida—as a general term in the 19th century, referring to many alien shores] (1844) and *La Guerre de Nizam* [The War in Nizam] (1847), the first and third of which are set in India, and the middle volume mostly in Africa. Those books and others in the same vein represented the core of Méry's contribution to the Romantic fascination with "the Orient," which was more an ideal quasi-mythical wonderland that a geographical location. Many of the leading French writers of the 19th century shared that fascination, although not all of them had Méry's Marseillais obsession with the sun, and few actually bothered to make the (usually disappointing) pilgrimages that Nerval, Flaubert, Rimbaud and several others undertook. Méry never went to India himself, and might not even have got as far as North Africa, so his own idea of such locations remained stubbornly fanciful, and became even more so when his attention moved further eastwards, as in such works as *Les Damnés de Java* [The Damned of Java] (1855). For a southerner like Méry, winter in Paris was always difficult to bear, and very conducive to dreams of his spiritual home—he appears to have had very vivid dreams of all kinds—and he might well have become accustomed to thinking of January in Paris as Hell if he had not had the misfortune once to visit Manchester, and realized how much worse things might have been.

Although there are features of Méry's prose that create difficulties for modern readers, there are also features that seem surprisingly modern. Almost all of his work for periodicals would have been paid by the line, and he and Alexandre Dumas were among the first writers to take full advantage of the fact that space could easily be filled by strings of curt and informal dialogue, although Méry never exploited that resource to the same cynical extent that Dumas did. While Dumas soon made the transition from short fiction to long novels, Méry's prose fictions remained fairly short, including numerous novellas and single-volume novels. During the 1930s and early 1940s he produced more non-fiction than fiction, but the boundary between the two was often blurred, and he experimented with various different rhetorical formats, in much the same fashion as his American contemporary Edgar Allan Poe. For the first half of his career the bulk of this offbeat endeavor remained buried in the pages of ephemeral publications, although when the opportunity eventually arrived in the mid-1850s to reprint the cream of that work, he did so with gusto; in many of the collections, little distinction is made between fiction, non-fiction and alloys of the two. Like Poe, too, Méry was interested in experimenting with new kinds of fiction, including various kinds of fantastic fiction for which there was little or no precedent.

Throughout the 20th century, all of Méry's work remained obscure and difficult to find. Thus, when Pierre Versins compiled the collection that formed the basis of his magisterial *Encyclopédie de l'utopie et de la science-fiction* (1972) he was only able to locate one relevant work by Méry, which he merely mentioned *en passant* in the encyclopedia, and evidently had no suspicion that there was more. In fact, there was—enough, in its bulk and its sheer eccentricity, to establish Méry as the nearest French equivalent to Poe as a groundbreaking pioneer, although Méry had deliberately spread the material thinly throughout his abundant collections, never placing more than one such item between the same covers.

The availability of Méry's work was, however, dramatically altered in the first decade of the 21st century, when the Bibliothèque Nationale began making old books that had previously been impossible to find available for reading on or downloading from its *gallica* website. That greatly facilitated the endeavors of a host of amateur bibliographers interested in identifying antique works of fantasy and science fiction, including those involved in building the gigantic Base de Données Francophone de l'Imaginaire [Database of Imaginative Fiction in French] website. Once Méry's name had been introduced to the website's Forum section as an author of possible interest, in 2006, it did not take long for the assiduous contributors to the forum to skim through all the texts available on *gallica*, identify more than a dozen items of potential interest and check them all out, arriving at a provisional summary of their findings in 2010.

There might, of course, be more items in collections that have not yet been electronically reproduced.

This research revealed that Méry actually made several interesting contributions to early French speculative fiction, the most significant of which are translated herein, along with a number of marginally-related items. Unfortunately, it is difficult to be sure exactly when most of the items were first published, because *gallica*'s periodical collection does not include very many of the outlets that Méry used most frequently in the 1830s and 1840s. Some certainly date back to the 1830s, because a footnote in one of the four stories assembled in book form under the heading "Les Lunariens," here translated as "The Lunarians," gives 1836 as its date of first publication, and all four items were clearly inspired by the *New York Sun*'s famous "moon hoax" of 1835, usually credited to Richard Adams Locke. These four items represent the author at his most farcical, but it is worth noting that Méry's interest in astronomy was genuine, as evidenced by the framing device he fitted to *Les Nuits espagnoles* (1859), in which a group of amateur astronomers hold elaborate discussions, and tell one another the included stories in order to illustrate myths regarding the nomenclature of stars and planets.

The first item in the present collection, the brief fictionalized essay, "La Verité sur la Création, grave plaisanterie d'un libre penseur," here translated as "The Truth About Creation: A Freethinker's Serious Joke," is more typical of the author's sarcastic stance, arguing in a mock-serious manner—on the basis scientific evidence that has been far outdated since—that there was nothing supernatural about God's creation of the world, which was always strictly in accordance with the laws of physics. I have put the item first not so much because it probably dates from the same period as "Les Lunariens"—although it probably does—as because it provides a neat introduction to Méry's world-view and general attitude to science, religion and rhetoric.

The second item, "Ce qu'on verra," here translated as "What We Shall See," is probably later, as well as being considerably longer and more elaborate; presumably, it first appeared as a newspaper serial. It foregrounds some of the key ideas of the bulk of Méry's work, especially his conviction that the Utopian prospects of future human progress are dependent on a drastic southward shift of endeavor, but it also allows Paris to continue its own evolution, under the guidance of science, and it includes some striking imagery—especially the symbolic statue of Prometheus Unbound—as well as some sociological speculations that are no less intriguing for being firmly tongue-in-cheek.

Although "Les Ruines de Paris," here translated as "The Ruins of Paris," is much briefer than "Ce qu'on verra," it is arguably the more significant work of the two, because it has the distinction of having prompted a whole series of further stories on the same theme, beginning with Alfred Bonnardot's "Archeopolis" (1857)[1] and continuing with Hippolyte Mettais' *L'An 5865* (1865)[2], Alfred Franklin's *Les Ruines de Paris* (1875)[3], Léo Clarétie's *Paris depuis ses origines jusqu'en l'an 3000* [Paris from its Origins to the Year 2000] (1886) and

[1] translated in the anthology *Nemoville*, Black Coat ptress, ISBN 978-1-61227-070-8

[2] translated as *The Year 5865*, Black Coat Press, ISBN 989-1-61227-100-2.

[3] translated in the anthology *Investigations of the Future*, Black Coat Press, ISBN 978-1-61227-106-4.

Edmond Haraucourt in "Cinq mille ans, ou la traversée de Paris" (1904)[4]. Méry probably knew Bonnardot personally, but Bonnardot presumably read Méry's piece for the first time when it was first reprinted in book form in 1856; his own reproduces many of its key features, which were then carried forward by the other writers, each of whom had either read Bonnardot or one of the other intermediate links in the chain. Méry did write at least one more futuristic item, "Paris futur" [Future Paris], but that is an unfictionalized essay preoccupied with rainfall and the possibilities of its avoidance, which I thought insufficiently interesting to include here.

Perhaps the most surprising of Méry's proto-sf stories is the longest of them all, an early contribution to the alternative history subgenre entitled "Histoire de ce qui n'est pas arrivé," here translated (borrowing a key phrase from its opening chapter) as "The Tower of Destiny: A Story of Events that Did Not Happen." This was probably the second significant exercise in alternate history fiction, following Louis Geoffroy's *Napoléon et la conquête du monde* (1836; reprinted as *Napoléon Apocryphe*), which presumably inspired it. Whereas Geoffroy imagined a history that deviated from ours during Napoléon's Russian campaign in 1812, avoiding the terrible losses of the retreat from Moscow, Méry, reinventing the hero-myth he had created in *Napoléon en Egypte*, imagined an earlier deviation taking place in May 1799, while the protagonist was still General Bonaparte. Although it is the most serious of Méry's exercises in speculative fiction, it is careful not to abandon light-

---

[4] translated as "A Trip to Paris" in the collection *Illusions of Immortality*, Black Coat Press, ISBN 978-1-61227-075-3.

heartedness entirely, especially in its whimsical entr'acte.

There is an inevitable temptation to regard "Histoire de ce qui n'est pas arrivé" as a celebration of the advent of the Second Empire, but it might seem even more fascinating if it turns out to have been written before 1851 (its book publication was in 1854). Whenever it was written, however, the argument of the story is a little more subtle than it might seem at first glance, and it contains several hints that the narrative voice is not reflecting the author's true opinions with complete accuracy (it makes gratuitously rude remarks about "Voltaireans," for instance, although Méry was a Voltairean through and through). At any rate, it is a fascinating pioneering endeavor that would undoubtedly have earned complimentary mention by Versins and other historians of sf had it not vanished from sight for a century and a half.

"Les Explorations de Victor Hummer," here translated as "The Explorations of Victor Hummer," combined two items in its book versions, the first of which initially appeared in the *Revue de Paris* in 1836. It is interesting both as a satirical representation of scholarly mentality and as a commentary on the development of archaeological endeavor in connection with the ongoing excavations in Egypt. It involves the supposed rediscovery of a mythical city, and is remarkable both for the hallucinatory sequence that precedes that discovery and for the sharply bathetic consequence thereof. The sequel is not as striking, but its parallel hallucinatory sequence also encourages some regret that Méry never got around to writing the collection of his nightmares that he mentions *en passant* in the explanatory foreword to "Histoire de ce qui n'est pas arrivé." The same Egyptian background is recapitulated in the farcical aeronautical fantasy that was initially reprinted as "La Pêche du lion" in 1844 before being reprinted again as "Un Voyage aérien," here translated as "An Aerial Voyage."

The final item in this collection, "Le Frère de Bertram," translated as "Bertram's Brother," is one of Méry's rare wholeheartedly supernatural stories. Although he wrote several comedies in which seeming supernatural events turn out to be more-or-less ingenious frauds, he seems to have been every bit as reluctant to make use of the supernatural as God, in the depiction featured in the first item in the collection, and he was prone to represent items of that sort as stories told to him by other people, thus denying personal responsibility for them. The long stories *L'Âme transmise* [The Transmitted Soul] (1837) and *La Dernière fantôme* (1853; tr. as *The Irish Widow; or, The Last of the Ghosts*) are both deceptively-titled—the second less so than the first—and one suspects that other suggestive titles to be found among books not yet made available electronically are probably similarly teasing. "Bertram's Brother," however, is a striking example of a full-blooded Faustian fantasy, and also an interesting contribution to the fugitive subgenre of theatrical fantasy, as well as a significant item of early "horror comedy" in a vein that was subsequently exploited to good effect by Paul Féval.

The translation of "La Verité sur la Création, grave plaisanterie d'un libre penseur" was taken from *gallica*'s version of *Les Journées de Titus* (Michel Lévy, 1866). The translation of "Ce qu'on verra" was taken from the Google Books version of *Le Château des trois-tours* (Michel Lévy, 1860). The translation of "Les Ruines de Paris" was taken from the version reproduced on the

Biblisem website. The translation of "Les Lunariens" was taken from *gallica*'s version of *Les Nuits parisiennes* (Michel Lévy 1855).The translation of "Les Explorations de Victor Hummer" was taken from the *gallica* version of *Nouvelles nouvelles* (Hachette, 1858). The translation of "Histoire de ce qui n'est pas arrivé" was taken from the *gallica* version of *Les Nuits d'Orient* (Michel Lévy, 1854). The translation of "Un voyage aérien" was taken from the *gallica* version of *Le Bonnet Vert* (Gabriel Roux, 1854). The translation of "Le Frère de Bertram" was taken from the London Library's copy of *Anglais et Chinois, suivi de Le Frère de Bertram* (Brussels: Meline, Cans et Companie, 1841).

Brian Stableford

THE TRUTH ABOUT CREATION
A Freethinker's Serious Joke[5]

At that time, there was no time at all. Space could have been accommodated in an atom. The universe was in a state of nothingness. Night, day, dusk, silence, noise and air had not yet arrived. There was nothing in the nothing. Even the void was empty, and nature could nor abhor it, because there was no nature either. The mind reels when it tries to sound that formidable NOTHING anterior to all creation.

That universal nothingness might have been eternal, and no one can tell what the physiognomy of that total absence would have been. Fortunately, God gave birth to himself and space was born with him.

Nothing could be simpler.

Everything became possible to the first inventor of the will, that ever-powerful mental level, who encountered no invincible obstacle at the commencement of his functions. The first to say "I want" got what he wanted;

---

[5] In the version reprinted in *Les Journées de Titus* this story is prefaced by a brief introductory passage that belongs to the collection's framing material. In translation, it reads: "One day, when everyone was arguing about something or other, and God himself had been called into question and reduced for the second time to the rank of Supreme Being, I dared to intervene in the debate and explained a host of mysteries, including the creation, with Titanic effrontery. Judge for yourself."

there as no one to contradict or oppose him. God gave himself the privilege of that primacy, and everything was successful.

In our century of verification and examination, it's good to explain these so-called mysteries, and to disengage them from their supernatural element.

The domain of space thus belonged by right to God, as its first occupant, *primo occupanti*, and God, armed with his virgin will, resolved to furnish his domain with unprecedented luxury.

Again, nothing could be simpler; the progress of modern science will assist us in this demonstration.

God took oxygen and nitrogen, the two inseparable elements constitutive of all fecund matter, and extracted therefrom the seed of the first sun. How many centuries were required to give the igneous embryo the incommensurable circumference of the first star no human calculation can determine exactly, but if one considers that the divine workman had all eternity ahead of him, the time devoted to that work is much less than a clockmaker requires to assemble a chronometer. Now, that minute having been devoted to the confection of the first sun, all creation was under way. Solar fireworks burst forth all the way to the limits of the four horizons of space, and within five minutes of the clock of eternity, every sun, spitting fire, gave itself a cortege of planets that set about rotating around it, in conformity with the law of gravity.

Life came into the universe, and again we owe that secret to modern science. How many errors and prejudices our ancestors incorporated into their theories regarding creation. Even the great Pascal nearly fell off the top of the Tour Saint-Jacques, in a fit of madness, on the day when he discovered his impotence. That was because Pascal was a mathematician, and not something else. He wanted to solve God like a Euclidean theorem or the problem of the square on the hypotenuse—vain efforts!

If Pascal had been a chemist like Lavoisier he would have kept his reason intact within his brain, and easily explained the creation that seemed to him to be inexplicable. Until Lavoisier, the philosophical world had piled stupidities on stupidities. The celebrated chemist pronounced his *fiat lux* in 1790, with his marvelous theory regarding phlogiston and vital air.[6] Thanks to Lavoisier, we now know how respiration was given to human beings in the early days of creation.

Thus, everything is explained; thus, one by one, the veils hiding the truth from us have fallen away; one more step forward by science and we shall see everything clearly. Let us admire the progress made already. Our forefathers only admitted seven planets in our solar system! We count seventy-two of them today, including the invisible ones. Seventy-two planets! And God knows whether Uranus conceals even more in its vortex! Monsieur Leverrier, the illustrious planetarian, affirms that we will reach a hundred—God willing! On that day, our fortunate descendants will have nothing more to demand of the sky or the government.

Let us rise up again, *in excelsis*.

Thus the life of God went by, in these grave occupations, with the aid of the science, whose primary elements he knew.

---

[6] Lavoisier put a conclusive end to the old phlogiston theory, which regarded combustion as a process of emission, by demonstrating that it required the absorption of a gas possessed of mass: oxygen.

One day, God deigned to cast his eyes over a large igneous ball that was orbiting our sun with a rather awkward rotational movement, and said:

"You shall be inhabited by humans, and you shall be named Earth, and you shall have the glory of giving birth to scholars who will clarify all the mysteries of the universe, and who will explain me to myself, with the aid of an algebraic proof, concocted with the science of Messieurs Biot and Gay-Lussac."[7]

That being said and decreed, God ordered time to accelerate its march, and advanced the clock of eternity by a billion years. That lapse of time was necessary to give our Earth the time to pass from a hot ember to the condition of cool clay. Nothing could be simpler than that petty task of mutation. The spongy mass that circles the circumference of the globe is detached, is unrolled into a ring, condensed, hardened and rounded out, and becomes a moon. Oxygen, which is in combustion around a seventy-two thousand-league perimeter, four times the present circumference, amasses vapors in the upper regions; those vapors are resolved as rain; as it falls, the rain battles fire, like Scamander and Vulcan in the *Iliad*, and, after five hundred trivial centuries, half the Earth is extinguished by the rain and the waves of the ocean invade the other half.

There is nothing astonishing in that confection. Any physicist can obtain the same result in his laboratory with a combination of oxygen and hydrogen on the cir-

---

[7] The names of the physicists Jean-Baptiste Biot and Joseph Gay-Lussac are coupled here because they made the first scientific balloon ascent in 1804 in order to collect air samples at different altitudes and take measurements of temperature and pressure.

cumference of a ball of clay or pozzolana,[8] with a temperature of eighty degrees above zero. The opposite temperature, which reigns in the interplanetary regions, is eighty degrees below. The atmosphere of life and the atmosphere of death.

Glory to science, whose torch illuminates the once-dark arcana of creation!

Meanwhile, the vital air infused over our globe with the power of ninety degrees, was obliged to give birth to a gigantic creation, in the same way that on the opposite scale, an atom of cheese expose to the ardent sun spontaneously gives birth to horrible insects, only visible to the solar microscope. Then God gave himself the most marvelous of spectacles, and was alone in contemplating it. Monsters, which would later serve Satan as models for the menagerie of Hell—the amphibious saurians, gigantic serpents, enormous flying lizards and tiger-fish—invaded the seas and the warm lands, and engaged in a battle for five hundred centuries: a battle that, unfortunately, deposited in the entrails of our planet a bellicose seed, the fruits of which the human species will taste eternally.

God, always reluctant to employ supernatural means, brought that battle to an end by means of simple methods of physics. Long before the beautiful experiments carried out in London by the illustrious chemist Priestley, God knew that latent and compressed oxygen was relentlessly making a subterranean effort to reappear at the surface. It was the light that wanted to escape from under the bushel, even if the lid had the high pressure of Etna, the cordillera of Quito or the Javanese mountain Mara-Api.

---

[8] Pozzolana is a fine volcanic ash.

God took advantage of this good disposition of igneous matter to let it intervene in the battle of the great saurian monsters. "Fire at will!" he cried—and a hundred thousand volcanoes burst forth all at once in the crust of the globe. Compared with that racket, which made the sun tremble, the duo of Solferino and Sebastopol is a melodic tune sung by the Marchisio sisters.[9]

The army of monstrous giants responded in unison. The entire globe became a battlefield that was carried away into space, furrowing the void with cataracts of fire, collected in passing by vagabond comets, those suppliers to the construction-yards of space. The monsters, united against the common enemy, rushed the volcanoes *en masse* to extinguish them, and the volcanoes swallowed them in their abysses, spewing them out again as blackened skeletons, to be picked up again and plunged back into granite reliquaries, where future ages would rediscover them.

God gave himself the egotistical joy of that fête, which lasted a thousand revolutions around the sun, and he said to the volcanoes: extinguish yourselves on the surface; retreat into the earth, and precipitate your fires toward its central axis.

A great and long silence followed, and after another thousand centuries, it was troubled by the murmur of the first ferns sprouting in the morning breeze. It was the first jewel of the habitable Earth. Another thousand centuries-long minutes, and humans were about to enter their house; God occupied himself with furnishing it.

---

[9] Carlotta and Barbara Marchisio, the first a soprano and the second a contralto, were the favorite singers employed by Méry's favorite composer, Rossini.

Admire how simple and natural all that is, in conformity with all the laws of physics, geology and Monsieur Cuvier's comparative anatomy! Let us take some examples of a very inferior order.

Sicily was once an immense volcano, an island in combustion, and look what it has produced: the most fertile and beautiful garden in the world. Fire and ash have been the compost of flowers and crops. Laborers, those physicists of nature, knew that in the era of the *Georgics*. Virgil, the famous agriculturalist, affirms that it is useful to make use of fire to fertilize the earth, and recommends that sterile fields be set on fire to turn them into nutritive gardens: *Saepe etiam steriles incendere profuit agros*. Further on he recommends that bushes be burned—*incendere vepres*—in order to give the furrows the compost of their ashes.

What the agriculturalist of Mantua did for his plot of land, God did on a large scale for the entire world: never a prodigy, never a miracle, nothing supernatural. Anyone could have done as much with a treatise by Monsieur Biot. Far be it from me to think of diminishing God's work; I recognize it as great and bow down before it, but while bowing down I dare to affirm, by virtue of free examination, that God has never set aside the primordial rules of nature, *natura mater rerum*, as one ancient put it, and that although the great workman has a right to our admiration, he has none to our astonishment. Modern science has erased the word *miracle* from its portable dictionary. The enigma of the world has yielded its key; the sphinx has spoken. We can finally breathe! It's high time!

The creation of the first humans passed for an insoluble mystery during the centuries of ignorance. Pascal himself, although full of faith in the first chapter of *Gen-*

esis, racked his brains over the apple of Eden. Another service rendered by science; analysis demonstrates that human flesh is of the same essence as the terrestrial crust. I'm a little disappointed by that, not on behalf of my own sex but that of women; their satin skin and vile gravel have the same origin. The voice of Ash Wednesday is right when it says: *Pulvis est in pulverum*.[10] That beautiful chemical discovery removes the mystery from the creation of humankind. We are all the products of the earth, like the trees, the plants and the flowers.

Undoubtedly, a more complete life has been given to us; that was just and merited, since we're the monarchs of creation. God owed us that. The trees, the plants and the flowers live a dead life, but they live; we live an intelligent life. Animals have instinct; we have reason, and a soul that is a spark from the hearth of universal electricity. We are now even fixed on the matter of the soul, that immaterial entity that all the doctors of the Sorbonne were never able to explain with their syllogisms *in barbara*.

The vault that God has given to the Earth to amuse the nights of humankind leaves much to be desired, but such as it is, it still has a certain merit. Orion and the Great Bear merit unrestricted eulogies, however; it's a matter for regret that the other constellations do not have the flair and grandeur of those starry masterpieces. Was that because of impotence, or a disdain for symmetry? No one can say.

Our impartiality imposed a duty upon us to introduce a word of just criticism into this eulogy on creation;

---

[10] This is a contraction of the liturgical phrase *Memento, homo, quia pulvis es, et in pulvrum reverteris* [Remember, human, that dust thou art and to dust thou shalt return].

we have now obeyed that duty. One always owes the truth to the great.

Today, we shall limit ourselves to judging God's work in its entirety, leaving it to the less intelligent to divine the thought that guides our pen. Perhaps it is time to get boldly stuck in to a subject reputed to be formidable, and to render to science that which belongs to science, and to God that which belongs to God. There ought to not to be any more burning questions today; there are just questions. God, highly placed as he is, must submit to the examination of human beings; too bad for troubled and pusillanimous consciences that claim the benefits of limitation! Philosophy does not know that clerical term.

God is an author who delivers his work to the public; we want to judge it, no longer with the old errors of scholasticism, but with the new enlightenment of sound reasoning. The supernatural has had its day; our compass has measured infinity with the aid of logarithms; we have discovered planets; our fingers have touched the star Vega, whose light takes twelve years to reach us; the Milky Way is our promenade; we play with the nebular mass in Orion; we joke with the comets; we have dismissed the sun from office and replaced it with masses of phosphorescent clouds—and it is certainly permissible for us to take legitimate pride in reforming the ancient theories of blind faith and finding new ones with the eyes of examination.

WHAT WE SHALL SEE

I

Bastien, prefect of the département of Good Hope, gave his blessing to his son Michel and said: "You're twenty-five years old; you own two mines of fossil ivory in the Val de Dembo and you're the honorary inspector of the African Electric Railway; you need to travel in order to learn, and marry in order to be virtuous. Bless you!"

Shortly afterwards, Michel, followed by his faithful guide Dornival, was at the railway station in Cape Town, the limit of France. It was June 15, 3845.[11]

The two travelers were wearing the fashionable costume of the day: a Crêpe-de-Chine dolman, a pair of trousers with multiple pleats and a wide-brimmed soft felt hat ornamented by a touraco-feather, all in conformity with the latest engraving in the Parisian *Journal des Modes*.

The steam orchestra, established in the prow of the electric train, played the fanfare from the opera *Adamastor* by the Chinese master Pe-tre-li, and the train departed like an arrow fired by an ironwood bow.

Let us hasten to say that the African railway line that traverses southern France from the Cape of Good

---

[11] This date implies that the story might have been originally published in 1845, as future projections were routinely undertaken by the addition of round numbers.

Hope to Algiers is the best line in the world. The average speed is eight hundred kils an hour. (People once said kilometers, but, as the illustrious mathematician Hopei has remarked, "Life is too short to use long words." The same scholar has demonstrated that, in this century of voyages, a man of eighty would waste ten years of his life saying "kilometers," the word being so common. The wise Chinese have measured distances in *li* since time immemorial.)

A train on the African line carries ten thousand passengers at the speed of electricity. A pretty quilted corridor allows it to be traveled in its entire length, communicating at intervals with various facilities recognized to be indispensable: a bathroom, a vaudeville theater, a gaming room, a reading room, a library, a dormitory, a restaurant and a café. One also finds two clothing stores there, in which male and female travelers can find all kinds of garments and necessary items, which liberates them from carrying, as in the past, the heavy items of luggage known as trunks or cases.

While walking along this corridor Michael perceived a young woman of rare beauty, and, love being the sweetest of remedies for the tedium of long voyages, became electrically amorous. Steam-generated passions used to be so slow, alas!

The female traveler's name was Himalaya. She was traveling alone, in accordance with the custom of well-bred young women, but she was, also in accordance with custom, under the protection of all the old men on the train—or, as one says, the mobile senate. Woe betide anyone who dares to give the slightest alarm to a woman traveling alone! He will be abandoned, alone and without means of existence, in the middle of the Dembo desert, where the last surviving panthers and lions still roam.

The Society of the Economists of Lupata,[12] who have rendered such great service to universal human-kind, made especially excellent usage of its sovereign authority when it placed women under general protec-tion, and then took the most ingenious and moral measures to popularize marriage and suppress celibacy. Those wise legislators understood very well that, in the present state of civilization, celibacy a scourge more terrible than the ancient plague of which historians speak. Birth prevention is a mass homicide committed by society. In 1857, for example, when the globe was almost deserted and making no effort to populate itself, celibacy could be an admitted profession—a sort of Christian pashalik—but things are different today. It was necessary to populate and purify our beautiful colony of Madagascar, as large as the eighty-six départements of ancient France; it was necessary to populate the vast African deserts, fertilized by the channeling of rivers, and the old domains inhabited by wild beasts, from the land of the Hottentots to the Atlas. That immense project could not be entrusted to bachelors. All the old excuses have been removed from those drones of ancient civili-zation; our opulent Electric Railway Companies, by ensuring concessions of land and cash endowments to poor marriages, have made celibacy an impossible vice in 3845.[13]

---

[12] There are at least two places in Africa called Lupata, but Méry was a great admirer of *Gulliver's Travels*, and probably selected the name because of its similarity to Laputa.
[13] Méry never married.

Thus, the moral laxity of the ancients slowed down the progress of true civilization for twenty centuries. Would you believe that a Cape scholar has discovered a comic opera performed two thousand years ago before honest families, in which this was sung:

"I've long traveled everywhere
"To lands both torrid and chill
"Courting the dark and the fair
"Loving and sighing at will!"[14]

And in another opera, miraculously discovered, is this other song;

"A child beloved by ladies.
"Wherever I cared to wander
"I was loved by Marias and Sadies,
"But husbands were much less fonder."[15]

Moreover, the same scholar offers evidence that, in the foremost theater of the ancient world, someone named Robert[16] surrendered a pretty young female vassal to fifty Christian knights, saying to them: "Knights, I

---

[14] The most familiar version of this popular song is the one recorded by Honoré de Balzac in *Le Père Goriot*; Méry was often in Balzac's company while the *feuilleton* version of the novel was appearing in the *Revue de Paris*, and Claudin alleges (presumably on Méry's own authority) that Méry made several useful suggestions to the author.

[15] A ditty from Louis-Benoît Picard's *Les Visitandines* (1806); I have taken some slight liberties with the exact meaning in order to preserve its doggerel quality.

[16] *Robert le Diable*; see the notes to "Bertram's Brother."

abandon her to you!" And that line was applauded in the hall of the Opéra by a multitude of knights.

What an epoch! What mores!

In consequence, the globe was populated by deserts.

Let us return to the African train to study and admire our modern mores, and take pride in progress.

II

Michel picked a lavatera[17] flower in the train's garden, and offered it respectfully to the young woman, who accepted it.

Acceptance signifies, as everyone knows, that a young woman has a free hand and that a young man has become a fiancé. After that short and decisive ceremony, if the voluntary fiancé does not marry within a week, he will be condemned to ten years in Zanzibar, where bachelor seducers dig up fallow ground with sweat on their brow. In ancient times there was a creature known as a rival, but the species has virtually disappeared. Today, if a rival dared to disturb the fortunate engaged couple, he would be condemned to discover three new planets in the system of the star Sirius. Our legal code intends, with good reason, that every condemnation is turned to the advantage of society, since the criminal has damaged it.

The train soon arrived at the superb station of Lupata.

That city, which has only existed for five hundred years, has reached the ultimate degree of prosperity. Instead of being surrounded by ramparts, like ancient cities, which only served to facilitate their seizure,

---

[17] The genus of shrubs that includes the mallows, noted for the breadth of their flowers.

Lupata is decorated over its entire circumference by a large gallery, high and cool; the neighboring mountain, called on maps the Artery of the World, had furnished stones to that immense circular portico, which serves as a promenade for old people. Canals of fresh water and tall trees refresh all the streets; the houses, built on the same level, have gardens, bathrooms and fountains.

One also finds four colleges in Lupata—or, more accurately, four squares shaded by tall sycamores, watered by pools and furnished with banks of grass. The municipality meets the expenses of public education. There are no professors. The final-year pupils teach French, English, German and Italian, but without books and dictionaries. These languages are learned by making use of them, currently and on the wing, for there are children from all countries in each college and they are good teachers. When an ambitious father, led astray by ancient history, wants his son to become a poet or a learned man, he provides him with a Greek and Latin scholar at his own expense. The galleys of childhood are thus suppressed in Lupata.

Young Michel sent an electric dispatch from the city, in his own name and that of his fiancée, to their two families, asking for their consent to the marriage. It was a simple respectful formality. The response was immediate and, as always, affirmative. *A marriage cannot be accomplished too soon*, the sage legislator Beny has written.

That evening, Michel's marriage was celebrated at the Town Hall in Lupata, in the travelers' hall, and the two spouses immediately rejoined the train from Algiers to Paris, swearing eternal fidelity.

Michael declared his love to his wife in calm and rational terms, which solidifies belief in progress. At one time, love began with *stretta* and finished in *andante*. Another evidence of progress toward true civilization.

At Timbuktu station, Michel and his wife got off the train to admire the triumphal gate of the great city and read its inscription. Latin has been banished from the lapidary style; every inscription is made in French, which permits everyone to understand it. Once, Latin enigmas were engraved on monuments.

On the gate of Timbuktu this simple sentence can be read:

To the memory of Noel Soggeron, who vanquished the wild beasts of the city of Kaisna, destroyed them in a single battle, and changed the forest into a garden.

Modern heroes only receive such honors for similar services. Once, it was necessary to kill many people, known as "enemies," to merit an inscription on a monument.

After a five-minute stop, the train took off again toward the great Atlas tunnel, a marvelous endeavor accomplished by means of electric drills within the space of five years.

The tunnel in question is illuminate by day by "lively lite." An orchestra plays the symphonies of Banton-Saib, nicknamed the Rossini of India. That melodious trilogy in known by its three titles: *The Wave of Ceylon*, *The Loves of the Flowers and Palms*, and *The Brahmin Wedding*. Once, travelers heard a shrill and strident whistling in tunnels, which ripped the ears and threw terror into souls. That frightful whistle tyrannized human hearing for ten centuries. How long it has taken to bring forth goodness in every last detail, and make our short lives agreeable!

The train stopped for two hours in Algiers, the chief city of the Mediterranean département. Algiers warrants its nickname, the Heavenly City. The magnificence of its seaside palaces, crowned by gardens overshadowed by forests of palms, has no equal. In that city, nature and human beings have joined forces to materialize a dream of happiness and render it visible to the eyes. The names of the streets seem to invite travelers to rest; at every corner one reads Rue de la Félicité, de la Tendresse, de l'Amour, de la Joie, du Sourire, du Bonheur, de la Fraternité, du Mariage, de la Douceur, du Doux-Sommeil, and others of the same kind.

An Algerian archeologist of Arab origin, the savant Ben-Aissen, has discovered that once, streets were given names like The Rue du Petit-Hurleur, aux Ours, de la Tixeranderie, des Vieilles-Écuries, du Chat qui pêche, Taitbout, Coquenard, Buffault, Cadet, Bleue, Ribouté, Verdelt, Pagevin, Tiquetonne and many others.[18] One might add that the properties found tenants just as prosaic to pay expensive rents in the streets that bore those names. However, antiquity had something called the Académie des Inscriptions. What did that academy do? The key to that mystery has not been handed down to us.

It was in the great bazaar of Algiers that Madame Michel bought her first married woman's costume: a Crêpe-de-Chine dress emphasizing the truth in all its pleats and all its seams; a headscarf with two little gauze wings; and a parrot-feather hat with the crowning dove's feather that is the distinctive emblem of married women, and invites respect.

---

[18] Most of these street-names can still be found in Paris; many presumably derived from argot terms.

A bridge of leviathans connects Algiers to Marseilles. What progress there has been since the boat-bridges of the Rhine! Kiel, Coblentz and Mainz no longer dare talk about their bridges today, and yet they were judged to be impossible before their construction. The word "impossible" has been consigned to the grave, with its sister "routine."

The embarkation-stage of the leviathan bridge is at Cap Ferrat. Its second point of support is on the island of Galita, the third at Cap Toulada on the southern tip of Sardinia. One then crosses the length of Sardinia by means of an ordinary railway to the Strait of Bonifacio; then one reaches Corsica, which one crosses to its north cape, where one finds the second leviathan bridge that ends in Marseilles. That magnificent structure, protected on both sides by indestructible breakwaters, was completed in twenty-five years—less than a second on the clock of eternity.

At Oristano Station in Sardinia, Italian artists came aboard the train to give a concert at forty francs a ticket; it was, therefore, effectively a free concert; it was crowded. The illustrious tenor Belleverini, from Florence, sang the beautiful cavatina from the opera that was all the rage in Europe at the moment, *The Life of the Hummingbird*. That great artiste is endowed with a very weak voice, which suits modern music by virtue of its marvelous tenuousness and its incomparable method. It is almost inaudible, and one is plunged into ecstasy by it; enthusiasm no longer knows any bounds when the artiste completes the *cabalette* with his mouth closed, *bocca chiusa*; it is a prodigy of the art. Belleverini is twenty-four years old.

During the concert, a young man exercising the profession of poet paid no attention to the tenor and kept his eyes fixed constantly on Madame Michel, without having the slightest respect for the dove feather the newlywed woman was wearing on her hat.

Michel, who was only gazing at his wife, according to the custom of husbands, was unable to notice the poet's crime, but his wife had three moments of distraction and met the criminal's eyes three times. At the end of the cavatina she took advantage of the universal murmur of enthusiasm to say these simple words to her husband:

"That young man dressed in the Greek style and holding a lyre looked at me three times with soft eyes."

"Is it possible!" exclaimed the husband. "In what century are we living? Perhaps it's an error. I'll try to witness the crime myself; pretend not to have noticed anything."

At the same moment, the baritone Musignano, the foremost artiste of the Italian Theater in Batignolles, stated singing the great aria from Rossini's *Barber of Seville*, and, from the very first bar, the guilty poet allowed his gaze to fall once again upon the face of the young married woman. Michel took his two neighbors as witnesses to the crime. One of the old men raised his eyes to the ceiling and said, sadly: That's something that was never seen in my time! A perverse century is beginning; better to die than witness the depravity of the future!"

The other old man did not have the strength to express his indignation; he was stunned.

They went into Corsica via the San Bonifacio bridge. It seemed that the mobile senate had to be convened urgently, in order to judge the guilty party before reaching the soil of ancient France, where virtue had reigned on the railway lines for fifteen centuries. After six thousand years, fathers had had enough of vice; their sons had had the fortunate idea of trying out virtue, and had found it good.

The young poet was summoned before the senate, and, having heard the damning evidence of the two old men, he began his defensive plea thus:

> *I'm not one of those who go everywhere*
> *Sighing at hazard o'er the dark and the fair;*
> *I'm not one of those...*

The president cut him off, ordering him to speak French like everyone else and to abandon the puerile game of rhyming, which is the libertinage of the ear and the ennui of the heart.

The young poet bowed and began the development of a long argument in which he tried to prove that music and song reach their full power when one listens to the while gazing at an unknown pretty woman.

"Have you no other excuse to offer for your crime than that?" the president demanded, in a severe tone.

"It seems sufficient to me," the accused replied.

A murmur of indignation ran around the audience. A rigorous sentence was anticipated.

III

At that moment, they arrived in the maritime station of Marseilles. It is an immense peristyle in Cararra marble, with four colonnades belonging to the order of the Graces, and a superb Greek arch ornamented with the inscription: *Gateway to the World*. The entire gulf is a harbor in which thirty thousand vessels with electric propellers can anchor, sheltered from the winds. The prison is built on the headland of La Joliette at

Miresipolis. It is a vast enclosure, in which the prisoners contemplate the beautiful Mediterranean, which inspires calm, meditation and concentration. Vast gardens are found there, maintained by the Durance canal, along with workshops of every kind, chemistry laboratories, a universal library, and an observatory with two Steinbach telescopes with their immeasurable lenses, which reduce Herschel's old instrument to the proportions of a set of opera-glasses. The moon is already our suburb.

The young poet was sentenced to prison and marriage.

"Young man," the president said to him, "you will be set free when you have, by virtue of labor, made a discovery useful to society. The prison of Miresipolis is provided with all the resources necessary to an inventor of genius. Think and find."

The condemned man thanked him, with his hand on his heart, and went to the prison on his own, where the jailer received him with all the respect due to misguided courage.

The train stopped in Marseilles for an hour before departing again for Paris, but the gallant Michel said to his companion: "We'll take tomorrow's train; today we'll visit this ancient city, founded by the Phoecians four thousand years ago.

The two traveling spouses booked into the Madagascar Hotel, a hotel as large as a city that occupies the entire breadth of the old harbor. One might say that Marseilles is a furnished hotel and a café; it is the world's caravanserai. The middle classes, people with private incomes and idlers live in the city of Le Prado, which covers the hills, the shore of the gulf of Montredon and the banks of the Bonneveine, and Le Roucas-Blanc.

The population of the three cities once rose to two million souls, according to the 2857 *Guide Marseillais*. There are nine theaters, four of which are Italian. The Chinese theater is the busiest of them all. It is built on the heights of the reserve and rotates on a pivot. Thus, according to the exigencies of the drama being performed, one discovers in the background of the open stage the magnificent horizons of the sea, the mountains or the three cities, which advantageously replace the ridiculous painted scenery of the old theater.

The Chinese dramaturge in vogue at present in the illustrious Li Hi; his imagination has broken all the boundaries and is only at ease in the infinite. Thanks to him, the theater has been liberated from those old bourgeois plays at which the audience swooned with delight on seeing represented on the stage all the things that its members had at home. That used to be called "observation," and writers who were able minutely to observe porters, imbeciles, peasants, innkeepers, valets, nurses, mothers-in-law, uncles and nephews occupied the first rank in the world of letters.[19] Today, real life is so noisy, so animated and complex that when the evening comes, one goes to the theater to see and hear things that one has not seen and heard during the day.

That evening, at the Chinese Theater of Marseilles, a drama in ten cycles was being performed entitled *What the Sea Says*. Three celebrated musicians were providing the music for the performance, but the palm had been

---

[19] The champion of Romanticism Charles Asselineau complained bitterly about the popularity in the 1840s, in novels and on the stage, of the "school of common sense" that reacted against the supposed excesses of Romanticism. Méry, unsurprisingly, felt the same way.

awarded to Golozzi the Palermian, who had made an authentic discovery in the domain of the art. In the seventh cycle the theater represents *au naturel* an admirably starry sky, a June sky; in the distance one perceives the sea and the crests of the mountains that extend toward Cap Couronne. A choir of nereids and tritons is celebrating that marriage of Septentrion and Africa, and the most melodious instruments in the world accompany those celestial voices. At intervals, the song ceases, and one hears the voice of the pines and the sea, which seem to be continuing the hymn of love, in the six-eight time orchestrated by the musician. Then the citra, the cor, the melophile and the erophone, the four instruments of choice, join in, accompanying the murmurs of the pines and the sea with a fortunate harmony that produces ecstasy. Nature plays a role in the work, as an artiste and as a collaborator.

Truly, that marvelous harmony, executed on the shore of the sea, on a night full of stars and perfumes, provokes no regret for the antique stages on which uncles quarreled with their nephews, mistresses with their lovers and wives with their husbands.

Our young travelers, seated in a box with four duck-down divans, took the greatest pleasure in that Chinese performance. In the entr'actes they went to breathe the cool night air, in the foyer on top of the edifice, which is the belvedere of the city and the sea. What people especially love to see from the height of that foyer is continuous spectacle of the merchant fleets arriving under full electrical power from Suez and Panama.

Michel and his wife would gladly have spent three days in Marseilles, but a name possessed of magical attraction was always resounding in their ears: the old and young name of Paris.

The next day, at noon, they took the northbound electric train, and at four o'clock they arrived at the two pyramids that are the gate of the ancient capital of France. All the voyagers bared their heads respectfully to salute Paris.

IV

Cities follow the movement of the sun; they go from east to west. Ancient Paris, so renowned in history, the Paris of the Palais-Royal, the Boulevard des Italiens and the Chaussée-d'Antin, is still a very habitable quarter, but the life, movement and wealth are no longer there. Twenty centuries have advanced the stones and the people; the pulse of the great artery of Paris now beats in the "West End," as the English say, in the maritime quarter of Grenelle and the vicinity of the Bois de Boulogne and the docks.

The names of quarters, promenades and streets are preserved by oral tradition, but when too many centuries go by, their origin becomes nebulous and archeologists begin researching etymologies with variable results. Thus, one often asks, in 3845, for the primary cause that gave the name Champs-Élysées to the vast quarter filled with palaces, hotels and pleasure-houses, the superb city that extends from the Place de la Concorde to the Étoile. A prize was even offered by the Archeological Society of Chaillot, and was won by Lucien Agénon, the etymologist *par excellence*, who proved that under the reign of Julian, in an epoch of paganism, the Champs-Élysées were a necropolis, or a graveyard.

Time has taken a step forward and the Champs-Élysées have become the city of life. Their vast portico, named the *Palais du Bon-Accueil*, stands at the entrance to the opulent city. When trains arrive, the heads of families crowd that portico, waiting for the married travelers, to offer them their most generous hospitality. Every day one sees the most touching scenes, whose origin goes back to the remotest antiquity, to the century of the patriarchs, which were suppressed in the epochs of avarice and egotism for more than two thousand years. Only the Arabs maintained the tradition, under their tents in the desert. Nevertheless, today, wealth and civilization give hospitality new forms, worthy of the Paris of 3845. People have even learned how to be rich, and wealth is no longer an annoyance.

Once, two young spouses arrived in Paris with a letter of recommendation, and presented themselves at the relevant address. A coldly polite millionaire opened the letter, gave the two recommended individuals an earnest smile and said to them; "That's all right!" The two spouses bowed and retired to the dingy numbered room of their unfurnished hotel. A week later they received a dinner invitation from the millionaire for "six o'clock precisely." The wife ordered a dress, a hat and shawl in the latest fashion. The husband dressed up like an engraving. They hired a carriage and answered the invitation, after having spent a thousand francs on clothes to do honor to the provincial correspondent.

They sat down to dinner at eight o'clock, because an invited guest had to wait. They ate badly; the food was cold, the conversation tragic; they were served fifteen drops of jaundiced Medoc with the roast; a guest with a head-cold sang a ballad at the piano; and, sat eleven o'clock the master of the house announced to the two spouses that he was leaving for the country in three days.

In 3485, at the Portico du Bon-Accueil, a Parisian bowed to Michel and his wife and said to them: "Welcome; my house is yours; I'm Gervais de Montreuil."

Michel shook the unknown man's hand and said: "This is my beloved wife, the woman to whom I have given my name. I'm Michel, son of Bastien. My father is a peasant from Poitou. He has changed the fever-ridden marshes of Madagascar into vast plains of rice; he has hollowed out the beds of the streams of water that descend from the Pakalaoe Mountains to the Mozambique Canal, which no longer stagnate. Because of his services he has been named Prefect of the département of Good Hope."

"We are brothers," Gervais replied. "I've provided electrical power to the orchards of Montreuil; I've given beautiful fruits to the world market in all seasons. The year is a perpetual autumn; people eat my peaches in January. My sun shines for twelve months and never sets."

While saying these words, Gervais directed the two spouses to a palanquin, where they were seated on very comfortable cushions. Gervais touched a spring and, in the blink of an eye, all three of them arrived at the arch of the Étoile, at the door of a charming palace veiled by trees and flowers.

An invisible orchestra in the garden composed of four instruments—the citra, the cor, the melophile and the erophone—played the hymn "A Stranger is a Brother," a masterpiece by the illustrious Javanese Sahapy. Gervais then escorted the French couple from the Cape personally to a delightful apartment, where their least desire was met.

Six o'clock in the evening chimed, and at the last stroke, a joyful carillon with a golden timbre burst out in the vestibule; it was the dinner gong.

Gervais' table was the work of the celebrated Milye of the Rue de Rouen in Meudon. Everything to charm the eye and dilate the bosom was admirably disposed on the tablecloth, in the form of a museum of exquisite sculpture. Once, according to archaeologists, people displayed in drawing rooms a bronze Charles Quint, a Sulla offering is resignation, a Galileo saying "But it does turn," a Hannibal crossing the Alps, a Marius at Minturnes, and other stupid forms adored by the ancient bourgeoisie. Today, only statuettes of women are admitted to the ornaments of a room; men in bronze and marble are not worth the trouble of looking at them. Even the Apollo of the Belvedere is a colossal ape who has stolen a quiver from an armorer in Claros.

One very curious innovation made a particular impact on the young traveler Michel. Before each guest, a crystal amphora rotated on a pivot, ornamented with nine figures of allegorical women with their attributes, whose feet were lightly suspended over urns of Bohemian glass. On these urns could be read: Burgundy, Bordeaux, Madeira, Cyprus, Constance, Champagne, Lamalgue, Ermitage and Malaga. The guests chose their wine themselves according to taste, and they were all within arm's reach. In barbaric epochs, a tremulous waiter, watched by his master, would pour an equivocal claret, drop by drop, as if they were rubies, into a glass fit for a dwarf. That was known as "knowing how to manage a household"; the managed died of thirst or drank water.

The centerpiece, representing young African sorceresses subjugating lions and tigers, was surmounted by the ancient Muta, the goddess of Silence, gazing at the guests while smiling, as to prompt them to soft table-talk, but she had a finger over her mouth, as if to invite them to shut up when they leave; nothing said at table ought to be repeated outside—an ancient moral rejuvenated by modern civilization.

Once, at table, conversation revolved around a melodrama that had had a lachrymose success, in which the eternal mother found her son in the fourth act, or the life of a fashionable woman, or the size of an actress's nose; these were known as "the charms of conversation." These frivolities and items of gossip are no longer seen today. People love to talk in order to say something, and, travel having given an education to everyone, important subjects of conversation are never lacking. One always has the resource of the prodigious news that arrives at every moment by way of a thousand electric wires, and which brings the conversation of the world to Paris, so to speak.

Every wealthy house has its tabularium on its external façade, as the wall of the Capitol once had, and it is there that the alert agents of the Central Telegraph Agency incessantly post all the interesting things that are happening in the world. An aide, alerted by the sound of a bell, runs to the door, collects the news item from the tabularium, and transmits it to the master of the house.

That day, during the evening meal, which lasted about an hour, the universal telegraph served four items of great interest to Gervais' guests and several minor items of planetary gossip, gathered that morning from the five continents of the world.

It was announced that Post-Captain Davis—an illustrious family name—had reached the eighty-eight parallel in the direction of the South Pole in his immense steel ship *London Afloat*, driven by four electrical propellers at high pressure, with four thousand elephant-power. That very morning, Davis ought to have reached the pole, melting ice-sheets contemporary with creation. No one in his crew, which constituted a people, had suffered from the cold, thanks to the warm artificial atmosphere with which electrical science had enveloped the *London Afloat*. The benefits the world anticipated from that navigation were incalculable; astronomy, in particular, would take a step toward infinity.

By way of dessert, it was announced thereafter that, at two-thirty that day, Ty-Hoang, the Celestial Emperor of China had married a French tourist who had arrived the day before on the express from Paris. The ceremony had just taken place at the imperial palace of Tsu-Kin-Tching.

When dinner was over, the guests were introduced into the ablution room. Two aides presented them with golden ewers, and ran an abundance of perfumed water into marble basins.

We have read in an old book of authentic appearance that in the barbaric centuries large cups of warm water were served, and that all the guests, bent over those frightful jaw-baths, would perform a symphony of gums with hoarse murmurs and little cascades that would nauseate a castaway dying of thirst. That atrocious habit persisted, it is said, for more than a century, even in the great halls of public restaurants; there, a family beginning their dinner often had a family that was finishing theirs at the next table, launching the splashes of their maxillary bath in all directions. When an innovator dared to criticize that odious ceremony everyone replied: "it's the custom."

At eight o'clock, Michel asked Gervais to take him to the residence of the Minister, and said to his wife: "I must report on my mission; one should not waste a minute when important affairs are at stake; at nine o'clock, I shall be all yours."

Gervais' eldest son, Delphin, offered to keep Madame Michel company during her husband's absence.

V

Delphin was charming young man of twenty-two; his one desire was to marry, for bachelors enjoy no consideration in Paris.

The coolness of the evening was delightful under the large trees in Gervais' garden. Madame Michel sat on a grassy bank and, according to the custom of women, spoke to Delphin, who was standing in front of her in a respectful attitude.

"Do you know our Cape département?" she asked, in the familiar tone that gives boldness to the most timid of men—which is to say, to all men.

"No, Madame," Delphin replied, his eyes lowered. "I'm still very young and have done very little traveling."

"What countries have you visited?"

"I'm ashamed to say, Madame, that I only know India and America."

"You don't like, traveling, then, Delphin?"

"I adore it, but I'm in love."

"With whom?"

"The most beautiful young woman in Valaparaiso."

"A South American?"

"Yes, Madame; I met her the other day at Lima Station in Peru, and my head has remained on the equator."

"Poor child! And you're waiting to be married in order to travel?"

"Yee, Madame; it takes two to wander around the globe."

"That's true; solitude is sad on the railway. And have you made any approach to her family?"

"This morning I sent an electric dispatch to the father asking for his daughter's hand in marriage, but I haven't had any reply. Imagine my despair; it only takes a hour to correspond with Valparaiso. It's so close!"

"Indeed," the young woman remarked; there's nothing between us but the stream of the Ocean. Le Havre has America for a suburb."

Delphin stifled his sobs, and, having nothing more to say, said nothing.

At the same time, Michel went into the Ministry.

It is said that the following atrocious verse could be read on that functionary's door:

*Ministère
des Affaires
Étrangères.*[20]

Today, a terrestrial globe has replied the inscription.

The Minister receives everyone between eight o'clock and midnight. In summer, the audience hall is a vast garden illuminated by a small electric sun and filled with marble side-tables; it runs along the river bank on a terrace with a sandalwood balustrade.

---

[20] The joke is untranslatable, because "Minister" does not rhyme with "Foreign" or "Affairs."

Michel, who had been instructed as to the etiquette, sat down in front of a free table and a ministerial aide immediately served his with water-melon ice-cream, a glass of Constance and a cake made of fire-gilded benafouli rice.

The minister, followed by an electric secretary, was going from table to table, collecting everything that people had to say to him: requests, replies and complaints, all as concise and laconic as a Chinese proverb.

Michel overheard what his two neighbors said to the Minister, and prepared his speech in the same style and spirit.

One said: "I'm Vincent the Senegalian, engineer. I want to canalize the River Cameroon in African France."

"Which descends from Mount Gebel?" said the Minister.

"Yes," the engineer replied.

"And empties into the Gulf of Biafra, almost on the equator?"

"Yes, Minister. All the land extending from the sea to Nimeanai is an immense wilderness; with a canal, it will be a garden."

"Granted," said the Minister.

The secretary stamped the seal of authorization on a counterfoil and handed it to the engineer.

"May God be with you, and get married," the Minister said to him, shaking his hand.

The other neighbor said: "I'm the Prefect of the Ajan Coast."

"Between the Gulf of Aden and the Indian Sea?" said the Minister.

"Yes," replied the Prefect. "I'd like permission to pierce the mountain chain..."

"That separates Bertat and Gingire?" the Minister cut in.

"Yes. We'll probably find a source of the Nile in some reservoir of the cutting, and we'll direct that fertile water into the wasteland of Gengiro."

"Granted, Are you married, Prefect?"

"I'm a widower."

"Remarry. Go, grow, multiply and canalize."

The Minister arrived in front of Michel's table, who said: "I'm Michel, son of Bastien. Our forests in Madagascar are full of wild oxen..."

"And excellent quail?" the Minister interjected.

"Yes. I can deliver a thousand oxen a day for consumption in Paris, at ten centimes a kil, but I need the concession of a small bridge..."

"Between Cap Saint-André and Mozambique?" said the Minister, briskly.

"Yes, and I request the right to charge a toll for six months."

"Granted," said the Minister, "and I name the son of Bastien Prefect of Cap d'Ambre in Madagascar. Are you married?"

"I have that good fortune," said Michel.

"May God give you all the others," the Minister replied. "Go, build the bridge, have children, and send your thousand oxen and four times as many quail on the same trains."

The secretary handed the certificate to Michel, who shook the Minister's hand and ran to rejoin Gervais.

As he went into the guest-house, Michel announced the great news to his wife, who manifested a great joy, for the rank to which her husband had just been promoted would permit her to wear a very simple dress without any kind of ornamentation.

The rich bourgeois of the Champs-Élysées almost all have a lyric theater at home, which procures them pleasant musical soirées when they do not go to the great Parisian theaters. Gervais funded an excellent Italian troupe and a German orchestra generously. The concert hall was adjacent to the house. There was only one row of two-seat boxes; the audience never exceeded thirty people, who only talked during the entr'actes. It was amicably forbidden to wear leather gloves, tight clothing—including cravats—and opera-glasses. One needs to be comfortable and mute in order to listen to music.

Gervais gave the box of honor to Prefect Michel and his wife. The performance was an admirable opera by Juliany-Miro, a masterpiece entitled: *Septentrion and Africa*, which serves as a kind of preface to another opera, *What the Sea Says*.

Miro's opera has no words, following a custom that is already very old, which goes back to a public insurrection at the famous performance of *Ninive*. Paris has conserved the memory in its dramatic annals. Two acts of *Ninive* had been completed; the Parisian public—the best-behaved child in the world—heard, after five centuries, the following words:

> *Douce espérance,*
> *Dans ma souffrance*
> *Quel doux espoir!*
> *… … … … … …….*
> *Mon coeur palpite,*
> *Il bat plus vite,*
> *… … … … … … …*
> *Douce chimère!*
> *En vain j'espère,*
> *… … … … … … … … …*

Funeste délire!
Je souffre, et j'expire,
… … … … …….
Mortel odieux,
Je fuirai ces lieux,
… … … … …….
Quel est donc ce mystère?
O moment fatal!
Je souffre et j'espère,
Mystère infernal![21]

Now, one evening, the public, finally wearying of this secular mystification, rose up *en masse*, like a single tiger, tore up the libretti, smashed the seats, demanded the head of the librettist and threatened to set fire to the Opéra if its ears were assaulted again, under the pretext of beautiful music, but that immutable and five-hundred-year-old poetry. The director was summoned and, recognizing the justice and the patience of the public, promised that henceforth, opera would no longer have any words. This promise was greeted with loud applause.

That fortunate revolution gave rise to another. It was recognized that music had not been put into the world to accompany words like:

---

[21] "Sweet hope/In my suffering/What sweet hope!... My heart palpitates/It beats faster… Sweet illusion/In vain I hope… Deadly delirium/I suffer and I die… Odious mortality/I shall flee this place… What is this mystery, then?/O fatal moment!/I suffer and I die,/Infernal mystery!" The vast stock of rhymes readily available in French lends itself to the production of great poetry, and also the most abysmal doggerel; the insatiable demand for new operas in mid-19th century Paris sometimes produced work that was closer to the latter than the former.

"Sit down on this chair."
"I'm all right, thank you." etc.

and people wanted to render to the sublime art its ancient nobility and dignity. From that moment on, reverie, amour and religious thought absorbed the genius of great composers; marvelous instruments were created that spoke the language of mystery and passion; the divine erophone was invented, which is the voice of love and has no need to accompany "Idol of my life" or "My flame answers her flame" to express all the emotion of the soul and all the tenderness of the heart in their slightest nuances. The symphony, strictly defined, has never had words, but it says everything; it is the melodious song of the infinite.

It required fifteen centuries to make the Parisian public the foremost artistic audience in the world. It would not be today that Paris would discard the ancient musical compositions of the divine Rossini, the Christian Orpheus: *The Siege of Cornith, Moses* and *William Tell*. The deaf flourished in those epochs; today, people can hear.

The subject of *Septentrion and Africa*, fortunately devoid of words, is self-explanatory to the eyes. Old Septentrion, white-haired and leaning on an oak-wood staff, crosses the Mediterranean Lake to warn himself in the sun of the Atlas mountains. A young woman passes by, seated on a lion and wearing a lotus in her hair, and is moved to pity on seeing the unknown old man, seemingly paralyzed. She touches his hand, and Septentrion wakes up with a start, and is rejuvenated. Then Africa puts a lotus-flower in the old man's hair and returns his ebony curls. She kisses him on the forehead, and the

Saturn changes into an Antinous. But the young woman's power is limited to these metamorphoses; she can do no more for the future of the land of Africa. Septentrion, rejuvenated, warmed up and amorous, changes that ancient savage domain in his turn. He sows, he builds, he fertilizes; he gives the genius of the North to the indolence of the South, and the great work of civilization is accomplished.

After the performance, Gervais said to Prefect Michel: "Tomorrow I'll give you an even greater surprise: I'll show you Paris."

VI

The next day, Gervais got up very early in order to show Paris to the two young travelers.

A pretty little city carriage was parked in front of the door of the house: an authentic promenade jewel, as light as a butterfly, as solid as bronze and as supple as fine steel. The traction device had the form of a hippogriff with blue wings. The steering mechanism was most ingenious. Paris excels in these fortunate inventions, which replace the perils of old with security.

In the barbaric centuries, cities were filled with an infinite multitude of horses, which put the lives and limbs of pedestrians in continual peril. Rich people launched their crazed and ill-tempered horses along narrow streets in order to satisfy a puerile vanity, furnishing the chronicles of Paris with an average of five equestrian catastrophes a day. Then thousands of public vehicles raced madly across the city, crushing, brushing and terrifying, and, above all, exhibiting the skeletons of poor automatic horses, martyrized at thirty sous an hour by coachmen who were always going to sleep and waking up again. When a good son left for Paris to complete his education and run up debts, his parents said to him between their tears: "Don't get crushed, child!"

Paris was a battlefield then, in which the cannonballs were called wheels and horses. It is said that a man who could certify, after thirty years of residence, that he had never been hit by one of these projectiles, received a medal, of honor.

With his hand on the ebony tiller, Gervais first took the two travelers to the ancient temple once known as Les Invalides. The denomination was slightly lacking in politeness, for it is not appropriate to say "you're an invalid" even to an invalid, but in antiquity, the inscriptions on monuments were not obliged to be polite. It is said that one could even read, on the door of a hospice in the Faubourg Saint-Martin: *Hospice des Incurables*, which is neither polite nor Christian. The unfortunate who set foot on the threshold of that hospital knew what would happen there; it was the inscription of the Inferno: "Abandon all hope, ye who enter here." Incurable!

The road that leads from the Champs-Élysées to that ancient edifice is one of the most beautiful in western Paris. Two covered galleries, sheltered from the rain and the sun, run alongside it, as in all the other streets, interrupted only by the mobile arch in the middle of the bridge, which rises up before the mast-less ships. On the causeway, the area is vast, and four rows of carriages are always coming and going along it, in orderly files to the left and the right, which never leads to traffic jams—an admirable system of circulation.

The painted mural is the principle interior ornament of the Temple des Invalides. Michel, who was in haste to depart to start work on his masterpiece at the Cap d'Ambre, regretted being unable to admire all the beauti-

ful frescos, masterpieces by the painter Koreb the Javanese, nicknamed Mara-Api, after the name of a volcano.
Michel contented himself with admiring the details of
The Battle of Dembo, painted with a brush with the fury
of an artistic demon. The veterans of that great day at
Dembo are always there before the fresco; they point to
the glorious scars of the battle and give strangers all the
desirable explanations personally; the story is told by its
heroes.

All ancient frescoes are miniatures by comparison
with *The Battle of Dembo*; that is because it required
prodigious dimensions to give even an incomplete idea
of the formidable ten-day battle.

The passage, painted according to nature, reproduces the plateau of Dembo, with its ring of rocks, enormous bushes ad virgin forests. It is there that an enemy
has found its last refuge; it is there that the army of lions
and tigers, continually driven back by the pioneers of
African civilization, has entrenched in order to defend,
one last time, domains inhabited since the creation of the
world, which stupid humans seemed to have abandoned
because of prescription and acquired right. On this supreme day, the feline races, forgetting their old enmities,
have been reconciled for the defense of their communal
territory.

In the crevices and caverns of gray rocks, in the
clearings of forests and the thickets of bushes, ember-
like eyes can be seen gleaming, wild manes bristling,
striped and spotted fur undulating, while monstrous serpents, which have also become the lions' auxiliaries, coil
their scales around palm-trees and threaten the usurpers
of the domain with their fangs. In the background of the
painting, these animals seem to form a reserve army for
the following day. In the foreground, battle is engaged

between humans, wild beasts and reptiles. It is a frightful mêlée, such as the sun has never seen. Our intrepid African pioneers have brought all the weapons of destruction to that battle: those that modern genius has invented for useful wars of pacification and legitimate conquest.

All of that hand-artillery fires smokelessly, and never veils the enemy after the explosion. The field of combat is always inundated by fluid golden light. No shot goes astray in a nebulous corner. And in that immense chaos of manes, pelts, stumps of reptiles, leonine teeth, foaming mouths and steel claws, wrath and life are expressed by the painter so vividly that we think we can hear the frightful concert of roars that filled the solitudes of the battle of Dembo.

Three paces from the fresco stands a colossal statue of Michali, the great hunter of Algiers, with this simple inscription of its stylobate: *To the Victor of Dembo*. Michali was the general of that memorable expedition.

The Rue de l'Océan leads from the Invalides to the Champ-de-Mars. Here the architecture of the buildings changes completely. The elegant and classic symmetry is broken. One sees unfolding on both sides a succession of Asiatic edifices of marvelous effect: pagodas, Chinese towers, verandas, chatirams, minarets and pavilions; all the fantasies of that painted, sculpted, decorated architecture, which seems to be laughing at the sky and launching for the from the earth to play with the radiance of the heavens.

The Champ-de-Mars is like the square of the Rue de l'Océan; the immense open space is bordered on is four sides by vast hostelries that the vicinity of Port Grenelle always renders too small, because of the affluence of travelers from the five continents of the world.

Four theaters stand in the center of each side and are the work of the same architect. The largest and finest is the Théâtre Rossini; there is nothing as gracious as its architecture. The columns of its peristyle are ingeniously composed of statues of women in the purest marble, whose groups overlap and support the entablature. The melodious heroines of the Rossinian oeuvre have been personified by the famous Athenian sculptor Dimitry Zapolous and ornament the façade. The theater in question, exclusively devoted to music, holds six thousand spectators and as many numbered quilted armchairs.

The other theaters are reserved for dance, grand pantomimes and equestrian exercises, combined with Indian juggling. The theaters in which people speak are two in number and relegated to the limits of the maritime quarter. In antiquity, comedy and drama justly enjoyed great favor; that is understandable, but the vices, farces, petty passions and all the gossip of the old world are of no interest today. The tiny breath of human beings is lost in the intelligent noise of the creation taking place around us.

The world is staging a drama, not in five acts but in five continents; a thousand electric links are recounting a thousand scenes, forming an eternal dialogue at every instant between the two worlds. Two actors recounting their affairs in front of a prompter's hole would no longer warrant attention. Only music has retained speech; music alone can still be understood by a public consisting of all the nations and languages of the world.

All the paltry satires of humankind, all the scenic exhibitions of our natural infirmities, all the pretended corrections that only serve to nourish hatreds by presenting humans to humans in a horribly ugly aspect, all those moral lessons fallen from the vicious flesh of the theater have lost their reason for existence and no longer find echoes in this century of universal communion, in which true civilization has said its two final words: Love and Charity.

VII

The two young spouses only paid scant attention to those streets and squares; they were impatient to see the port of Paris, which is the world's port, and it marvel.

Feats of engineering once almost impossible, but rendered so easy today, thanks to the electric agent, have hollowed out the bed of the Seine and broadened out its banks, and have rendered the river navigable by the largest ships fall the way from Le Havre to Paris. It required two centuries to complete the work, but what are two centuries in the eternal life of Paris? The former plain of Grenelle has been changed into a harbor, and there is no sight as moving as that immense basin of active water, where the flags of all the friendly nations fly, framed by palaces of commerce, with their cornices of Indian marble, surmounted by statues of all the illustrious navigators.

The harbor wall, built with enormous slabs of Himalayan granite, is ornamented by two superb fountains in Rhine porphyry, a hundred feet high. One supports a triple row of conch-shells with statues of blue marble representing then ten incarnations of Brahma; another reproduces the same workmanship, but the figures are in Paros marble; one recognizes the nine Muses and the god of poetry and. Two aerial rivers bound, play, foam and stream over those two sculpted hills, distributing waves of humid dust and an atmosphere of sweet freshness all around.

Between those two fountains stands a statue of Prometheus in Caucasian granite; it is a tribute to the prophetic genius of Greek antiquity. The gigantic Titan is crushing the vulture upon the rock, and holds in his hand the electric sun that reignites daylight over the immense zone of Paris when the other has set. The statue is a lighthouse, and the rays of its vast luminous fire eclipse the brightest constellations on summer nights. On the pedestal, these lines can be read:

> *L'electricité, c'est la vie!*
> *Enfin, Promethée, à son tour,*
> *Tenant la flamme au ciel ravie,*
> *Au roc enchaîne le vautour.*[22]

At the entrance to the harbor the Rue Christophe-Colomb begins; it runs along the river as far as Rouen, a noble city that fully deserves to be a suburb of Paris one day. It is necessary to go back to ancient Egypt to find as a long a succession of edifices built on two banks, for Herodotus tells us that Egypt was a long street of cities whose gutter was the Nile.

On the other side of the harbor, going up the Seine as far as the old Louvre, one still finds docks for ships, but they are of medium size. An auxiliary harbor has been hollowed out for these small merchant fleets in the place where the Institut once stood. Archeologists have recovered a rather curious ancient fact on this subject.

In 1806, the emperor Napoléon I, who would have done great things with steam or electricity, submitted

---

[22] "Electricity is life!/Finally, Prometheus, in his turn,/Holding up the fire stolen from Heaven,/Has chained the vulture to the rock."

Fulton's discovery[23] to the scientists of the Institut. The scientists, who did not believe in inventions then, and who had not invented anything, replied to Napoléon's envoy with an outburst of Olympian laughter. Never had there been such hearty laughter beneath the severe and dull dome of the Institut. The Emperor had faith in the official science that he funded; he did not believe in Fulton and his discovery, and civilization was set back a century by the scientists' fault. Now, this is what time has wrought: the Institut has disappeared, as something unnecessary in an epoch when the world is full of scientists and learned people, and fleets of steamships are seen smoking with all the force of their boilers over the site where the scientists of 1806 laughed so hilariously.

On the right bank of the Seine, opposite the great port of Grenelle, Paris has an incomparable monumental splendor; the heights of Chaillot, Passy and Auteuil are, so to speak, dressed with palaces and gardens; it is the quarter of commercial opulence. Thousand of counters are open there, which maintain correspondence with the world. The Quai de l'Abondance, formerly des Bons-Hommes, is occupied along its entire length by an immense granary, where the rice of Madagascar and the wheat of Africa and Oregon are stored. Thus, bread is so cheap that one can say that the people receive it virtually free; there is no complete civilization without that.

The Bois de Boulogne is the park, the public garden and the promenade of this port quarter. The people find all possible amusements there, free of charge: theaters, circuses, hippodromes, naumachias, concert-halls ball-

---

[23] Robert Fulton demonstrated his submarine on the Seine, but could not obtain funding for its further development and manufacture, and took the plans to his grave.

rooms, firework displays, aerostat ascents, steeplechases, menageries, libraries, regattas, aquatic tourneys, Indian jugglers, bayaderes, greasy poles, magnetizers, gymnastic displays, roller-coasters, lyric cafés, wax museums, Alsatian giants and Lapland dwarfs, all the zoological phenomena of the world—and it is the Universal Bank of Maritime Credit that pays the expenses of so many exhibitions that are so dear to the people, especially when the people do not have to pay for them.

The district known as the Étoile crowns all the magnificences of the port quarter in a worthy manner. There is nothing as grand and splendid as the triumphal Rue de Neuilly. It begins at the ancient monument erected by Napoléon I to the glory of the French *grande armée* and ends at the river quays at Neuilly. The arch of the Étoile finds its glorious pendant at the extremity of that street: those two gigantic granite orators announce to the traveler that civilization, begun by war, has been accomplished by peace; thus, our final peaceful conquests have their own triumphant monument; the arch of the Étoile has a brother: it is the Arc du Soleil, at the end of the ancient avenue that is today's Rue de Neuilly.

The Arc du Soleil is divided into five parts, like our globe; it has five faces, or five marble tablets, on which are engraved the names of the heroes of peace, with the names of their victories. No base national jealousy has excluded any foreign name. There are no more frontiers; our little glove is a city, the fatherland of all its inhabitants. The astronomical discoveries of Steinbach, in bringing the frightful revelations of the infinite within the range of our eyes, have taught us how pitiful the exiguity of our planetary atom is, which we no longer dare divide into nations that separate us by means of rivers that are streams, mountains that are pebbles, and oceans that are lakes. Our voyages in space, through the monstrous lenses of the latest telescopes, have deprived the world of its old pride.

One may cite the principle names inscribed on the five faces of the Arc du Soleil, along with their entitlements to glory. These few give an idea of the others:

Xavier of Nantes, ploughed up Oregon, the granary of France.

Sebor of Canterbury felled the first trees in the forests of the Segalin peninsula and constructed the most agile vessels therewith.

Steinter of Cologne fertilized the largest islands in the Maldives and Laquedives.

Paulus of Antwerp restored to Egypt, by means of intelligent canalization, its ancient fecundity.

Chartier of Toulon discovered the gold mines of Borneo and the mountains bordering the Mer Vermeille.[24]

Gaetano, gardener of Genoa, fertilized the immense Australian wilderness extending northwards from De Witt Land to Arnhem Land.

Constantin of Auteuil naturalized the fruits and vegetables of northern Europe in the savage interior of Guinea.

Adamson of Dublin got rid, by means of the electric agent, of all the reefs close to the surface that rendered navigation so dangerous in the Coral Sea.

The five catalogues of the Arc du Soleil are already almost full of these titles of nobility, but the triumphal

---

[24] Mer Vermeille [Red Sea] was a name applied to various stretches of water in 19th century France.

street of the Étoile will be extended as far the crest of Mont Valerien, and a third triumphal arch will be raised to the glory of future benefactors of humanity.

Michel and his wife particularly admired the Arc du Soleil, and took an exact copy of it with their portable camera obscura.

When they passed in front of the Théâtre du Jour on the heights of Passy, Madame Michel manifested a desire to hire a box to see the magnificent spectacle that has the sun for a chandelier. At that moment they were presenting the ballet *Océanides*, danced by a thousand young women from every land and all the possible shades of skin and hair color.

Very tenderly, Michel said to his wife: "My angel, your wishes are mine, but the performance last five hours and I have imperious duties to fulfill. First we have to go to Valparaiso to arrange poor Delphin's marriage; he has received no reply, so it's a matter of urgency. Thereafter, I mustn't neglect my Prefecture at Cap d'Ambre. Since yesterday evening, I am no longer my own man; I belong to the colonists of the Sakalava and the merchants of Nosy-Be.[25] Five hours devoted to frivolous pleasure would weigh heavily upon my heart, like a remorse."

Madame Michel bowed, and aid: "You're always right."

The two spouses took their leave of Gervais at the American dock at Bougival, where the steamboats with electrical propellers are stationed that go downriver to Le Havre and race to Panama. They are floating cities; their mass does not impede their agility, thanks to the

---

[25] Nosy-Be is an island off the north-west coast of Madagacar, most of whose inhabitants belong to the Sakalava ethnic group

irresistible power of the locomotive agent. Today, such excursions to the other world are regarded as mere strolls, there are pleasure-trips from Le Havre to Panama.

Michel succeeded in his expedition beyond all expectation. The electric telegraph between Valparaiso and Yucatan had been broken, so the response, good or bad, had not been able to reach Delphin.

On arriving at the first telegraph station in Chile, Michel sent the following dispatch to Gervais' son: *Depart; you are expected.*

With that important duty fulfilled, Michel boarded another steamship to go to St. Louis and take the branch-line of the African Railway to Lupata. That was a second excursion.

After having devoted a few hours to the sacred duties of the family in Cape Town, he took the train too Zanzibar and, having reached the shore of Mozambique, embarked for Cap d'Ambre, where he was awaited with all the honors due to his rank, for the Minister's dispatch had announced his appointment.

Michel is a model Prefect and a model husband; he deserves a numerous family and God will give it to him.

THE RUINS OF PARIS

The Atlasian Phalanstery is indubitably the most charming creation of African Fraternity. That corner of the earth only harbors three thousand families, but it is proposed as a model residence to all the peoples of New France, from Algeria to the sources of the Nile.

The love of archeological studies has driven two travelers from the Phalanstery to visit he ancient land of France, where civilization displayed its first glimmers, and whose physical and mental history is no more today than a chaos devoid of guide and enlightenment.

Denis Zabulon and Jérémie Artémias are the guiding lights of modern science. The first has for an ancestor the immortal physicist to whom the human race owes unalterable peace. Everyone knows that in the year 3509 or thereabouts the great philanthropist in question invented the admirable machine that two fleets of five thousand steamships and a hundred and thirty-three thousand combatants in less time than it takes a clock to chime midday. The sublime inventor had discovered that the maritime atmosphere is inflammable over an extent of a hundred square leagues, and catches for spontaneously by means of a brand of pulverized asbestos. Before that discovery, ships armed with simple Paixhans cannons[26] of an improved model could only vomit forth a

---

[26] The Paixhans gun, developed by the eponymous French general and first demonstrated in 1824, although it did not

73

thousand incendiary bombs per minute, with the result that a third of an enemy fleet was still afloat after a battle. Zabulon's ancestor, by popularizing his philanthropic secret of destruction, obliged two fleets to burn naturally, down to the last launch and the last sailor. Thus for three centuries, no one in the world has gone to war; the excess of evil has engendered good.

The world has rewarded that generous discovery by according to the Zabulon family in perpetuity, until the Last Judgment, a pension of ten thousand gold phalansters, secured on the treasure of the human race, the Quito mine. Denis Zabulon spends that hereditary fortune nobly, in making it serve, the needs and pleasure of the Mappemondian Brotherhood.

The two brothers traversed the stream that separates Africa from ancient France by steam-table. Slightly inconvenienced by the winds, they did not land until midday, although the departed at four o'clock in the morning. The provisions for their voyage comprised a block of racahout,[27] four lion chops, a wild boar pâté and five jugs of Constantine wine. They ate their first meal on the deserted shore where it is said that a city once stood called Marseille, Marsyo or Marsyas.

They took off on the steam-table and discovered, from high in the air, eighty kilometers of mossy ruins, which, according to their calculations, ought to belong to the ancient capital of France—named Paris according to some and, according to others more learned, Parigi or

---

enter into service until 1841, was the first naval gun designed to fire explosive shells.

[27] Racahout is an Arabic word referring to a generic foodstuff, normally stored as a powder, whose basic components may include acorns, potato, rice, vanilla and caçao

Lutétia, a word that signified "mud" in an ancient language. Another scientist, Brother Dalhia-Dream, opts for Parigi, being unable to reconcile himself to admitting that, in antiquity, a city might call itself Mud in order to attract inhabitants.

The family-aides set up a beautiful tent on the plateau of a vast ruin, which had to be one of those monuments called triumphant arches by the ancients. The furniture and provisions were deposited there, and the exploration of the ruins put off until the next day.

The two voyagers went through a vast forest in which creepers veiled the trees and long grass hid the ground, and they discovered the ruins of a Greek or Roman temple that appeared to belong to the time of Pericles or Augustus.

Denis Zabulon is one of the rare scholars who still have some notion of the old Greek and Latin languages. In the various cataclysms to which the earth has been subjected, either on the part of humans or that of the elements, only a few books have survived to conserve the filiation of languages for us. Denis Zabulon knows those books—or, to be more precise, the skeletons of those books—and that is sufficient for his marvelous sagacity as a commentator.

Digging in the ruins of that Greek or Roman monument to the west of Paris, Denis Zabulon discovered a fairly well-preserved mosaic: a large picture representing a young woman dressed in a white tunic, surrounded by young men offering her golden bracelets and rings. Without paying the slightest attention to the young men and their gifts, the young woman is looking into the distance at three crosses planted on the summit of a mountain, and seems to be forming an important resolution. That mosaic, says Zabulon, gives us an exact idea of the costumes of the period, whose date it retains: 1848. What antiquity! The young men of Paris are wearing an almost Roman costume, a breastplate, armbands, a helmet and sandals; the young woman is only clad in a loosely-hanging chlamys; she has bare feet and her long blonde hair inundates her shoulders and bosom.

We shall see by what ingenious procedure the archeologist Denis Zabulon has reconstructed these ruins and demonstrated the ancient purpose of the monument.

By arranging in a single line several fragments of stone inscribes with letter, Zabulon succeeded in reconstituting this votive inscription:

DOM. SUB. INV. S. M. MAGDALENAE[28]

Which clearly signifies: Madeleine has found her husband under her house: *Sub dom invenit suum maritum Magdalena.* The E that follows doubtless commences another word of the sentence devoured by the centuries, but what remains to us of the inscription is sufficient to prove to us that the temple was dedicated to the glorification of the domestic virtue and virginal meditation of the gynaeceum—a monumental lesson given by the ancients to young women! The temple tells them to avoid public places, circuses, festivals and excursions, and also informs them that a wise person, without leav-

---

[28] The notional author inserts a footnote: "Inscription on the fronton of the church of the Madeleine, a renovated Greek temple." The Latin dedication in question actually reads "D. O. M. SVB INVICAT S. MAR. MAGDALENAE" [To God the All-Powerful and Great, under the invocation of St, Mary Magdalen]. The construction of the present Neo-Classic building was completed in 1842 and consecrated in 1845.

ing the domestic hearth, might very well find a husband in her house, as did this Madeleine, who merited a temple by her virtues. The mosaic completes the inscription and develops its meaning with the most expressive relief. Thus, the mores of that epoch—1848—were not corrupt, as certain historians have insinuated too lightly. It was, on the contrary, a noble century, one that elevated a temple to solitary virtue, to the cenobite virgin and to pious meditation: *Sub domo invenit.*

Denis Zabulon and his friend moved eastwards, and discovered, a short distance from the monument of the Madeleine, under masses of lichen and ivy, the stumps of a triumphal column, which, according to all appearances, had been lined with bronze when it was standing. The stylobate was not broken up, four eagles attesting to the Roman origin of the column still surviving in a reasonably good state of conservation at its four corners. What completed Denis Zabulon's joy, however, was a Roman inscription that was still very readable, although ripped apart, so to speak, by the fingernails of the northern barbarians. The illustrious scholar succeeded in reconstructing the inscription in its original order, but bringing together the debris of the marble plague on which this Latin sentence was engraved:

NEA POLIO. IMP. AUG.
MONUMENTUM BELLI GERMANICI
ANNO 1805
TRIMESTRI SPATIO DUCTU SUB
PROFLIGATI EX AERER CAPTO
GLORIAE EXARCITUS MAXIMI DICAVIT[29]

---

[29] The notional author inserts a footnote: "An absurd inscription, fundamentally and in form, which one is ashamed to read

This inscription, although written in very mediocre Latin, casts a great deal of light on an ancient history shrouded in darkness. That triumphal column was dedicated to the glory of an exceedingly large army, *exercitus maximi*, by Nea Polion, a general of Augustus Nea Polio, *imperator augusti*. Nothing could be clearer. It was the time of the war against Germanicus, *monumentum belli Germanici*, ended within a trimester, *trimestri spatio*—very bad Latin but perfectly clear. The column was constructed with bronze taken from the vanquished, *ex oere capto profilgato*—which is to say, with all the copper coins found on enemy territory, or with their treasure, *oere*.

Nea Polion, Augustus' general, thus had the glory of ending the war against Germanicus, and he erected that column in Paris, probably under the reign of the King of Rome, whose realm was located on the banks of the Seine, according to one historian. The inscription is all the more precious because it corrects a chronological error of approximately sixteen centuries; it fixes the reign of Augustus in 1805; gives us the exact date of the end of the war against Germanicus; and, finally, proves that in 1805 the Latin language, although somewhat degenerate, was spoken in Paris. It was, therefore, not until the end of the 19th century that the French language was formulated by the putrefaction of Latin.

---

on the stylobate of the Vendôme column—and there was an Académie d'inscriptions et belle-lettres in 1805!!!" The quoted inscription resembles the actual inscription very closely, the differences probably being misprints, but the translation is absurd; the monument actually commemorates Napoléon's victory at Austerlitz.

Denis Zabulon and Jérémie Artémias experienced a very natural joy in confrontation with these great discoveries. That consoles many tribulations. To draw a ray of light from a ruin and illuminate history—what an endeavor! And what service rendered to humankind!

Doubtless the wise King Spirigh, who flourished in 3245, fully deserved to rule the world by virtue of ordering the burning of all the books and libraries of Europe, Asia and America. The world was on the point of no longer being habited by anything but books; the insects and rodents that lived on printed papers were multiplying in an alarming manner, and it would soon have been necessary for humans to abandon the cities of libraries and worms.

Wise King Spirigh, the enlightened conqueror off three continents, therefore rendered humans a valuable service in putting those innumerable mountains of books to the torch, which no longer served any purpose by infecting the atmosphere, for they had become so numerous that their formidable mass was discouraging science and education. Wise King Spirigh wasted to give the history of the world a new point of departure, and cause everything that had happened before his glorious era to be regarded as a void, but, while rendering homage to King Spirigh's decree, we also owe thanks to the scholars who, by means of a few scraps of paper snatched from the flames, and a few nebulous inscriptions, have captured some of the historical secrets of antiquity.

Denis Zabulon has served the cause of science well, since, with the aid of three lines of Latin, he has filled in the immense lacuna that the burning of all the libraries had opened prior to the present epoch, 3844.[30]

Continuing his explorations, Denis Zabulon succeeded in proving that in the 19th century the French spoke a degenerate Latin, under kings clad as Caesars. This theory, however, soon encountered a singular contradiction, and our savant voyager was obliged to meditate for a long time to reconcile his ideas.

In the middle of a circular enclosure of ruins that that still preserves the form of a public square, Zabulon discovered the fragments of a bronze equestrian statue, linked by sticky moss to debris of inscriptions and bas-reliefs. The costume and head-dress of the statue left no doubt as to the national classification of the hero represented. The cloak with broad pleats, the buskins with bandlets and the crown of laurels advertised at first glance a Roman emperor.[31] The name had disappeared

---

[30] Stories of this kind are usually set at dates different from the date of composition by a round number, so this implies that the story's original appearance might well have been in 1844, although a different reprint carries a subtitle dating the mission to 3846 rather than 3844. If the story was first publish in 1844 or 1846, the dates 1848, 1853 and 1875 associated with the rediscovered monuments would all be fictitious—but 1875 clearly is, as it postdates the story's reappearance in book form (not to mention Méry's death), and I can find no evidence that the either of the other two dates actually appears in association with the monuments in question.

[31] The notional author inserts a footnote: "The statue of Louis XIV on the Place des Victoires. The king, on his horse, is costumed as a Roman emperor, and on the bas-relief in a French wig." The statue, by François Joseph Bosio, was commissioned after the Restoration in 1822 to replace an earlier statue destroyed in the 1789 Revolution.

from the inscription, but the following words could still be read there: *inter reges magnos.*

Zabulon and Artémias, with common accord, recognized the emperor Hadrian, the only Caesar whose image has been conserved until our day, amid the geological and historical revolutions by which the globe has been ploughed up in all directions. The bas-relief beside the statue however, apparently belonging to the same era, represented the same hero as the statue in a costume that would have provoked violent outbursts of laughter among travelers less earnest than our two scholars. The emperor Hadrian was wearing an enormous, overflowing wig, with a fake and comic opulence, beneath the vat brim of a hat, hanging down over the collar of a strangely-tailored coat. Zabulon and Artémias explained these differences of costume by means of a theory as natural as it is ingenious.

"Hadrian," said Zabulon, "made a seven-year voyage across Europe and Africa; when he wears the light costume of an emperor, it is because artists are representing him as he was when traveling along the banks of the Nile; when he is wearing his vast borrowed hairpiece, he is presumably visiting the cold and rainy climates of the North."

"Indeed," added Artémias. "The people inhabiting those lands must have worn enormous wigs in order to protect their heads against an atmosphere that was perpetually damp or glacial. Civilization had demonstrated victoriously, since the ancient epoch in question, that humans, with their delicate flesh, were not born to receive Niagara Falls upon their heads, bit by bit, throughout their lives. All these monuments that surround us have not all been destroyed; they have melted like sugarlumps under a perpetual deluge. It is incomprehensible

81

that there was a Pharamond sufficiently amphibious to found a city here and to make it endure the rainwater and snow for twenty generations. How belatedly wisdom comes to the human brain! It required centuries to extract so many barbarians from their natal cataract, their snow, their fog, their dull sky, their squalls and hailstorms and finally to persuade them to seek, in the regions of Algiers, Constantine and the Atlas, a habitable land and a climate fit for humans! Truly, one cannot understand that long aberration of antiquity!"

Denis Zabulon had two of his family-aides clear an area covered by vulgar ruins, in order to be able to read a Latin inscription of which he could only see the first word. That work of excavation brought to light the fragments of a fountain almost melted by rainwater, which had only conserved the following words on the stump of a pilaster:

NIMPHA...FLUCTUS...CREDIDIT ESSE SUOS[32]

"That's a precious revelation," said Zabulon. "Nimpha! The Parisians, in 1805, had not yet renounced the mythological worship of nymphs. If we had encountered that word in a book we would have had every right

---

[32] The notional author inserts a footnote: "The fountain of Jean Gourgeon in the market-place of the Innocents; the verse of the inscription is from the Latin-French poet Santeuil, a priest who believed in nymphs." The fountain bears the title *Fontium Nimphis*, followed by two lines supplied by the 18th century poet Jean-Baptiste Santeuil (*Quos duro cernis simulatos marmore fluctus/Hujus Nympha loci crediditis esse suos* [The fruits you see on this cold marble hewn/This Fountain's Nymph believes to be her own]) but actually much older in origin, probably originated by Giovanni Campani.

to regard it as the belief of one writer, but this is a public monument speaking, a national monument; it's the profession of faith of an entire country.

"*Nympha fluctus credidit esse suous*: The nymph believed that these waves belong to her. The nymph of this place is claiming her property; the divinity is demanding her rights. Nothing could be clearer. Thus, Catholicism was unknown in Paris in 1805. Moreover, all that we have seen, and all that we can see around us, confirms the verity of this discovery. Brother Artémias, these ruined temples, these domes and colonnades, belong to pagan art. The Greek and Roman styles are predominant in these ruins. National and Catholic art is not manifest anywhere."

As he said this, Zabulon looked southwards, and discovered the ruins of a Greek temple on the summit of a hill.

"Let's go see that Greek temple," he said to Artémias.

They went through about four kilometers of mud and liquefied ruins, and reached the summit of the hill. Zabulon was transported by joy. Fifteen fluted columns were standing, like the peristyle of an absent temple. Half of a cupola, surmounted by a genius, lay a little further away, and on the debris of a fronton the word *Panthéon* was legible, in all the exaggerated height of its letters of bronze, under the date 1875.

"Zabulon, my brother," said Artémias, "Your theory is accurate, and more accurate than you thought. Paris maintained the worship of the gods in 1875. This looming monument summarized in the sky the religious beliefs of that epoch. The Christian cross was unknown in Paris in 1875; if it had been known, we would certainly see it on the most elevated of all its edifices, and on that dome on which a pagan genius is mounted. In 1875, Paris still believed in genii. A genius was something that had one foot suspended, two arms extended forwards and flaming hair."[33]

"Oh!" cried Zabulon. "This is decisive! Look at your feet, Brother Artémias; this is a marble plaque detached from a wall of the neighboring monument that once stood facing the Panthéon. Read these two words: JUS ROMANUM 1853."[34]

"*Jus romanum!*" said Artémias, crossing his hands over his breast. In 1853, Paris was governed by Roman law! Fathers here cut off their children's heads, and slavery had not been abolished! Great God, how long the world persisted in its errors!"

As dusk was about fall, our two travelers climbed back on to their steam-table with their family-aides, in order to spend the night in Marsyo or Marsalias, opposite Algiers.

Denis Zabulon has invented this maxim: *to travel is to scorn one's house*; so our scholar did not undertake any further excursions for a few days. "Life is short," he said, "to live in to protect one's family; any external attraction is a commencement of death."

The Society of the Portico of the Friends of Truth had instructed Denis Zabulon to undertake that excursion to the ruins of Paris, and the scholar had been

---

[33] The notional author inserts a footnote: "The Panthéon or Sainte-Geneviève, according to the hazard of revolutions and restorations." The Panthéon, constructed on the site of an old church dedicated to St. Geneviève, underwent numerous changes in design and title after its completion in 1790.

[34] The notional author inserts a footnote: "The school of Law beside the Panthéon"—i.e. the Sorbonne law school.

obliged to obey. Four days after his departure, however, he embraced his family and friends, who were waiting for him on rocky causeway that Algiers harbor projects for six kilometers from the African shore. It is a superb piece of work; its accomplishment required the demolition of several mountains and their submersion by means of the invincible action of refined fulminating powder.

The prodigious causeway gives the mariner a pleasant illusion; it seems that Atlas himself is reaching out his hand toward the horizon. At the extremity of the causeway, as everyone knows, rises an immense portico in which the Friends of Truth assemble to talk about the nature of things, between the infinity of the sky and the infinity of the sea.

Denis Zabulon offered a report on his mission in a very detailed discourse, whose peroration we shall quote.

"Brothers," Zabulon said, by way of conclusion, "the general aspect of the ruins of Paris has something heart-rendingly desolate about it. You have seen the ruins of Calcutta, Madras and Canton: charming ruins gilded by the Indian sun, bristling with aloes, nopals and palm-trees, edged everywhere by verdure and ardent mosses, animated by the leaps of tigers and the spindles of boa constructors twisting in the air. Those are adorable ruins, and woe betide the hand that might attempt to resuscitate their monuments! But the ruins of Paris— Great God! Oh, a fog of irritations covers my eyes and heart as I report my memory of them. Imagine an ocean of black mud, raised in enormous waves by a tempest and suddenly frozen in its mad insurrection. The eye has difficulty distinguishing the house of a citizen from the dwellings of kings and gods. A uniform complexion covers those artificial hills, and the air there does not ring with any other sound than the continual plaint of drops of water on the leaves, and the croaking of crows circling in the fog.

"Ought we to be astonished that the inhabitants of that uninhabitable zone lived and died in the darkness of paganism, generation after generation, perhaps for twenty centuries, without knowing the true God? That is because the true God only manifests himself in splendid regions by the light of the stars, the daughters of God. The Parisians, as my brother Artémias will attest, and our discoveries forbid us to doubt, lived in the shadow of death and error. Physical darkness is the sister of moral darkness. Yes, Brothers, our explorations confirm that in 1805, a temple was built there to all the gods; you know that God alone has always been excluded from pantheons.

"Our historical discoveries outside the religious domain are not without interest. The Parisians erected columns to Né Polion, the general of Augustus, to celebrate the fortunate outcome of the war against Germanicus; they built a temple to the modesty of the gynaeceum, which proves, at least, that paganism did to lead to the corruption of their mores. They erected an equestrian statue to the emperor Hadrian in 1816 or thereabouts, and a bas-relief on that monument had told us that the Parisians wore enormous wigs to protect them from the perfidious dampness of their climate.

"When one returns from an excursion to the ruins of Paris, one experiences a just sentiment of pride in casting an eye over the present state of our civilization. How lucky we are, my brothers, to live in 3844, when everything that could be great, useful, agreeable and beautiful has been accomplished. Ruins are the landmarks of the groping of humankind. When a planet attempts to live, its attempts last a long time; the childhood of a nine-thousand-league giant is long; at the age of forty centuries, it is still at the breast of its mother, Experience. Let us congratulate ourselves for having received life at the best of times, and in the interests of our children, let us work to take care of the wealth we have, in order to change it for the better."

This speech was greeted by a solemn silence, an indication of profound emotion, and the great artist Albert Segor, whose domicile is on the third floor of the Atlas, sang the hymn of the Mappemondian Brotherhood. A hundred thousand voices repeated the famous chorus:

"Sing, Brothers! This is the time foretold;
"God has made an earthly paradise."

THE LUNARIANS

What's the point of loving the moon?
She's too high up and we're too low down.
(Popular song)

I. First Glance

Dr. John Herschel is continuing his admirable lunar discoveries at the Cape of Good Hope, in company with two or three of his friends, whom he calls his associates. They are the moon's publicists.[35]

We know that he has already discovered green lakes, crimson mountains, gray valleys, pink trees, seas made of a single diamond, rivers made of a single piece of amethyst, sheep that have visors of flesh to protect them from earthlight, humans with wings who resemble conscripts, whose feet are small at the tip and swollen at the heel, as if they were wearing polished boots.

One does not stop on such a good road. The marvelous telescope, with the aid of three hundred men, has been moved on the spot and turned toward the part of the moon known as Blagavion.

---

[35] The improvised term I have translated, very loosely, as "publicists" is *éditeurs-unis*; *uni* can mean "smooth" or "even", but also means "joined" and is sometimes used with respect to closely bound couples, as in "honeymooners."

The moon's publicists were struck with amazement on seeing humans running across the field of the telescope clad in short trousers. On their backs they had written 75,000 francs.[36] They were browsing grass like animals.

Further away, they plunged their gaze into a valley that is made neither of gold nor silver but of fine rubies. It is the valley of shareholders; it is full of dividends placed at great heights, at the tops of trees. The dividends are white in color. The color of the shares is not known, as yet, on earth.

But what delighted the moon's publicists was the sight of the land of Virtue. It is a small region, about the size of the estates of the King of Sardinia. The men have no hands and are the color of eighteen-carat gold; the women only have torsos and are very ugly, although swarthy in hue. The women and men appear to get on well together, perhaps because of the eccentricity of their nature. The women see for the men and the men speak for the women; the children are made of fine stone. They are all well-behaved, and are carved into facets.

It was a thunderbolt for the publicists of the moon when, in the public square of a city they had just discovered, in they perceived a crimson man who was looking at them through a telescope. The man appeared to be an astronomer of good family. On a piece of paper placed next to him he was making fun, by means of ingenious caricatures, of the physiognomy of the English astronomers. It appears that the astronomers of the moon have a

---

[36] The author includes a footnote: "In 1836 the figure of 75,000 francs represented the prize that a lottery organized by publishers promised its subscribers."

sense of humor and that caricature is allowed there.[37] A rainbow having passed between the two telescopes at the moment of the astronomers' mutual observations, those of the moon wrote that terrans have tricolor rings on their heads, while those of the earth noted that lunarians wear colored clouds as cravats. The moon's seamstress is the aurora borealis.

The lunarian city that is in question here is blue; the sidewalks are in the middle of the street and the carriages pass by on the mezzanine. The mezzanines are brown. Signs are positioned in such way that the characters face the walls—a position that gives rise to the supposition that no one in the city reads signs. But what use are they, then?

The roofs of the houses are in the cellar. Mr. Herschel also assures us that the city pays no taxes, but, on the contrary, receives them. The King of the Moon pays every inhabitant direct contributions and rights of entry.

The King of the Moon is made of fine pearls.

II A Drama on the Moon

Assuredly, Monsieur Arago is a man of eminent intellect, but he seems to us to have denied Mr. Herschel's discovery rather lightly.[38] Thus, we are sure that, when he has taken cognizance of new information that has been transmitted to us, he will take back the declaration the he felt obliged to make to the Académie des Science.

---

[37] Louis-Philippe's government took the unusual step in the mid-1830s of banning political caricatures.

[38] Dominique Arago, the director of the Paris Observatoire, was one of the first scientists publicly to denounce the *New York Sun*'s moon hoax as an insult to Herschel and science.

Mr. Herschel has just read in the lunatic language, and has translated and entire drama into French. He was able to devote himself this magnificent work while an inhabitant of the moon was reading his work to the actors who were going to perform it. Mr. Herschel followed it line by line and dictated to six stenographers while the author was turning over the pages.

It appears, moreover, that there are no manuscripts on the moon; the people having bat-like wings and no quills, as a book is printed as it is composed; that is all the easier because one can take, at a single stroke of the press, sixty thousand copies of a page.

The method is easy to explain; the lunarians have a paper so thin that our bank paper would pass for ignoble cardboard. Because the moon has no atmosphere no one is afraid that the wind might blow sheets of paper away, no matter how light they are.

The characters with which they print are stamps that have no less than three feet of relief. They resemble in their length a comb for combing hemp. Beneath that stamp are placed a hundred or a hundred and twenty reams of the paper of which we have spoken, and the press is operated with a force of two thousand horsepower; immediately, the punches pierced the whole from top to bottom, and one obtains a cut-out impression of infinite delicacy and lightness.

This procedure is much neater and faster than ours, and involves no expenditure of ink.

One reads these printed pages by looking at them sideways, which also gives the coquettes of the land the advantage of being able to peer at their lovers without needing to raise their eyes from their book, which is a marked superiority over our earthly civilization.

At the moment when Mr. Herschel was able to follow the lunarian author in the reading that he was about to make, it appears that the cast had assembled. In fact, there was a species of creature there, somewhat resembling a sarigue[39] but much more complete than that interesting animal. Instead of the single pocket that the sarigue has on its abdomen, the lunarian creature had them all over its body. Mr. Herschel observed that all these pockets were empty, and rightly concluded that it must be the director.

Beside it was another creature, more reminiscent of a she-monkey than a sarigue; this one was half-lying on a kind of slender monkey with Z-shaped arms and legs, part of whose hair was so magnificently curly that did not doubt for a moment that the she-monkey was the sweetheart of the troupe and the slender monkey the sweetheart's lover.

A little further away a kind of ball of flesh that has no analogue in our world, except among the big drums of our orchestras, seemed to Mr. Herschel to be the *basso cantata*, or grand old man of the place. Another little she-monkey who embraced everyone there and even left the reading to embrace those who were passing by was evidently the theater's money-spinning actress, who boosted the takings. To begin with, Mr. Herschel was quite embarrassed by the employment she held, but on seeing that she seemed, at any rate, to be in clover, he decided judiciously that she must be a Dugazon.[40]

---

[39] A South American marsupial similar to an opossum.

[40] The Dugazons were a well-known dynasty of French stage performers, who name translates literally as "of the lawn" and therefore connects with the previous euphemism, "se couchait sur l'herbe" [literally, to lie down in the grass, although the

Behind all the others, a face as wrinkled as an old apple was visible, pierced by two ardent eyes, grimacing like a clown, fidgeting, writhing and posing, who was doubtless the chief comic. To judge by the glances he directed at a red lady-apple, tense, cold and motionless, she was obviously the second half of the double-act.

A tall muscular fellow incessantly showing off superb teeth and a passable leg but who seemed to have no more understanding of the author than a donkey understands a sermon, was placed by Mr. Herschel among the minor parts.

Before the reading, the aforementioned inhabitants devoted themselves to all kinds of chattering, which was visible by virtue of the increased movement of all the jaws in the assembly. When the author arrived, the leading players saluted him with their fingers, and those with lesser roles bowed all the way to the floor. The author saluted the minor players with his finger and bowed deeply to those with major roles.

Finally, the director made a gesture and the reading began.

The reading was as hard to decipher as the Apocalypse.

III. An Amour

The English newspapers, which arrived today, contain elegiac articles about the young and handsome Blifil Morton, the nephew of the governor of the Cape of Good Hope, and unfortunate young man who became a poignant victim of the Herschel telescope. The stories

---

nearest English expression I could find to carry a similar implication is "in clover"].

are heart-rending. Not since the story of Paul and Virginie has anything similar been heard in the romantic school of the Indian Ocean. The official censors established at the Cape, comprising four Hottentots as in Paris, initially demanded the suppression of the story of Blifil Morton in the long lunar voyage that we have read. It was said that they wanted to protect the sensibilities of his uncle, the governor; then, the uncle having consoled himself, the local press was permitted to recount the following anecdote.

Blifil Morton, having approached the telescope at the moment when it was providing a view of the Ruby Coliseum and the delightful valley of the *Vespertilionum hominum*,[41] discovered, under a tree bearing a strong resemblance to a *Magnolia grandiflora*, a *Pinus italia gigans*, a *Fagus linnensis* or a *Quercus spongiosa fluviatilis*,[42] as well as a host of other conically-shaped trees somewhat resembling a *Qualis populea moerens Philomela sub umbra*[43] or a *Quantum lenta solent inter viburna cupressi*,[44] not far from a little rock of basaltic form not much different from a *silex tertiae formationis* or a *saxum igniferum*, on a couch of grass reminiscent of

---

[41] The fourth episode of the moon hoax—the first three having been relatively sober and modest—described the supposed discovery of the moon's humanoid inhabitants, allegedly dubbed "Vespertilio-homo, or man-bat," allegedly living within the "Ruby Colosseum" not far from the "Sapphire Temple."

[42] Mangolia grandiosa exists, but the other species, attributed to the genera of pines, beeches and oaks do not.

[43] A famous line from Virgil's *Georgics*: "So the mourning nightingale, in the shadows…"

[44] Another line from Virgil, from the *Eclogues*: "As cypresses loom up among [some kind of shrub]"

Formix vitrea, Gramen aphrodisiaticum, Ligustrum eburneum or *Citisus capreolus...*[45]

It was one o'clock in the morning; the Southern Cross was shining over Lion Mountain...

Oh, a thousand pardons, I forgot to tell you what discovered under that tree, which closely resembled so many others. He discovered a young maid about sixteen years of age; she was asleep in the attitude of the Borghese Androgyne,[46] and was no more and no less dressed than that ravishing statue, whose marble seems to have softened under five centuries of desire. She was asleep, the beautiful child! Her face was also visible. What a face! Raphael's Madonna della Seggiola would have died of jealousy. Coral was less coralline than her lips, purity less pure than her forehead; her left cheek, slightly inflated by her slumberous respiration, resembled the full moon, when she blushes to forecast wind.

Pallida luna, pluit; rubicunda, flat; alba serenat.[47]

She awoke, and shook her splendid golden hair; she took a bath in the grass (there is no water on the moon); she frolicked—the innocent!—as is her modesty had nothing for fear from any indistinct gaze. What a lesson

---

[45] *Gramen* means grass, *Ligustrum* privet and *Citisus* broom (the plant). The suggestiveness of *aphrodisiaticum* is obvious enough, but one would probably have to be a very good Latinist to pick up any other veiled sexual references

[46] Méry has "Farnèse androgyne," apparently referring to the collection of antiquities assembled by Alessandro Farnese in the 16th century, but the description strongly suggests that he is referring to a famous statue contained in the Louvre usually known as the Borghese Hermaphroditus

[47] A popular saying adopted from the *Georgics*: "Pale moon: rain; red: wind; white: calm."

for our terrestrial ladies who talk of love in our parks by moonlight!

Mr. Herschel, the eldest son of the astronomical dynasty, observed a considerable agitation in young Blifil's bosom.

"What can you see?" he asked

"Me? Nothing... I... see... let me... another... minute... a thousand pounds for one more minute!" Such was Blifil's reply.

Mr. Herschel the eldest son made the observation to him that it was not decent to monopolize the telescope thus. Blifil, without budging, took his wallet out of his pocket and said to Mr. Herschel: "Here's two thousand pounds in cash for five minutes of monopoly."

Mr. Herschel, in his capacity as a disinterested scientist, took the wallet and whistled the tune of *Clair de lune*, with Weber's variations.

Poor Blifil! Love had fallen upon him from the clouds, and what love!

At that moment, a slight shadow passed over the field of the telescope; the divine forms of the celestial maiden shrank. Blifil perceived that she was about to escape him.

"Lunarina!" he cried. "Adieu!"

And he gave the concave lens a kiss. The unfortunate fellow fell unconscious on the grass, which bore a strong resemblance to *Gramen saxicolum Alpense*.

The next day, Blifil was truly delirious. How pityingly he gazed at the sun! How dull it seemed, that sun which ripens the grapes of Constance!

"Oh, my dear uncle," he said, to the English governor, "I shall die if I don't marry Lunarina!" And the unfortunate fellow wept.

For his part, the governor said: "I don't know any damsel of that name at the Cape. She's and Italian, no doubt."

"Yes, an Italian who lives in the Ruby Coliseum."

"In Rome?"

"On the moon."

"Poor child!" said the worthy governor. "Constance wine has addled his brain."

That evening, Blifil took a set of dueling pistols, paper and quills, and climbed to the top of Table Mountain in order to be closer to his beloved. He was hampered by lions, but he reached the summit. There, he wrote this quatrain:

> *I have two mistresses at the Cape*
> *My love for both I've eschewn;*
> *I've come armed from ankle to nape*
> *To carry off a girl from the moon.*

He had prepared a rope-ladder, made with the *Scolopendra*[48] that closely resembles a liana and less so a fistful of wheat, *flagellum vitium.*[49] At that moment, the moon rose over the incommensurable horizon of the Indian Ocean. Then Blifil, who had cleverly stolen Herschel's telescope, placed it on its pivot and threw himself head first into the moon.

First he saw three insignificant districts pass by— Endymion, Cleomene and Langrenus. He stopped momentarily on the edge of the well of Galileo in order to

---

[48] *Scolopendra* is a genus of centipedes.

[49] Not the correct Latin term for a fistful of wheat; *flagellum* implies a possible unorthodox use for one, provided that the stalks are long enough.

cool his fiery blood somewhat. Having completed his journey he made contact with a few bat-men and a species of animal that resembled a kangaroo; he walked, involuntarily, through a valley where a multitude of nameless beings were fluttering around, which did not resemble anything at all. Only a few of them appeared to have any analogy with Earthly objects; there was a troop of bald heads walking on lizard's feet, and a quantity of pairs of black eyes linked by a connecting shaft, with pretty butterfly wings attached to the tear-duct. These eyes were fluttering around the heads, and appeared to be deriving a great deal of pleasure from the game.

Blifil soon tore his eyes away from those eyes. "Oh, Lunaria!" he cried. "Where are you?"

He searched every mountain and every valley; he parted the reeds that bordered the lakes; he descended into the depths of extinct craters. Orpheus did not put so much effort into searching for Eurydice. Finally, Morton saw the Ruby Coliseum in a fog, which was advancing toward him quite rapidly, borne by the movement of rotation.

When Blifil was no more than fifty paces from the Coliseum, his heart leapt so sharply that he nearly fell over. It was there that Lunaria lived! Oh, people who have truly been in love will comprehend Morton's ecstasy! He drank in the atmosphere of Lunarina, devoured the Coliseum, took the moon in his teeth, and was happy.

The ravishing maiden soon appeared, on her bed of grass. How beautiful she was! How much love, how much sensuality, how much perfume there was around that body, so supple and so graceful! Aphrodite emerging from the Ionian waves; Helen damp with the water of the Scamander; Nerea asleep in her coral palace; our first mistress at her first revelation—nothing equaled Lunaria, lying on the grass in the Ruby Coliseum. Morton dare not breathe, for fear that the slightest imprudence might alarm her and make her run away into the nearby forest, formed of bushy trees bearing a strong resemblance to the purslane *Hortolaia.*[50]

Alas, misfortune is always the sworn enemy of happiness on this earth! The amorous Blifil Morton savored those delights, and the improvident young man had no suspicion of the catastrophe that was about to fall upon him from the heavens.

"Oh, my God!" he cried, and his arms shivered, his hair stood on end and groaned in the breeze from Lion Mountain. "Oh, my God!"

He was unable to say any more.

What had he seen, poor fellow?

From an arcade of the Ruby Coliseum a figure six feet tall had just emerged, quite similar to Apollo in his Belvedere costume—but this figure was even more beautiful that Apollo's. Besides which, he was alive; he could walk; he could love. Blifil looked at him scornfully, but he did not appear to notice.

The Colisean figure leaned over the beautiful Lunaria. The young woman smiled and allowed herself to be looked at; it was easy to understand what the two lovers were saying.

The figure said: "You're more beautiful than the full earth when it rises at midday."

---

[50] The apparent generic name does not exist, and is seemingly incomprehensible,

Lunaria replied: "You're more beautiful than Madroglion. I want to live for you; I shall only cease to love you on the day when I'm inluned."[51]

The figure sat down beside Lunaria and threw his arms around her neck.

Blifil was dying; delirium disturbed his brain and a tempestuous jealousy distressed his heart. He yielded to a horrible inspiration, so true is it that love often counsels crime, even to the most virtuous! Blifil took a single-shot pistol from the side pocket of his jacket, took aim at his rival, and fired...

A thick cloud suddenly spread through the valley of the Coliseum. When it dissipated, Blifil could no longer see anything but the grass, softly hollowed out by the smooth impressions of Lunaria's body. Close at hand, he noticed a field of grass resembling saxifrage, *Saxifraga*, or cochineal, or vermilion. Blifil looked more closely. What he had mistaken at first for red plants was alas, blood!

At the same moment he saw a squadron of bats emerge from the Coliseum, which bore a striking resemblance to policemen.

At that sight, Blifil became anxious; the horror of his crime confused his thoughts; he saw the scaffold loom up before him.

"No, no!" he said, in a hoarse voice. "I'll prove that there was no premeditation. Great God, forgive me!"

He let himself fall on to the rock. The cool night air soothed his delirium; he went to sleep under the guard of

---

[51] The author inserts a footnote to suggest that Madroglion might be a planet unknown to us, and adds "interred" in brackets after "inluned" in the text, to emphasize the wordplay.

an old lion that he had previously encountered in his uncle's residence, and to which he had rendered liberty and a few services.

He had a dream, poor Morton—a dream that did not come from the ivory gate nor that of ebon horn; a dream such as has never been glimpsed from the pillows of earthly beds. To have a similar one it would be necessary to dream that one were dreaming, and to go to sleep after swallowing a concoction of verbena, poppies, nenuphar lilies, holly, grave-dirt, mandrake, poisonous orange, basil and opium.

In that dream, he inhabited the uninhabitable, a region where the bare feet flow over cotton-wool clouds, where the body is clad in light, where life is easy to carry, like the evening breeze that runs through one's hair after a summer bath in the gulf of Baia. He floated in the vicinity of suns; those stars were singing an unusual concert that relieved the tedium of God's eternity, a hymn that died away thirty million leagues from terrestrial eras. Blifil asked the names of the stars that passed before him, and they said, smiling:

"I am Ibis of the blue flame."

"I am one of the twenty-five thousand wheels of Eloa's chariot."[52]

"I am Immerio; I have opaline rays."

"I am Abrida, I sometimes disguise myself as a comet in the carnival of the Heavens."

---

[52] Eloa is the heroine of a narrative poem by Alfred de Vigny, in which the eponymous angel sets out to comfort Satan and is seduced by him. This might be a coincidence, as the other names cited are dubious in their significance, but the subsequent reference to Vigny suggests otherwise.

"I am Pieria, the ring-star of the little finger of Sabaoth."

"I am Bimmo, the diamond encrusted on the footstool on which God's heel rests."

Blifil saluted them with his hand, and his hand received radiance in exchange for the salute.

He heard a voice that said to him: "Blifil, sit down here," and the seven stars of the Great Bear, which are designed like an armchair, offered him their luminous back. He said down.

From a heavenly abyss, he then saw a cataract of young women flow, arm-in-arm with cherubim. Soon there was an immense ball, danced on a carpet of rosy clouds, with suns for chandeliers and the horizons of the infinity for limits. The invisible orchestra intoxicating that ball gave every note as many mysterious sounds as rise in the Gulf of Tissiau when the birds, the wind, the palm-trees and the waves perform their magnificent quartet for the solitary pleasures of the Southern Ocean.

The celestial bacchanal went on, spreading over the vermilion zones, and every time a cherub's kiss descended upon the forehead of a dancing girl, Blifil felt in his breast the frisson of a young bridegroom to whom the matron-of-honor has just said: "She's waiting for you!"

By degrees, a dark vapor descended from the depths of infinity; the rosy tints faded; the divine phantoms of the ball dissolved into smoke; the suns went out; Morton could no longer see anything but their cadavers, floating heavily at hazard, like spherical mountains of coal. The Great Bear, which had served as his armchair, withdrew, and he fell upon a thorny nopal stem.

He heard a lugubrious voice saying to him: "Where is Gremio's murderer?" He saw large hands groping, searching.

"There he is! There he is!" said a soft voice.

Morton recognized the beautiful Lunaria, radiant in the shadow, like a glow-worm. Beside Lunaria was a king's prosecutor, and Lady Jane Grey's executioner. The latter took hold of Morton and led him to a scaffold. The unfortunate placed his neck in the lunar crescent...

He woke up; the moon was still full.

Can you imagine the state that Morton was in when he awoke? Never had fever desolated a human brain as much. He had an old lion by his side; he had emerged from a ball beyond the stars; he had seen more women than all the seraglios of the Orient would ever see if God granted eternity to the empire and religion of Mohammed; he had been executed by Jane Grey's executioner; he had sat in the armchair of the Great Bear; he was a murderer; he had woken up two thousand fathoms above sea-level, no longer remembering the previous day; he was confused with the earth, the clouds and the sky.

At intervals, the memory of his crime shook him out of his lethargy; he dared not look at his hands, for fear of seeing them stained with Gremio's blood; Gremio's phantom rose up before him and he closed his eyes in order not to see.

It was in the midst of the anguish of this terrible crisis that Morton saw dawn break beneath his feet, in a river of the Black Land. What a day that dawn promised!

Blifil Morton could not consent to live at the Cape. He was seen again in Europe after ten years of insensate peregrinations in the former corners of the world. One day, in Nubia, he opened his travel notebook and saw that he had already covered three million five hundred thousand leagues (he had not yet become aware of kilometers). Blifil said to himself: "I've seen enough countries."

He left for England, where he arrived on the frigate *Coroner* on the first of April 1846, in the fishing season. Six weeks later, he married a blonde and pale-skinned quaker, a daughter of the sweet Kitty Bell whose stormy chastity was celebrated by Alfred de Vigny in a temperate prose drama.[53]

As prolific as all Englishmen, Blifil Morton has already has six children, all of whom have the same character, the same height, and dress in the same manner. He never lets a day go past without making this invariable recommendation:

"Children, never look through a telescope at the moon."

IV. Farewell to Lunarian Poetry

What beautiful names, and what invective, have poets and lovers not received? The star of the night, the star of silence, the star of meditation, Phoebe, Diana; Homer consecrated more verses to her than the number of times he had seen her; Virgil sang of her in a thousand ways. And paintings! The walls of Paris could be covered with all the moonrises and moonsets with which canvases have been blanched; they would cover the moon herself.

That is yet another poetry that has been banished; the moon is henceforth dishonored, since the discoveries of the scientist John Herschel.

---

[53] *Chatterton* (1835).

"This evening, I shall wait for you under the great oak, when the département of the moon is perpendicular to the département of the Seine."

On what discretion can they count now, when they think that the focusers of telescopes in the lunar regions are following them everywhere in their tender effusions?

There is more; if the husbands of the moon will correspond with the husbands of Earth by way of telescopes, with the aim of reciprocally revealing to one another the solitary excursions of their wives, adultery will become almost chimerical. The full moon will have avenged the crescent.

This is what one of the Lake poets wrote before the discoveries in the moon: "the two rays of Phoebe silver the dying foliage of sycamores; her pallor glides over sparkling networks of lakes." And the same poet wrote on the same theme this other phrase imposed by the recent observations of John Herschel, one of the moon's copy-editors: "The houses built of chalk, very numerous on the moon, are silvering with their reflections the dying foliage of Earthly sycamores; the glare of the lunar seas glides over the sparkling networks of lakes."

How can one invoke the moon, that sister of Apollo, when statistics have confirmed that it is composed of crimson mountains of silicious quartz, and plains covered with water-cress, and cities of three million sheep-like souls?

THE EXPLORATIONS OF
VICTOR HUMMER

I. In Egypt

In 1810 there was much talk in Munich of Victor Hummer, a young student newly emerged from the university. A few friends tried to drag him into a national association for the extermination of the French. Victor Hummer replied that he did not want to exterminate anyone, that his inclinations were devoted to science, and that he proposed to spend his entire life peacefully in his study in Munich, in order to raise a monument to his fatherland and the world. He spoke all languages ancient and modern.

Hummer had made a special study of history at the University. No one knew more than him about the causes of the grandeur and decadence of all empires. He knew Greek like Monsieur Gail[54] and read Xenophon like a veteran of the Ten Thousand. One day, he was asked unexpectedly to name the roman consul who flourished in the time of Alexander of Macedon. Without hesitation, he replied: "Papirius Cursor." The twenty quarto volumes of Catrou and Rouillé were consulted,[55] and the verity of the answer recognized.

---

[54] The French Hellenist Jean-Baptiste Gail (1755-1829)
[55] There are actually twenty-one volumes of François Catrou's *Histoire romaine* (1725-1737), annotated by Catrou's fellow Jesuit, P. Rouillé. The work is notorious for the pomposity of

Hummer isolated himself from society, dedicating himself body and soul to a translation of Herodotus. He held that historian in great esteem, and wanted to testify his affection in a solemn manner.

Hummer was not distracted from his task by all the noise of contemporary battles. A lover of antiquity, he had a sincere scorn for German and foreign soldiers, abhorred the shako and the white dress-uniform. Everything that was not a Macedonian phalanx was wretched in his eyes.

After ten years of work he had devoured his petty patrimony, but Herodotus was translated. He offered approximately a hundred kilograms of manuscript to the publishing house of Cotta[56] for ten thousand florins. The Leipzig publisher wrote him a charming letter and refused to print his translation. Hummer had studied philosophy for three years, and it served him well on this occasion. He recalled al the aphorisms of the sages regarding the vicissitudes of life, and kept his manuscript in order to savor its delights in the domestic hearth. He read fragments of it to his friends. After a year, he had no more friends; only Herodotus remained to him.

By virtue of rereading, his individuality melted into that of Herodotus; sometimes he thought he was Herodotus, and thought in Greek.

"What my work lacks," he said "is commentaries and footnotes; the publisher Cotta was right to point that out to me. It's necessary to complete the work. Let us commentate and footnote; I shall have a hundred editors

---

its style, and its English translation as *The Roman History* was harshly criticized.

[56] Johann Friedrich Cotta (1764-1832), a leading promoter of German Romanticism.

instead of one. If Germany lets me down, I shall go to Paris, and any publisher in the Palais-Royal will give me a hundred thousand francs for my translation. O Paris!"

He still had a small house worth four thousand florins. He sold it in order to compile his commentaries. "Happy are those who invest their money in posterity!" he said, as he accepted a letter of exchange drawn on the Maison Patré in Alexandria, in Egypt. Free of all care, he left for Egypt on the fifteenth of March 1822.

On arriving in Cairo, he was struck down by the plague, but, knowing that he must not die because the commentaries had not been written, he allowed himself to be tormented by the scourge and consulted no physician other than hazard. He lost an eye, however. "That's exactly what happened to Hannibal in the Etruscan marshes," he said. One can see that his character as a historian sustained him to the end.

Scarcely convalescent, he took German vellum paper, which is gray, and a Hungarian pencil, hired a camel and left the city by the Kalib Gate.

"Let's begin by examining Lake Moeris," he said. "Herodotus extended himself obligingly with respect to that lake. He saw the two pyramids that rise up in the middle of the lake; they were six hundred feet high, half of which was under water and half in the air. They were surmounted by two statues in gilded bronze, and lined on all four faces with beautiful polished marble extracted from the quarries of Mokatan."

Hummer addressed himself in Arabic to the fellahs drinking in the shade beneath the gate of Cairo, and asked them the way to Lake Moeris. The fellahs started at the stranger and did not reply.

"Well," said Hummer, "I'm addressing myself to stupid peasants; I'll easily find the lake without them.

Lake Moeris was eighty leagues in circumference, according to Herodotus, who saw it as I see my camel. One doesn't lose such a lake like a glass of water." And he urged his mount toward Mokatan.

The sun was shining directly over the head of Herodotus' commentator, but science does not stop at forty degrees Réaumur.[57] Hummer even thanked the sun, which he called Horus, for showing him the plain so clearly. The day was so bright that one could have spotted a sacred scarab within a distance of two leagues. That transparent clarity only served to prove to Hummer than he could not see anything at all.

After four hours journeying through the sands, he saw two pyramids appear in the direction of Sakkarah. All fatigue was forgotten.

"Those are the pyramids of Lake Moeris!" he exclaimed. "I recognize them—but it seems that the lake has dried up. No matter; I'll see its bed, a bed eighty leagues round! If I'm not mistaken, I believe I'll also discover the ruins of the Labyrinth. Oh, how many beautiful things I said about the Labyrinth in my work on Herodotus! The Labyrinth, I said, was a palace composed of a hundred palaces; it had been built by the architect Cramris, under a Basileos-Ptolomeus—I don't know which. That prodigious edifice, I added, occupied as much land as a city; it bathed in Lake Moeris like an Oriental king in a porphyry bath. O palace of palaces!"

As he finished this sentence he discovered the top of a third pyramid. The camel stopped.

---

[57] In the Réaumur scale of temperate the boiling point of water is eighty degrees and the freezing point zero.

"Three pyramids in Lake Moeris!" he said. "That's odd; I was only expecting two, and I thought I'd seen them. Perhaps that one's a shadow—forwards!"

As he went forward, he discovered fourteen of them.

"Fourteen pyramids in Lake Moeris, where there ought to be only two!" Hummer said. "That merits a particular commentary. Perhaps the alignment is causing me to make an arithmetical error; let's examine the phenomenon at closer range."

Having arrived at the feet of the pyramids of Sakkarah, he counted seventeen. They were not six hundred feet tall; they were pyramids of bricks. Sixty feet tall, and in very poor condition; they had probably been built unceremoniously to bury seventeen bankers from Memphis.

"This must be the small change of Herodotus' great pyramids," said Hummer. "Behold the demolishing genius of peoples! It destroys a palace to construct a hundred paltry houses! It destroys two pyramids to construct seventeen! Thus great things are extinguished. Behold, then, the two famous pyramids of which I spoke. How beautiful they must have been when there were only two! Let's write that commentary in my notebook."

Hummer cast a circular glance around the desert, and said to himself: "Behold the ruins of Lake Moeris. This really is our lake; it only lacks water. My descriptions are perfectly accurate. I'm in the middle of the lake, at the feet of these seventeen pyramids, and I only have the Labyrinth still to find."

He had spent a great deal of time in these explorations; dusk was falling rapidly. In searching for the Labyrinth he had gone astray.

After wandering for a long time in one direction and another, he discovered an Arab hut.

"Let's knock on that hospitable door," he said. "How gladly the child of the desert will take me in!"

He knocked three times; the hut was empty. Hummer lay down on the sand, making his camel into a four-poster bed with a roof.

The first ray of sunlight woke him with a start, as if a firebrand had burned his face. He made a fugal meal, and, orientating himself with the aid of a map and the sun, he established that he was not far away from Lake Natroun and the "waterless river."

"Herodotus mentioned Lake Natroun," he said. "It's an unimportant lake, but I'll be very glad to explore the waterless river, Anhydropotamus. Let's start with the lake; the river is close by."

Indeed, he found a mass of salt, firmly crystallized, extending over half a league. It was incontestably the lake. He took a specimen of it and wrote a commentary. Then he plunged into the desert, following a valley formed by small prolonged dunes. Hummer recognized that valley as the river-bed. There was not a drop of water, and the sand was warmed to eighty-five degrees.

Before going back to Cairo, he visited Arsinoe, now Faioun.[58] Herodotus called Arsinoe the Province of Roses; he had traveled through the province, always between to hedges of rose-bushes. Herodotus added that the perfume of Arsinoe reached all the way to Memphis.

---

[58] Arisonoe was previously known as Crocodilopolis, although Hummer is clearly unaware of the fact, as he later deems Crocodilopolis to have been lost. I have retained Méry's Frenchified spellings of Arabic words; his Faioun would nowadays be represented as Fayyum.

Hummer followed the direction of the perfume, his nose in the air; he found forests of nopals, which were exceedingly thorny, but no flowers; they were inhabited by green lizards. The German voyager understood that Herodotus' denomination was merely a profound allegory, and admired the Greek historian's common sense.

He returned to Cairo carrying precious documents, but with sunstroke.

"Now," he said, "encouraged by my first successes, I ought to extend my explorations to the Upper Egypt that Herodotus knew so well, and of which we have given such marvelous descriptions together."

Upper Egypt was, at that time, devastated by war. The Wechabites were in revolt against Mehmet Ali, and Ibrahim Bey was going up the Nile with an army to subdue them. It was necessary for Hummer to obtain a firman[59] from the Viceroy or wait for the rebels to surrender. Down to his last few piastres, Hummer resolved to ask for the firman. He went down the Nile to Alexandria, where he asked for an audience with the Viceroy.

When the scientist from Munich went into the palace, Mehmet Ali was smoking his eternal pipe, as painted from life by Horace Vernet in the charming picture in which the janissaries are being so horribly massacred. He was resting his feet on and old stuffed lion fashioned into a footstool. Hummer prostrated himself before the redoubtable footstool, and struck the floor three times

---

[59] In general terms, a royal mandate, but in this specific context, a permit to conduct scholarly research and carry out archaeological excavations. Mehmet Ali handed out a lot of them—far too many, according to critics of the manner in which European adventurers looted Egyptian antiquities on a massive scale.

with his broad forehead, which caused the grave Mehmet to laugh until he cried.

"Here's another one," said the Viceroy, who'll compare me to a serpent or a phoenix, to Pharaoh or Joseph in Egypt. Explain yourself without any preamble, my friend. What do you want?"

"Star of the Prophet's Heaven, Sun of the new Memphis, Scarab..."

"Enough of that—get to the point. What can I do for you?"

"I want to travel the sacred ground of your Estates and converse with the genius of dead nations..."

"Well, travel then, my friend, since it amuses you. They're all avid to take a walk in the desert, these people! And to see what? Stones, sand and lizards."

"I've written an ancient history of your Estates, O sublime Pasha, and am yearning to visit the lands I have described in such detail..."

"I don't understand, my friend. You say that you've described my country before having visited it..."

"Personally, I haven't visited it yet; but Herodotus, the father of historians, described your kingdom about two thousand years before the founding of your glorious dynasty, and..."

"This is taking too long; I've got a hundred audiences to grant. If we go back two thousand years, we'll never get finished today. Let's get things clear: you want to wallow in the sand; if that's your fantasy, go—I'll give you a firman. You're not the first Frank I've received. I've seen Belzoni, the tightrope-walker who opened the second pyramid, which was already open. I've seen Cailliaud, the goldsmith, who found the Oasis of Memnon, which doesn't exist. I've seen Rossignol, who proved that the Nile ought not to bed flowing where it flows; the Nile went its own way and didn't listen to him. I've seen Champollion, who explained the hieroglyphs my little brother buried under a stone after having painted them in Indian ink. I've seen Lord Elgin, who asked me for a pyramid to break up. Every day I'm harassed by that miserable desert, which brings me not an ounce of wheat or cotton. Well, take my colossi, my mummies, my pyramids, my sphinxes and my crocodiles, and leave me in peace! Go get your firman. May Allah preserve you from pleurisy and the jackals!"

Hummer, in his capacity as a German, admired the Pasha's pipe but deplored his ignorance. Armed with the firman, he shook the dust from his feet and launched forth into the desert.

He went up the Nile as far as the first cataract, contracting ophthalmia on the way. An Arab operated on him, restoring the clarity of the heavens to him. Hummer abandoned his skiff and obtained a camel and a guide to go and examine the famous cataract.

"I talked a great deal about the cataracts in my history," he said, "and everything I said must be true, like the rest—except, perhaps, for the Labyrinth. I have the Labyrinth on my conscience, unless it was another allegory making allusion to the hundred detours of that terrible desert, in which the simoom, a monster more terrible than the minotaur, devours stray voyagers. I'm ready to adopt that view. The Labyrinth is an allegory, like the roses of Arsinoe. As for my chapter on cataracts, I take it literally. The Nile isn't an allegorical entity; it descends from the Mountains of the Moon. It encounters precipices on the way; then it falls in cataracts, like Lake Erie and Lake Ontario, which collaborate in forming the deluge of Niagara.

"I've said, and I affirm it on my honor as a historian, that the cataracts of the Nile make such a racket that they deafen the unfortunate inhabitants of the locality; I've even mourned the inhabitants struck by endemic deafness in a touching manner. 'O unfortunate Africans,' I cried to myself, 'why do you not abandon those inhospitable ruins, where the eternal thunder of the cataracts of the Nile deprives your children of a precious sense at the dawn of their lives? Why not inhabit the tranquil oases that the Nile caresses and crowns with its placid waves?'

"When I arrive at the village of the deaf, I'll pin up those words, in the form of a proclamation, on the trunk of a palm-tree."

He continued his monologue, saying: "Cicero consecrated a beautiful page of *Scipio's Dream* to the same unfortunate inhabitants of the village of the cataracts. In the dialogue he established between Scipio Africanus and his nephew, the inventor of clepsydras, the former says, in speaking about the stars, that they make such a noise as they rotate on their axes that the inhabitants of the Earth are all deaf without being aware of it; and, in that respect, Scipio—who knew Africa, because he was African—cites his compatriots of the Nile, afflicted with deafness because of the cataracts…if I'm not mistaken, I believe I can hear them from here."

At the extremity of the horizon, Hummer perceived a clump of palm-trees isolated in the desert. It was the little oasis of the first cataract. He felt that he ought to take precautions against deafness, so he blocked his ears with wax, like Ulysses at the approach of the Sirens. Protected henceforth from the scourge, he accelerated the pace of his camel and defied the thunder of the Nile.

As he went forward, he searched the clouds for the summit of the mountain from which the Nile precipitates itself into the ears of the inhabitants. The desert and the bank were as uniform as a calm sea. The river ran over a slightly inclined surface strewn with little mossy stones; the murmur of the interrupted water was delightful to hear in the silence of the desert.

Hummer watched the water flowing, and then said to himself: "What a horrible din the Nile must generate in echoing from that bank! So I'm not surprised that the entire village has finally followed my advice and moved away. The cataract isn't falling from a great height, though. Let's pass on to the second one. The second one must be the rival of Niagara."

The scientist and his guide slept in abandoned huts after a light meal composed of dates and Nile water. Hummer could not sleep, because of the noise, which he could hear through the wax. At dawn, the indefatigable commentator was already up and about.

As he traveled in the direction of the second cataract, he testified to his regret at not having made an incursion into the ruins of Thebes, which barbarians call Karnak. "Of the colossi of Memnon," he said, "only one remains standing—which is to say, sitting. Those colossi, as I have proved, are monuments raised to the glory of the two Ozymandiases, who governed Thebes of the Hundred Gates nineteen hundred and forty-three years before the birth of Christ and three thousand seven hundred and twenty-four years before my own birth. Ozymandias the son has fallen face down, like the idol Dagon; Ozymandias the father has resisted. I've forgotten to pay him a little visit, but I shall. He's the colossus known to the world under the name of Memnon. At sunrise, he makes a harmonious sound like the sigh of a lyre. Herodotus heard that harmonious sound; Diocletian heard it; Hadrian heard it; we've all heard it.

"Diocletian, going to rejoin his army camped at the third cataract—but some distance away, because of the racket—paused in front of the colossus and spent the night at its feet, waiting for dawn. The illustrious emperor was pleasantly surprised to hear, at about four o'clock in the morning, a delightful melody that incontestably emerged from the pink granite lips of the colossus Memnon; and, to testify his satisfaction to Ozymandias, he took his stylet and inscribed these words on the pedestal: 'I, Diocletian, son of Diocles, have heard the song of Memnon.' And he signed it.

"The prefect Mutius, commander of the tenth legion, provided a similar certificate. Hadrian, when he was building Antinoe, often went to Thebes, and always found further pleasure in hearing the matinal song of Memnon. His favorite, the beautiful Antinous, knew the tune by heart, and sang it at table when prayers were said there. Those are so many reasons for me to spend at least one dawn in the company of harmonious Ozymandias, and to add my signature to that of Herodotus, in order that there should be no lacuna in the works of antiquity."

After this monologue, the addressed himself to his guide. The latter was a young Arab of twenty-five, with a gaze full of intelligence and fire; he was reputed to be a very well-informed guide.

"My friend, do you known the colossi of Ozymandias?"

"No, Master, but I know all the others."

"Have you heard mention of the colossi of Memnon?"

"No, Master, but I've heard mention of all the others."

"Do you know the city of Thebes?"

"No, Master."

"See how ignorance is desolating this unhappy land! But you know Karnak?"

"Ah! Karnak, yes. There are hills and ruins; I've killed waterfowl there."

"Have you heard mention of a stone statue that salutes the sun by singing?"

"Yes."

"Ah! There we are! Where is that statue?"

"In the Yellow River, in the kingdom of the great Brededin-Assem, which has mountains of gold."

"Go take a walk," said the scientist. "One might as well talk to the sphinx as to these Oriental fools."

While chatting thus they arrived at the second cataract, which flowed as tranquilly as the first; two crocodiles were asleep on a bed of moss between the two principal currents of the cataract. "Those animals are deaf," said Hummer, "but let's go on, lest we wake them up."

The third cataract resembled the other two, and offered the voyager no new incident but a graceful family of ibises, asleep with their beaks beneath their wings on a little green rock that divided the waters. Hummer set his ears free, and embarked on a skiff for Dongola.

As they sailed upriver he said: "My expedition to the three cataracts will be a great help to science. To begin with, I've established the existence of the cataracts—an essential point. Secondly, I've recognized that the advice we had given to the inhabitants has been rigorously followed, since I've only encountered deaf crocodiles and ibises. The only objections that can be raised relate to the height of the cataracts, but they're not serious. The falls have a height of two thousand fathoms, although they seem horizontal to the casual observer. In physics and hydrology, one calculates the height of waterfalls with reference to the mountains that serve as their reservoir. Now, the Mountains of the Moon being the cradle of the cataracts, these cataracts have a drop of two thousand fathoms. Niagara is a dwarf. Everything we wrote in that chapter, and everything Scipio Africanus dreamed, is in conformity with the truth. Now it only remains for me to make one last observation, the most important one. I want to visit the peninsula of Meroë."[60]

On arriving at Dongola, Hummer had a truly scientific emaciation, and his guide, who was also his doctor, advised him to get some rest and drink camel's milk.

"Get some rest!" cried the heroic Hummer, "When Meroë is reaching out to me with the arms of its peninsula, when I can see on the horizon the cradle of the illustrious gymnosophists whom Herodotus admired so much! To the camels right away, and to Meroë! Where is Meroë?"

The guide repeated "Meroë?" while gazing at the sand and the sky.

---

[60] The city of Meroë was in the Sudan, north-east of Khartoum; it was once the capital of Kush. The site of the city, notable for the presence of more than two hundred small pyramids, was discovered in 1821 by Frédéric Cailliaud, whose description of the ruins in *Voyage a Méroé* (1823-7) Méry had presumably read, although he misrendered the name as "Caillard" in Mehmet Ali's speech above (where I have corrected it) and called him a "goldsmith," although he was actually a mineralogist and naturalist. Hummer seems to have no knowledge of that discovery, even though he set forth on his journey in 1822.

"What!" said Hummer. "You call yourself a guide and you don't know how to take me to Meroë, the cradle of the gymnosophists,[61] where Herodotus lived for three years!"

The guide remained mute.

"Well, let's go on. What do you call this desert?"

"The Sennaar."

"So this is the Sennaar? Forwards! Meroë isn't far."

"You want to go across the Sennaar, Master?"

"Why not? Am I the first? Cambyses crossed it at the head of four hundred and thirty-two thousand infantrymen and twenty-seven thousand horses, as I've said. It's true they all asphyxiated out there, in a valley that leads to Ethiopia, but I'm not going to have anything to do with that valley—it's sufficient for me to know that it exists."

"It doesn't exist, Master."

"The valley doesn't exist?"

"No, Master."

"Ah! You think you know better than Herodotus! Cambyses didn't choke to death in a valley that links Nubia to Ethiopia?"

"Master, it's possible that Cambyes choked…"

"What! Cambyses wasn't choked…?"

"He was if you want, but not in that valley."

"The bones of Persians were found in the sand."

"One finds bones everywhere in the sand."

"Of Persians?"

---

[61] The Greek writer Plutarch appears to have coined the term gymnosophist [naked philosopher] to describe a group of men taken captive in the Punjab by Alexander the Great. One of Hummer's other sources, Strabo, also locates them in India. I cannot find any evidence that Herodotus used the term.

"Of Persians, giraffes, ostriches, jackals..."

"That's all right, my friend, that's all right. Are you going to come with me or not?"

"No, Master."

"I'll go to Meroë on my own, then. I know the country better than you do. Goodbye."

Hummer took up his mathematical instruments and established that he had reached the nineteenth degree of north latitude and the forty-eighth degree of longitude, based on the Île de Fer meridian.[62] Traveling by night under the stars, and sleeping by day, relying on the proverbial hospitality of the Arabs, he crossed the Sennaar Desert alone and found the Nile again.

"Good," said Hummer. "There's my river, and I have Meroë within my grasp. The Nile, after having received the Tacazze, bends back on itself and forms the peninsula of Meroë. I can see a caravan that's probably heading for Meroë; I need to question its leader."

Hummer approached the leader of the caravan and said: "May the light of the Prophet be with you and guide your brothers through the desert."

The other was an old man entirely clad in white, beard and hair included. "Has my brother been led astray in this wilderness by the evil spirit of the desert?" he asked.

---

[62] The island of El Hierro [Île de Fer in French] in the Canaries was used as a longitudinal reference point on many ancient maps because it was then considered to be the westernmost point if the Old World. It was considered (inaccurately) to be exactly twenty degrees west of the Paris meridian, the other reference point considered standard in France.

"I'm looking for Meroë, the cradle of the gymnoso-phists and the terrestrial paradise of Nubia, Can you point me in the right direction?"

"For sixty years, my son, I've been crossing the Sennaar, and I've never heard mention of Meroë. Last year, I sold an Abyssinian woman of that name to his lordship Ibrahim Bey."

"Do you believe, my father, that the Nile turns back upon itself in this direction."

"It's possible that it bends back out there, toward the east. That's not on the caravan route."

"My father, may the Prophet protect you from the ambushes of the crocodile, and give you fresh water in the middle of the day!"

Hummer turned away from the caravan, saying: "Have such idiots ever been seen? When I get back to Munich I'll write a fulminating note about these stupid people who don't know their own land. Shade of Herod-otus, guide my camel!"

Full of confidence in this invocation, he resolved to go along the Nile as far as the Tacazze. There was no lack of water and fresh dates, and that was sufficient for him. Every morning, at dawn, he cast a rapid glance over the desert, his gaze following the eternal Nile, which descended into abysses on the horizon, exhaling a gray mist.

On the two banks, the white desert extended as far as the eye could see, allowing a few nopal bushes to be glimpsed at intervals, or a clump of sterile and agonized palm trees. The sun only allowed itself to be glimpsed through a atmosphere heavy with floating sand, each grain of which as a spark; one could not smell, see or breathe anything but fire.

In order to refresh his burning head, Hummer had recourse to his scientific monologues, and said to himself: "The Earth must have been subjected to a cataclysm since Herodotus, and this climate has certainly changed, for its proven that we saw two thousand cities here—two thousand, neither more nor less; Herodotus saw them, and, in consequence, so have I. Egypt was then, as Herodotus said, one long street traversed by a gutter. The street was the two thousand cities, the gutter was the Nile. To be sure, some of these cities still remain—seven or eight, in ruins—but what has become of the rest?

"It's here that a commentary is indispensable, and yet a schoolboy could make it. What has become of them, these cities? Dare you ask, O frivolous voyager? There they are, there they are, everywhere, in front of you, beside you, beneath your feet, in your sandals, in your hair, under your eyelids! Those cities were dust, like us; they have returned to dust; time has ground them down like grains of barley in a mortar. Look how many cities it requires to make a desert of sand! Two thousand. O Herodotus, your pen was never anything but the conduit of the truth."

Hummer paraded his melancholy gaze over all those cities changed into sand, and contemplated in the emptiness the temples, the palaces, the pylons and the galleries that stood on both sides of the river, making a monumental border of granite for its waters.

The beautiful spectacle delighted Hummer; he leapt for joy on his camel. Meanwhile, the heat of the day rose to its homicidal maximum; the Nile was fuming like a thermal spring; the sand was radiant with fire, like Archimedes' mirror; the ibises were roasting in mid-flight; Hummer's brain as boiling in his skull.

An incendiary zephyr gripped the voyager; one might have thought that the sun was rolling through space in fusion, or that aerial lava was descending from a celestial volcano.

"How sweet it is," said the scientist, "to breathe in the shade of those sycamores that one grew, like plumes on the temples of that city! Hail, Crocodilopolis, superb city where the holy reptile was adored! You have no rival among your two thousand sisters but the city of Hermes, Hermopolis, because divine Hermopolis has the most beautiful of porticos, a portico whose ceiling is azured like the sky, and starred with gold by night. The barbarians call you Achmounain today, O city of Hermes—and you, Crocodilopolis, they do not name at all; they say that the Nile has washed away the last of your foundations! Oh, the sacred river does not devour his daughters! He waters them, he caresses them, he fills their thousand porphyry baths, in order that they may bathe their beautiful bodies, polished like ebony or the bosom of the virgin of Meroë!

"How powerful they were, the hands of the people who tore those two thousand cities from the quarries of the Libyan mountains and sowed them thus, graceful and strong, from Gondar to Memphis! I can only admire that infinite succession of temples so profoundly rooted; those pylons flaring from their bases; those obelisks lavished like seamstresses' needles over the mosaic of the gynaeceum; those colossal mountains sculpted in place; those galleries running along the Nile, like avenues of palm-trees, where the virgins of Isis and Osiris stroll; those pyramids which present one face to the sun and offer a triple shadow to the pilgrims of the caravans; those palaces in which kings and sager converse; those hostelries where the mages of the Orient stayed; those caravanserais blossoming at the city gates to give the joy of hospitality to the indigent voyager!

Who could count so many marvels? What eye could be patient enough to read all of that symbolic history, written in a mysterious alphabet on pages of granite: an inexhaustible arabesque, always sealed with the azure scarab, the image of the infinite King who holds the world in his fingers? Count those hieroglyphs? Rather count the atoms of sand that compose this desert, or the drops of water that the Nile holds in reserve in the Abyssinian mountains."

Hummer fell silent in the ecstasy of his contemplation. He could not tear his eyes away from that magnificent spectacle of Egyptian nothingness. He was then at the fifth degree of north latitude and the fifty-fifth of longitude. "Oh!" he cried. "I can breathe! Meroë! The Nile is flowing eastwards! To me, Meroë!"

This new region was frightful in its solitude; one could easily believe that one were traversing, before any other voyager, one of those zones of the African interior where no human foot has ever left an imprint.

Meroë has no road indicated by milestones; it is necessary to make one's way there by instinct here; it is a pearl for which one searches in the sand and the immensity; only a German could discover it.

At five o'clock in the evening, the scholar found himself in the open sand, as one finds oneself in the open sea; a perfectly circular horizon extended around him, and everywhere, at those infinite distances where the desert melts into the molten azure of the sky, he perceived, as the sun began to set, the black milestones that mark out the road to Abyssinia for caravans.

That wilderness is saddened by the uncanny silence that reigns in the vicinity of clouds, and makes such an impact on travelers in an aerostat. Hummer recognized by all these indications the proximity of Meroë; his camel was giving signs of joy, as if it had divined the terminus of the voyage.

As the sun descended into the red clouds and crevices of the western horizon, the entire sky exhaled the vapors of the day to the east. The atmosphere resumed its transparency and permitted the gaze to distinguish objects in a distance resplendent with a serene purity. Hummer was like a voyager who is dying from hunger and seeks in the air the providential bell-tower that promises him a hostelry; by dint of interrogating the horizon he perceived a dark dot surging from the hillocks of sand. It was not an illusion.

The dot became pyramidal; Hummer descended into a valley and, on scaling the opposite dune, made out a collection of pyramids that stood out like a field of snow. The camel was breathing the air with a violent agitation of its nostrils, and began to run at top speed, like an Arab stallion.

Hummer wept with joy. Like Adam, he was witnessing the creation of a world. Antiquity was revealing itself to him in the inaccessible and unknown wilderness. Meroë, that noble daughter of Isis and Osiris, abandoned like Ariadne, had rediscovered a worshiper.

"How many centuries have gone by," said Hummer, "since she surrendered herself thus to the sole caresses of the sun. No one, before me, has dared to lift up the funereal shroud that covers her—the shroud of the desert!"

And the voyager leaned toward the adored image like a lover, and he threw the name of the holy city into the air. The cry expired without any echo in the immense plain; nothing but the great Nile could be heard babbling in the desert.

"Forty pyramids!" Hummer shouted.

And he raced his camel over the sand. He kissed that august sand; he contemplated, in that rapture, the first traces of his feet, which were finally opening a furrow in that ocean of dust. He paused to lend an ear to the applause of invisible beings, supernatural witnesses to his heroic courage. Sometimes, he thought he glimpsed the shade of Herodotus seated and draped in a shroud, at the foot of a pyramid. It was an old palm-tree devoid of leaves, which the last simoom had blanched with sand; pale sycamores, inclined and lifted by the wind, appeared to him as a group of gymnosophists excited by discussion and seeking wisdom collectively.

Hummer stopped in front of the forty gigantic tombs, build in quincunxes and quite well preserved. Around them, the ground was strewn with ruins, heaped up as at Thebes. The voyager was searching for a place to sit down and contemplate these marvels at his ease when, on going around a pyramid, he saw a four-wheeled berlin in the English style.

Robison Crusoe perceiving a human footprint on his island was less terrified than the scientist Hummer before that berlin. At first he considered it for a long time with fearful eyes, then drew nearer to it on tiptoe, and startled two ostriches entrenched in an aloe bush.

Hummer recognized at first glance that the berlin was not ancient; he circled around it, admiring the work of a carriage-maker far superior to the industrial genius of the gymnosophists. A copper plate fixed under the seat bore the inscription: MILNE. EDGWARE ROAD, LONDON.

Hummer crossed his hands and raised them above his head, like an adept uttering a cry of distress. Momentarily, he thought that ophthalmia might have extinguished his sight for a second time, and that what he saw was a blind man's dream.

"An English berlin in Meroë!" he said. "Milne, London!"

After a long pause, he made a decision. "Let's go on," he said. "Perhaps I'll find the horses."

Indeed, twenty paces further on, he discovered two beautiful black horses, which were eating oats from an ancient basalt bath. The oats were modern. The horses looked at Hummer, and were not astonished.

"Is it Herodotus who, touched by my fatigue, has sent me this magnificent present?" He said, raising his eyes to the heavens.

That idea pleased him, and he was amusing himself by caressing it when a third surprise nailed him to the spot beside the pedestal of a sphinx that he had been about to step over.

He had seen three elegantly-dressed Europeans sitting on the eastern side of a pyramid. Two of the gentlemen were playing chess; the third was reading a pyramidal newspaper. A little further away, two ladies dressed in white were walking under their parasols; a third was sitting to one side, embroidering a tapestry in a melancholy fashion. Hummer could not suppress an exclamation of surprise, which ricocheted from the pyramids in forty echoes. At that cry, the European reading the newspaper got to his feet; the other two remained hunched over the chessboard.

No longer being able to remain incognito, Hummer marched courageously in pursuit of his cry and extended his hand to the stranger, who also came toward him, laughing.

"I'm sorry to have disturbed you," Hummer said, in German. "Excuse me for having troubled you in your solitude."

The reply he received, in English and German, told him that the region belonged to everyone, and that anyone was free to walk there. Hummer was introduced to the chess-players and the three ladies and invited to dinner—an invitation that he accepted gladly.

The Englishman with the newspaper struck up a conversation with Hummer to fill in time while they waited for dinner.

"Have you come here alone, sir?" the Englishman asked.

"Alone, with my camel."

"You're doubtless making a scientific voyage?"

"Yes, sir. I'm visiting the region in order to complete my commentary on Herodotus."

"Ah! I'll reserve a copy of it. Here's my address: John Mawbrick, Regent Circus, London."

"I'll send it to you from Munich—count on it. Are you and your family making a scientific journey?"

"No, it's a pleasure trip; we've already been here for a week."

"In Meroë?"

"You call this Mereoe? We've named this place Mawbrick Town."

"Has it been a long time since you left London?"

"No—five years."

"You must have seen many countries in five years!"

"Not that many. We rived at the Cape of God Hope, where we have vineyards; one must look after one's property. On our return from the Cape, via Paris, we made a little detour to Egypt to amuse the ladies—my wife and my two beautiful sisters-in-law; you're looking at the three Mawbrick brothers. In stages, we came this far. Our guide promised us a simoom at the new moon, and we're waiting for it. One can't leave Egypt without having seen a simoom."

"You're right. Have you encountered any traces of the sect of gymnosophists here?"

"We've found a lot of mummies—these pyramids are full of them."

"Mummies of gymnosophists?"

"Oh, they're not signed; they're anonymous mummies."

"Can one take them away?"

"You can do what you like with them. In that other carriage over there we have the famous pharmacist-chemist Fallon White of the Strand with us. He's packed a supply of mummies in his trunks."

"For the National Gallery at Charing Cross?"[63]

"No, to make family remedies: mummies mixed with essence of rhubarb make a sovereign digestive aid; that's well-known."

"A digestive aid with mummies!" cried Hummer, taking three steps back. "A digestive aid with the ashes of gymnosophists! Is nothing sacred to pharmacists?"

"What do you expect? It's the fashion. White has patented his discovery; he's already come here four times to choose his merchandise personally; his agents cheat him, sending him mummies of janissaries fabricated at Boulaq by an Italian. The head of a company ought to come to the place. From London to this pyramid is

---

[63] Méry had visited London, and knew the difference between the National Gallery (in Trafalgar Square) and the British Museum (in Bloomsbury) well enough, but Hummer clearly has not.

only a little further than from Regent Circus to Richmond. Our globe is very small. Shall we go to dinner? The table's laid between these two sphinxes."

Hummer brought to dinner a face upset by surprise and indignation. He bowed to his fellow guests and sat down at the place indicated to him. John Mawbrick said: "Excuse the ladies, Mr. Hummer; they're tidying themselves up a bit, having been in traveling costume."

John was the only English conversationalist in the party, travel having Gallicized him. His two brothers were still meditating the king's gambit, and had deposited two pawns on their plates, which they were pushing with their knives. Two domestics in full livery brought the dishes. The places had been set on a large slab of pink granite posted on the corners of four sphinxes.

"We're giving you an informal dinner, Mr. Hummer," said John Mawbrick. "In the country, as in the country. Would you like to begin with these fillets of beef in Madeira, or these roe-deer supremes?"

Hummer cast a fearful glance over these mysterious foodstuffs and refused, in spite of his appetite, which was speaking to him imperiously. He thought he could see fillets of gymnosophists; it seemed to him that Herodotus himself was being offered to him under the pseudonym of roe-deer.

"Sir," he said to the Englishman. "Permit me to ask you where your provisions come from?"

"Chevet, in the Palais-Royal in Paris; they're conserves that we bought when passing through. It dispenses with the difficulties of cooking while traveling. Ah! Here are the ladies!"

The ladies were in evening dress. They sat down on folding chairs, took off their mittens, bowing graciously to the guests, and were served claret in beautiful glasses of Bohemian crystal.

"And here's our chemist," said John Mawbrick. "Always late, Mr. White!"

The chemist asked for water in order to wash his hands; a domestic brought him a silver ewer.

"From what horrible mysteries is he emerging?" Hummer murmured.

Fallon White was an Englishman about sixty years old; his face was pink, symmetrical and commonplace. He was bald, like all London pharmacists.

"Mr. White," said John Mawbrick, serving him roe-venison, "we have a new guest, Mr. Hummer of Munich, who is honoring us with a short visit."

Hummer and Mr. White bowed to one another.

"Is it curiosity that brings you here?" asked White.

"Yes, sir, for the sake of science."

"There's nothing much to see, as you can see. When you've gone past these forty bats' nests you can say goodbye to the company—it's a matter of forty minutes."

"Has your work gone well today, White?" asked Mawbrick.

"I've started on the second well, but the merchandise there is damaged. Of forty-eight subjects I've unwrapped, I've only found two of commercial quality. I'll start on the third well tomorrow."

"Infamous," whispered Hummer.

"It's necessary to make haste to exploit this old junk," the pharmacist went on. "Colleagues will soon be arriving, and I don't want to leave them anything but the rubbish. I'm quite content with the two subjects I butchered this morning; they must have been very distinguished individuals of the epoch. They were under glass, and embalmed with aloes and bitumen of the finest quality."

"Under glass, did you say, sir?" cried Hummer.

"Yes, under glass. Does that astonish you? I've found a hundred like that."

"They're gymnosophists! Only the gymnosophists were embalmed under glass. They're gymnosophists! Ah!"

"Well, what difference would it make if they were Tories?"

"Did you find scarabs in the cases?"

"Green ones."

"Green ones! That's it—the sacred scarab! There are no more of them in Egypt. Only Meroë has retained the scarab. You've seen these green scarabs, then?"

"I ate some of them this morning."

"Shocking!" cried one of the ladies, melodiously. "Can't these gentlemen find another topic of conversation for the table?"

This censure put a stop to the dialogue. The meal became silent. Hummer had crossed his hands and was meditating profoundly. At dessert, he was allowed to leave.

Having attended to his camel, Hummel explored the ruins of Meroë. Nightfall took him by surprise; from the abysms of the desert the moon rose, large and red, giving the ruins a desolate tint. The voyager felt his heart constrict on seeing, at every step, the recent sacrilegious violations of the tombs.

"What horror!" he said. "Who says that the sanctity of the sepulcher lapses after a time, that what is sacrilege after a century becomes licit after a thousand years? O morality! You are no longer anything but a name! The Elysium of the gymnosophists is now a pharmacist's shop! Holy and virginal Meroë, you are delivered into the claws of barbarians! Cambyses is vanquished by the English! What a commentary I'm preparing on these profanations!"

He fell silent in order to listen to mysterious noises that were passing through the air, and thought that he could hear the shades of the gymnosophists, who were demanding vengeance and complaining about entering as aperitif elements into the pharmaceutical composition of anti-indigestion powder.

John Mawbrick emerged from a pyramid in a brocade dressing-gown and accosted Hummer cheerfully.

"I've had your apartment made up," he said. "39 Pyramid Street, on the entresol. I'm next door. My servant has been to fetch you a feather-bed from the boat. Would you like a cup of tea?"

Hummer made a gesture of negativity full of nonchalance and melancholy.

John Mawbrick continued: "We're expecting the Sappleton family this evening, by way of the Nile; they've been spending the season in Dongola—a charming family! They're paying us a short visit; we'll be dancing. My God, one has to kill the time somehow, eh?"

"You're dancing in Meroë!" said Hummer, in a tone of consternation.

"Why not? Since we'll have eight ladies and a violin, and a charming ballroom in pyramid number 7. I'm on my way to the boat now to choose a few fabrics from our floating store to hang up. Our whole Regent Circus house is traveling with us, as you can see. See you later."

Hummer made a firm decision. "If I stayed here," he said, clenching his fists, "I'd be the accomplice of these frightful profanations. My camel has had enough rest and nourishment for ten days; me, I'm proof against anything. Let's go; let's flee this Meroë, so despicably violated! They're demons, these English! They install themselves everywhere as if they were at home; they number the pyramids; they call Meroë Mawbrick Town; they purge themselves with gymnosophists; they dance on the tombs; they mock Herodotus, God and me! Let's go denounce these sins to Europe. Let's go!"

As he crossed Pyramid Street to go to his camel Hummer perceived the other two Englishmen, who were putting on their evening suits in front of a mirror suspended from the neck of a sphinx, between two chandeliers with diaphanous candles. The ladies were taking tea behind a windbreak.

"Oh, if only the heavens of Meroë had a single thunderbolt in their arsenal," said Hummer, "I'd pay with my life to see it fall on these Cambyses in white gloves."

Under cover of darkness, however, he gathered up some debris of Chevet roe-venison and beef filet. To soothe his conscience, he said: "I'm following the example of the Hebrews, *in exitu Aegypto, de populo barbaro*.[64] They took vegetables; I'm taking meat. God will forgive me."

He mounted his camel again and plunged into the desert illuminated by the moon, that mild sun of Egyptian travelers.

As he made his way over the sand and on the Nile, Hummer shut his eyes to everything he saw. One sole

---

[64] Derived from a Psalm numbered 114 in the King James Bible: *In exitu Israel de Aegypto, domus Iacob de populo* [When Israel went out of Egypt, the house of Jacob from a people of strange language...]

and constant thought absorbed him: the sacrilege of Meroë. By night, it gave him frightful dreams; he saw Herodotus weeping into a chemist's alembic, and Fallon White butchering a gymnosophist and suspending the blackened pieces from Chevet's display-shelves. Oh, how he regretted being cured of his ophthalmia!

"What use are eyes, then?" he said, and looked into the sun, like an eagle, in order to restore his blindness— but his eyelids closed again.

It was not until his departure from Alexandria that he started work on his commentaries. By the time he arrived at Genoa he had written two volumes; at the customs-post the Sardinian police confiscated them, because certain passages raised doubts regarding the infallibility of the Bible.

"I'll write them for a second time in Munich," he said, "with a new commentary on the Genoese police." On hearing which, two policemen took him to prison.

After two months of captivity, he was allowed to return to Germany. Having returned to Munich, he wrote his commentaries and, once the work was done, offered his new manuscript successively to all the publishers in Europe. He received letters from all of them, congratulating him on his fine work but refusing to print it because Herodotus was getting a bit old.

Hummer has given his manuscript to the Munich Library, where anyone may consult it. It is a work that proves, along with a hundred others, that history has been written by fabulists, and fables by historians.

II. In Gaul

In 1828, the King of Bavaria[65] requested a private audience with Victor Hummel, and was granted one.

"Sir," the king said to him, "you know how interested I am in ancient history, since I continue it in the person of my son, the King of Greece and the successor of Leonidas. I've heard about your courageous explorations in Africa and I want to reward them; it is high time that your precious manuscript, buried in the Munich Library, was brought into the light by way of printing. I'll buy your translation of Herodotus for fifty thousand florins and declare myself your publisher."

Victor Hummer threw himself at the king's feet and struck the floor three times with his head, in the Persian manner.

"Believe, Sire," he said, "that I shall employ the money I receive from you in the service of science. With that sum, the world belongs to me, and I shall translate Strabo.

"That's good," said the king, with a charming laconism.

The king shook the scientist's hand, and left like a simple commoner.

Victor Hummer found himself in possession of a letter of exchange drawn on Herr Reighanum of Frankfurt, a fantastic banker who built castles in Spain for Germans. However, an honest broker in Munich accepted the letter of exchange at a fifty per cent discount, in order to honor the endorsement of the Bavarian finance minister. In the eyes of a scientist, nothing resembles fifty thousand florins more closely than twenty-five

---

[65] Ludwig I (not the mad one).

thousand; fundamentally, it is the same thing for someone who has nothing.

Hummer threw himself head first into Strabo's folio; he reduced himself to a skeletal state and became diaphanous, but completed his task. The venerable scientist, eaten away by late nights, was no longer anything but an illusion, who vanished from the public squares of Munich at the slightest breath of wind. When he looked at himself in a mirror he could not see anything—but what does the absence of the body matter, if the soul remains? Knowledge only comes at that price.

Hummer's soul, clad in a light twill frock-coat, left to explore Gaul in the spring of 1828. It only paid half-price for the interior of the diligence; there were seven passengers in perfect comfort, including Hummer.

On the route to Marseilles, that queen of Gaul, Hummer said: "I'm going to see the ancient city, founded six whole centuries before Christ, a city contemporary with the Tarquins, which Strabo loved most of all the Gallic cities."

So saying, he booked a room at the Croix-de-Malte, on the Cours.

The next day, when he woke up, he was in a quandary.

"I don't know where to begin my excursions," he said. "I have to choose between the temple of Neptune, the temple of Delphian Apollo, the temple of Diana of Ephesus, the temple of Lacinian Juno, the temple of Venus Victrix, plus the Lacidum, the Necropolis Paradisius, the castle of Julius Caesar, the house of Milo, the thermal baths, the Julian Gate and a host of other antiquities, some of which are modern, like the famous tower that sustained the siege of the Constable of Bourbon in 1539, and the beautiful Gothic church of Las

Accoas, mentioned by Papon and Grosson, who wrote continuations of Strabo."

He called the hotel's bellboy and said: "Which is the nearest temple to here?"

"Saint Martin's," the bellboy replied.

"Good!" said Hummer. "It's the same here as in Rome, where Catholicism has inherited paganism. What was Saint Martin's called in antiquity?"

"I don't know, sir. If you want to see it, go along the street and turn left at the end."

"That's all right, my lad. You aren't educated."

Hummer set off toward Saint Martin's, and saw a rather ugly church, very dingy and dirty, and not ancient at all.

"My friend," he said to the sacristan, who was passing by, "can you give me some archaeological information regarding...?"

The sacristan turned his back on him abruptly. Hummer went out, to wander at random in search of ruins.

He saw magnificent streets, opulent neighborhoods, picturesque and animated people—a city larger, more beautiful and more cheerful than Munich—but none of that made any impression on him. He had a horror of the modern; he was in search of *Massilia civitas*, not the city of Marseilles. He was in search of ruins, but could see nothing but architects building edifices. The architect is the born enemy of the antiquary; he demolishes ruins and makes use of the ancient to make the new.

As he crossed a street as broad as Dublin's Sackville Street he saw a map of Marseilles in the window display of the bookshop of Joseph Chardon, the author of the *Guide Marseillais*.

"That's what I need," he said. "Let's go in."

Monsieur Chardon regards Marseilles as his own daughter; sixty years before, he had appointed himself the historiographer of the daughter of Phocea. On the first of January every year he publishes a very elegant summary of the progress of Marseilles, ornamenting the work of serious statistics with a host of moral reflections addressed to women and young people.

"Monsieur," Hummer said to him, "you have written about Marseilles, if I can believe your sign. Would you be kind enough to identify the most remarkable localities to visit, and sell me copies of your map and your *Précis*."

Monsieur Chardon paid homage to Hummer's works by referring to him as "my colleague," and offered to accompany him in his explorations. Hummer thanked him profusely, and took out his notebook, either to sketch the imposing ruins he was about to see, or to make notes in pencil.

"Let's begin with the nearest," said M. Chardon. "This is the Rue Saint-Ferréol. What do you think of it?"

"Very nice," said Hummer. As straight as an I."

"How do you like this square, with its chestnut-trees?"

"A lovely square, but I don't like chestnut-trees."

"Would you believe, Monsieur, that there was a superb church here?"

"An ancient church—a basilica? Is it possible, Monsieur?"

"Not a single stone of it remains, as you can see."

"That's true; there are chestnut-trees. That's very curious. Damn! People don't destroy things by halves here. Let's pass on to another curiosity."

"Now I'm going to show you the Necropolis Paradisius. I talk about it in my book."

"So do I, in my Strabo. Permit me to prepare a sheet of paper in order to make a sketch of the famous Paradisius."

"There it is," said M. Chardon. "The cemetery no longer exists, but it would have existed if that street you can see hadn't been built, which is rightly called the Rue Paradis.

"That's all right. Let's pass on to another marvel; the cemetery is well and truly buried."

"This road that you see leads to the famous mountain immortalized by Lucan."

"What!" cried Hummer. "It's the road to the *Silva Sacra*?: 'That forest sacred throughout human times, and at all times revered.' The forest in which the druids made human sacrifices, and where Trebonius, Caesar's lieutenant, cut down enormous oaks for the galleys of his fleet, the shade of which covered the marble temple of Sidonian Neptune? Oh, let's run!"

"The forest would still exist, if humans and time hadn't destroyed it..."

"The Silva Sacra, destroyed! Nothing remains of it?"

"Not a single tree—but you can see the stripped mountain where the holy forest stood from here..."

"We can still go see the ruins of the temple of Sidonian Neptune..."

"The temple has followed the forest. We can pass on to other antiquities, if you wish."

"What! That beautiful temple has fallen into ruins, its ruins into dust and its dust into nothing! Let's hasten to find consolation elsewhere."

M. Chardon was consternated by Victor Hummer's distress; he walked ahead of him in the direction of the old city, and seemed to be saying by means of his gestures: "Wait; I'll try to show you something; don't despair."

As they went through the docks in the harbor, the city was radiant; the entire world had sent its representatives there: America, Africa, Asia and Oceania were strolling under the tents slung like Chinese bridges from the windows of the houses to the masts of ships. All the languages of the Earth intersected in that naval Babel; it was an ambulant mosaic of all costumes known and unknown, all complexions nuanced by the sun between the tropics, from ebony to bronze. The atmosphere did not have enough echoes to respond to so many voices, so many cries, so many songs; the water of the harbor had disappeared under ships; the sacred forest, stripped of its foliage, seemed to have descended from the nearby mountain to give its innumerable masts to al the fleets in the world.

Hummer did not deign to cast a single glance at that extraordinary scene; he would have given all of Strabo to see before him, instead of the animated harbor, the tranquil Lacidum, deserted and silent, and two of Trebonius' triremes at anchor, having arrived from Ostia that morning.

M. Chardon took the foreign scholar to the Rue des Grands-Carmes, and brought him to a halt in front of number 55. It was a newly-replastered house whose façade was gleaming with bright ocher, like the main room of a village inn.

"There," said M. Chardon, "is Milo's house."

"Milo of Crotona?" Hummer asked.

"Milo, the assassin of Clodius."

"Forgive me, Monsieur Chardon; I regard Milo as a man more unfortunate than guilty. Milo killed Clodius, it's true, but Milo can't be called an assassin. You know very well that Milo was accompanied by his family, and that he was draped in his cloak—*paenulatus*, as Cicero puts it—when he had the misfortune of finding Clodius under his sword. Now, if Milo had premeditated his action, he would have left his wife and his cloak—things that are very inconvenient for committing murder—in Rome. Monsieur Voltaire made the same mistake as you in his translation of a passage in Homer when he said, in talking about Achilles: 'Hector's murderer in that tranquil moment.' Achilles fought Hector fairly, and was not a murderer. The words *murderer* and *assassin* always carry an implication of infamy."

M. Chardon apologized for having insulted the memory of Milo.

"You're saying, then," Hummer continued, "that this house belonged to Milo?"

"Yes, Monsieur—number 55."

"It appears that someone has committed the sacrilege of restoring it."

"No, Monsieur, it's been rebuilt. The other fell into ruin."

"It was rebuilt with the ruins of the ancient house?"

"No, with the ruins of a modern house that was a hundred years old. Milo's house is rebuilt every hundred years; there have been twenty like that since the vanquisher of Clodius. No one was able to find a means of conserving that precious antiquity."

"You're joking, M. Chardon?" said Hummer, pale and indignant.

"Oh, I rarely joke; I'm a bookseller."

"You're a bookseller, and you don't shiver on the threshold of this house! And you don't smash it with a hammer, as one does with a sacred vase profaned in the tabernacle! Come, Monsieur, lead me to other antiquities."

"At present, we're on the Boulevard des Dames, and..."

"The boulevard made famous by the Marseillais during the Constable of Bourbon's siege! Oh, it's as beautiful as it's ancient. I only know of one other feature of that sort in history, and that was in Carthage. Alas, the ramparts of Carthage have disappeared with the heroic Carthaginians who defended them! At least, here, the rampart has survived as a monument to virtue. Let's see the boulevard."

"This is the boulevard; it's in front of you."

"I can't see anything."

"There is indeed, nothing at all—but this is the place in which you would have seen the rampart, if it hadn't been demolished."

"Your ancestors must have been enthusiastic demolishers, Monsieur Chardon."

"Oh, the Saracen and Father Time's scythe!"

"Bah! The Saracen and Father Time's scythe! Pathetic excuses! The Saracen is a useful scapegoat, and Time too. Humans have a rage for destruction, and then they put it all down to Saracens and Time! Time! Don't you know that Time, avid as it's said to be, doesn't eat the outer layer of a column in a thousand years, if it doesn't have human collaborators?"

"What do you expect?" said M. Chardon, tremulously. "I'm very sorry not to be able to show you the boulevard, all the more so because one of my ancestors, Madame Vivaux, was appointed sergeant-major of the breach on the fortieth day of the siege, I can show you her portrait."

"Show me, I beg you, the two famous temples of which I speak in Strabo: the temple of Ephesus and the temple of Delphinian Apollo. You know that I've said that those two magnificent temples were within the encircling wall of the citadel. Show me the citadel."

"There's the citadel built by..."

"Protys."

"No, by Louis XIV. There's nothing in it but two spiked cannon and a dead mortar."

"And my two temples?"

"Your two temples no longer exist."

"Oh, that can't be; I need at least a few ruins, a few stumps, a few stones! Why, in Egypt, I've seen the ruins of the temple of Hermes, which the barbarians call Achmounain, and which flourished two thousand five hundred years before Christ, but I can't find a stone of my *Ephesium* or my *Apollo Delphicus*? I shall denounce your European ancestors, and compose a *Misogallo* about them, like Alfieri.. Think hard, Monsieur Chardon..."

"I'm in despair, believe me, Monsieur. All that I can show you of that place is the castle of Julius Caesar; we call it the Joliette now."

"Ah! Let's see that..."

"Caesar's castle was built there, in front of you..."

"Well, where is it?"

"Where is it? I beg to you excuse me, Monsieur; it's another lost treasure..."

"Oh, Monsieur Chardon, if I can't hold myself back, if I can't stifle the god that is groaning in my bosom..."

"We have a temple of Diana over there," said M. Chardon, rapidly, increasingly afraid of the scholar's wrath, and wanting a diversion.

"A temple of Diana!" Hummer cried. "Where?"

"Come, Monsieur, come...can you see that church?"

"Yes, it's very ugly."

"It's the Église Majeure, the *Major*. There are scholars who say that it's the temple of Diana."

"Those scholars don't know anything. Diana has never passed this way."

"That's what I told them; but other scholars have established the location of the temple of Diana over here, in this direction...follow my finger..."

"In the sea?"

"Yes, in the sea. The sea has worn away the land and brought down that beautiful temple, but one can still see it."

"One can see it?"

"One can see it, the same scholars say, when the water is calm, on the sea-bed."

"And what can one see?"

"One can see stones covered with algae and marine moss, which undoubtedly belonged to some monument. One can't make out the stones very well, but the algae and the moss can be distinguished clearly. Other colors also affirm that the same sea bathes the temple of Venus Pyrena..."

"Where do they locate the temple of Venus Pyrena?"

"Follow that chain of mountains to our right with your eye; its ends in a cape. That's Cap Creus..."

"Cap Creus! And the temple of Venus Pyrena! O Strabo! Consult my first manuscript volume, and you'll see that the temple of Venus Pyrena was built in the mountains that separate Gaul from Iberia. I have two ancient maps in my study engraved before the invention of maps and engraving. One is named the Theodosian Map, the other, the Map of Eratosthenes. Eratosthenes' geographical system flourished in the time of Strabo; he was the one who determined the true location of the temple of Venus Pyrena. Your scholars, who place it at the end of the mountain chain, are ignorant."

M. Chardon was consternated; he folded his arms nonchalantly and gazed at the sea, like a man who has reached the limit of his erudition and has nothing more to say or show.

"That's all that you have in your ancient city, then?" said Hummer.

"That's all," said M. Chardon, emotionally.

"Which is to say that you're resigned to having nothing at all?"

"Well, Monsieur, what can you do?"

"A city that has had the honor of seeing the Tarquins, but which hasn't a stone the size of a fist to show me! Munich will never believe it. Come on, we'll have to revert to modern antiquities. Would you care to show me the famous tower of St. Paul, which blasted the Spanish encampment with its culverins."

M. Chardon lowered his eyes.

"That too is destroyed?" Hummer exclaimed.

M. Chardon nodded his head sadly.

"Destroyed! Why?"

"Because it was too old and hampered the alignment."

"I shan't spend another quarter of a hour here. Thank you, Monsieur; I'm leaving immediately for Arles, and I shall shake the modern dust from my shoes. Goodbye."

An hour later, Hummer was rolling along the road to Arles in a mail-coach.

That evening, he crossed the Rhône over the iron bridge, and, sure that he could not be far from Ugernum, asked for directions to Ugernum from all the cavalrymen of the 17th Chasseurs who were walking under the trees along the river bank. None of the soldiers or civilians had heard of Ugernum.

"It's odd how cities go astray in this land," said Hummer. "Let's go visit the desert of the *Creus*, or the Crau; we'll see whether the desert too has got lost in the desert."

That same evening, at the inn in Beaucaire, he learned by chance, from the mouth of the curé, that that Beaucaire was Strabo's Ugernum.

"Are there any antiquities here?" Hummer asked.

"Only the ruins of the château of the Seigneurs de Beaucaire," the curé replied. "They're not worth a glance."

At dawn, he went into the Crau on horseback.

"This reminds me of Egypt," he said, recommencing the monologues of a lone traveler. "It's a desert—a true desert—with the difference that in Egypt there are grains of sand, whereas here there are large pebbles. Let's see—what did Strabo say in talking about the Crau? I said that the desert was a hundred stadia from the sea, that it was circular, that it was a hundred stadia in diameter, which makes its circumference triple that. It's necessary to take Strabo's word for those measurements; he always walked with compass in hand.

"Posidonius thought that the Crau was once a lake; I think so too. I'd even add that the lake was salty, alimented by the sea—or, in other words, that the sea covered the whole of this extent of pebbles, and has since retreated. On my opinion and that of Posidonius one can base a sound judgment. I'd have more difficulty with regard to Aeschylus, although it pains me to be in contradiction with the great Greek poet. In his fine tragedy *Prometheus Unbound*,[66] the great Aeschylus mentioned the Crau, which proves that Aeschylus know the Crau.

"In the tragedy, Prometheus says to Hercules: 'Listen Hercules, You'll arrive among the intrepid Ligurian people to fight and subdue them, but soon, you'll have no more arrows for your bow or stones for your sling. Then Jupiter, touched with compassion for you, divine son of Alcmene, will make a hail of round stones fall at your feet, with which you'll defeat the Ligurians.'

"I'm quoting that passage literally. That's the origin of the Crau, according to Aeschylus. Strabo, ordinarily so serious, permits himself a joke in that regard. 'Jupiter,' Strabo sways, 'would have done better to crush the Ligurians with those stones himself.' Fundamentally, Strabo was probably right, for, since Jupiter had cited to work a miracle, he ought to have rendered it more complete. Hercules must have taken a long time to kill one Ligurian after another with stones from a sling; it wasn't the least of his twelve labors. So this is the desert where Hercules stoned an intrepid people! How sweet it is to charm the ennui of travel with such memories of reading! Let's continue.

---

[66] Méry renders this title as *Prométhée delivré de ses chaines*. The only surviving element of Aeschylus' trilogy is usually known in English as *Prometheus Bound*, but the plot of the second part, *Prometheus Unbound*, is known from secondary references, as is the (apparently comparatively disappointing) plot of the third, *Prometheus the Fire-Bringer*. The allegorical image of Prometheus freed from his chains is central to the vision of "What We Shall See," which was probably written after "In Gaul."

"Now, it's written, in my master Strabo, that the desert of the Crau so closely resembles an Egyptian desert that it offers travelers the phenomenon of the mirage. In Egypt, I never saw the mirage; that's not surprising, since it's a phenomenon. Strabo saw the mirage in the Crau; he saw out there, to the south, an oasis of green hills, palm-trees, sycamores, fountains, cascades, jasmine and young Arlesiennes wearing the headbands of Isis, with amphoras on their heads, chatting to one another about love under the fig-trees near the well. Strabo spurred his horse in the direction of that charming oasis, and at each stride of the gallop he saw a palm-tree, a cascade, a sycamore or an Arlesienne disappear; when he arrived at the oasis, he found nothing but pebbles. That's one of the ingenious jokes than benevolent nature can play on poor weary voyagers. Let's see whether I can discovery any symptom of the mirage on the horizon."

Hummer got down from his horse and looked around, searching for Strabo's mirage; he saw nothing but a perfectly circular zone of pebbles, of which he was the center. The sky resembled an azure dome thrown over the desert, as if to protect Hercules' ancient arsenal with a bell-jar. The sun gazed perpendicularly upon Hummer and the pebbles, like an antiquary's eye glued to a crystal globe. Hummer was proud of being the only man at whom the sun was taking the trouble to stare at that moment. He thought he owed it the politeness of a respectful bow. The grateful star insinuated thirty-five degrees Réaumur between his flannel and his skin. The northern scholar jumped in response to that fiery needle.

Hummer quickly got back on his horse in order to set out in search of another phenomenon identified by Strabo.

"It is in this desert," he said," he said, that Strabo places the famous black wind, known in French as the *bise*, from the Greek *bis*, which means black, as we say 'black bread.' The black wind, says Strabo, lifts up the pebbles of the desert, suspends them in mid-air, and causes them to fall back like rain, dispersing them at its whim like pieces of flying straw: *stipulas volantes*. The wind knocks over a horse and rider, as in the canticle in *Moses, equuum et ascensorem*; it picks up a soldier— any kind, a *veles*, a *hastatus*, a *vexillaire* or a *prince*— strips him of his weapons and his clothes, including his helmet, rendered him naked, and then carries him away like a vain shadow, from pebble to pebble, and leaves him dying on a grassy knoll. Strabo has seen these things, since he talks about them, and I believe them, since I have translated them. Get up, black wind! Get up for the translator of Strabo!"

The air maintained its innocent serenity. The black wind, asleep since Strabo, and as feeble as all old scourges, got up toward midday under its modern name, the mistral, and whistled through Hummer's hair. The pebbles remained in place, and the rider on his horse. Hummer made every effort to allow himself to be carried away; he opened both flaps of his vast jacket to the black wind, but he only lost his hat, which bounced from pebble to pebble, rising up like an aerostat a hundred times, to fall back a hundred times like an aerolith and vanish like an extinct planet into the depths of the desert.

Hummer only regretted his hat at the gate of Arles, for he could not salute the city beloved by Constantine. He had an invariable habit of taking his hat off to ancient cities, out of respect.

"Here I am now, in my domain," said Hummer. "I don't know whether to begin my explorations on the *promenoir*, at the theater or in Constantine's palace. Let's go take a walk on the promenoir first. All the author's talked about the promenoir of Arles; but what I love most of all, with regard to that promenoir, is an epigram by Martial. Oh, how pitilessly that malign poet mocked a certain Cliton, who had a lot of creditors, and always put a statue between himself and his creditor when he was walking on the promenoir. My God, how densely packed the statues must have been in that one part of the city, since the debtor Cliton had so many creditors! Alas, the debtor and his creditors are dead, but the statues remain. What a lesson for creditors! Will they profit from it?"

He booked a room at the hotel in the Place des Hommes, and asked to speak to the proprietor. The latter, tall and antique in stature, presented himself, *linteum* in hand, as if to conduct the travelers to the bathroom. Hummer was delighted with that welcome.

"What's your name?" he asked.

"Pinus," relied the hotelier. "You can read my name on my sign."

Indeed, *Pinus* could be read there in golden letters, on a black marble background.

"Pinus!" cries Humer. "Good! That changes things. Pinus—that suggests *Pinus sacra Jovi*. There's an Arlesian name! Monsieur Pinus, be so kind as to point me in the direction of the promenoir."

The hotelier repeated the word twice, looking at the sky.

"The promenoir of which Martial speaks," Hummer added, "with regard to Cliton and his numerous creditors."

"Oh, I don't pay any attention other people's business," said Monsieur Pinus. "Too bad for those who are owed money."

"Oh, ancient creditors, dead and buried for sixteen centuries; creditors of whom nothing remains but a letter of exchange."

"Listen, Monsieur, take the trouble to ring that bell and ask for Monsieur Rigoul. He's a commissioner for oaths."

"What the Devil? It's not a matter of lawyers! What do you call the place where there are as many statues as a man might have creditors?"

"All we have here is the Place des Hommes; it's possible that there are creditors, but no statues, as you can see."

"What's that cornice that I can see over there?"

"It's called Constantine's palace."

"That cornice is Constantine's palace?"

"Yes, Monsieur; everybody says so."

"Oh! What have you done with the rest of it, O Arlesians?—for the great Constantine didn't live on a cornice."

"The rest was destroyed by the Saracens."

"Here's the Saracens again! And your Roman theater, what have you done with that? Have the Saracens destroyed that too?"

"If you want to see the Roman theater, I can take you there."

"It exists, then?"

"It doesn't exist, but we know where it was located. Would you care to come with me? I'll show it to you."

"What are you going to show me?"

"Nothing, but all foreigners want to see the nothing in question; it's rather curious. Recently, one traveler wept on seeing it."

"On seeing what?"

"The Roman theater."

"The one that no longer exists?"

"That's exactly why the traveler wept; he wouldn't have wept if the theater had still existed."

While chatting thus they arrived in front of two columns, the only surviving debris of the theater of Arles.

"There," said Monsieur Pinus. "That's what the Saracens left us."

"Two rather massive columns," said Hummer. "They're covered in nails."

"That's because the columns once belonged to a cobbler who displayed his merchandise on those nails."

"A Saracen cobbler?"

"No, Monsieur, an Arlesian, who put the columns in his shop—a perfectly honest man, anyway."

"A rascal who would have been crushed by those columns, like Samson, if the immortal gods had any Capitoline blood left in their veins! Provide me with dinner, and then I'll leave."

"Monsieur doesn't want to see the Arenas?"

"I'll see them after dinner, by moonlight. These Arenas exist, then?"

"After a fashion—you won't find them in very good condition—because of the Saracens."

"That's all right; in the meantime, would you be so kind as to tell me how many mouths the Rhône has?"

"There are seven, Monsieur. Seven, or eight. Or six."

"You're not in agreement with Polybius."

"What do you expect. One can't be in agreement with everyone."

"Polybius only counted two. It's true that Polybius was not in agreement with Timaeus, who counted three, and Artemidorus didn't agree with either of them, counting five. All that's very difficult to reconcile. I'll have to write to the prefect of the Bouches-du-Rhône, who'll give me a definite answer. Come on, mine host, give me an antique dinner; it won't be any trouble, I think—you don't have many travelers staying with you."

"Oh, that's all right with me. Travelers are getting so much more demanding every day that innkeepers ask for nothing better than never to receive any."

"Well, it's a theory. And what will the innkeepers live on without travelers?"

"One always gets by, Monsieur. It's the travelers who ruin us and prevent us from living. Fortunately, they don't come here. Why would they?"

"Very original! As for me I won't ruin you; I rarely eat. Give me some frugal local specialty. Do you have Arles sausage?"

"No, Monsieur; we're waiting for a delivery from Marseilles."

"Well, let's chat while waiting for moonlight. How do you spend the time in these parts?"

"We take the fresh air in the doorway, play *boule* and hunt."

"There's game in the region?"

"No, there's no game, but we hunt for the pleasure of hunting."

"Forgive me for questioning you like this; I'm collecting observations of modern mores in ancient cities, in order to establish the progress or decadence of the human species. You can see that my curiosity has its source in a strict principle, more important than frivolous idle interest. One more question: How do you spend your evenings?"

"We let them go by; we go to bed after supper. We sleep a great deal."

"That's good! All your replies will be sent to the secretary of the Munich Academy."

The hotelier bowed.

"Now that it's past dinner time, let me have some coffee and take me to the Arenas."

"Could you skip the coffee this evening?"

"Why not? While traveling, I have a habit of living on privations. Let's go to the Arenas."

Hummer allowed himself to be led through a labyrinth of back streets and, when he reached the middle of a chaotic mass of buildings, in which the moon shed hardly any light, the hotelier say to him: "Here's the Arenas."

"Where?" asked Hummer.

"Shh!" said the hotelier, in a whisper. "You'll wake the people who are asleep."

"Eh? Who's asleep here? Are these buildings inhabited?"

"Certainly, Monsieur."

"And why are these buildings in the amphitheater?"

"Still because of the Saracens, you understand."

"I don't understand."

"Our ancient predecessors took refuge in the Arenas in order to defend themselves against passing Saracens."

"Well, why don't the moderns come out again, now that the Saracens are no longer passing by?"

"They've got the habit; they're all right here; they don't pay any rent and they have no fear of the mistral."

"The black wind—the *bise, bis, noir*. But they're preventing the Arenas being seen; they're masking antiquity; they're changing the amphitheater of the emperor Gallus into a sewer! Who would recognize in these wretched hovels the famous distich that Martial composed here: *Omnis Caesareo cedat labor amphitheatre; Unum pro cunctis fama loquator opus.*"[67]

"Oh, my God! Lower your voice. You'll wake the poor dock-workers who are sleeping."

"I respect sleeping workers, but why have they put their dormitory in this venerable Coliseum?"

"The Saracens..."

"Go take a walk, with your Saracens! The Saracens are those who are asleep here; the Saracens are the cobblers who nail their shoes to the columns of a *proscenium*; the Saracens are those who suspend their washing from the august *podium* of senators; the Saracens are those who hollow out drains in the *altae praecinctiones* where the plebeians dressed in brown came to sit; the Saracens are those who have cut antiquity into slices to build huts that are not worth a *denier parisis*. The Saracens..."

A hurricane of voices emerged from a hundred open windows and cut off Hummer's speech; the former rolled from porticos in *vomitoria*; the latter was consigned to oblivion. The hotelier briskly slipped away in a ray of moonlight, on hearing the terrible word *marrias*[68] sounded on a scale of irony and fury. Hummer thought

---

[67] The quote from Martial's *De Spectaculis* actually refers to the Roman Coliseum, and suggests that it's reputation will be preserved by posterity (as, indeed, it has been).

[68] A Marseillais argot term meaning something akin to "naughty boy" or "little bastard."

his ears were filled with the roaring of all the lions that the prefect of Barca had sent to the Arlesian proconsul of the Emperor Gallus.

The labyrinth of buildings in the amphitheater was soon filled with white phantoms searching for the imprudent antiquary, the disturber of public slumber. Hummer, who was not obliged to have courage in his capacity as a scholar, understood the danger and took flight with the marvelous agility that a diaphanous body and dialing fasting provide. Fortunately, he was able to say, like Bias[69]: *Omnia mecum porto*; fortune was with him.

Fear shortened the route. Hummer had left Arles far behind, but he could still hear those Colisean voices, and he could still see the phantoms that were searching for a scholar in order to devour him. As he ran, he had traversed an immense plain, with all the more facility of flight because the black wind had risen from its bed and was carrying the scholar away like the *paille volante* of the *Georgics* or Strabo's horseman.

Sometimes, Hummer, flying with his jacket deployed over a ruin pierced by daylight, was afflicted by a roaring that might rip a human ear apart. It was the black wind, blowing through the ruin and animating it like an orchestra of a thousand instruments, tearing from that clavier of hazard a symphony comparable to the tempest of desolation that rises up from a city taken by storm. The stones, mosses, ivy, lichen, cracks and projections were weeping, howling, laughing, wailing and vibrating, as if Beethoven or Meyerbeer had confided the partition of an infernal nocturne to that frightful conductor that Strabo called the black wind.

---

[69] Bias of Priene, one of the "Seven Sages of Greece."

Victor Hummer, carried away through the air like a sylph, was deposited by an pause in the wind's organ at the entrance to a great dark village, which seemed to have descended entirely in living stones from the mountain in order to receive him; it was the village of Les Baux. In France, people know of Timbuktu, but they do not know Les Baux. France is a little known country.

Bruised by the wind, tattooed by the pebbles, stunned by the din of the tempest, and dying of hunger and thirst, Hummer searched by means the rays of the red moon for an inn-sign, or one of those lights that shine behind a window like a smile of Providence.

He walked along a street bordered by tall and beautiful houses, whose doors and windows were open to the black wind, resounding as if they were made of brass. Hummer dared not utter a cry of distress, for fear of seeing a renewal of the terrifying scene of the phantoms of the Coliseum of Arles. He stopped in front of each house; he climbed high steps with disjointed and convulsive paving-stones and darted a gaze of terror and amazement into the vast and sonorous staircase, vertically illuminated by the moon through the cracks in the roof.

These houses had atrocious physiognomies; one in particular, with its two bull's-eye windows in front, its tall casement in the middle, wedged over a destroyed balcony, its large doorway opened on a jagged stairway, resembled a gigantic mask of the ancient theater, and infernal bursts of laugher driven by the wind screeched over the steps, shaking the long grass like a giant's beard.

Hummer searched for a closed door, in order to knock on it like a pilgrim; unfortunately for him, all the doors were open—or, to put it more accurately, there

160

were no doors; it seemed that the population had carried them away over the mountain, as Samson did in Gaza.

The unfortunate scholar who populated that incredible solitude stopped in a deserted public square where a green oak was weeping, a gray and leafless old man. He lay down on a grassy tumulus and permitted him to make this reflection in a low voice:

"If this isn't Herculaneum, it's Satan disguised as a village."[70]

Having said that, he lost consciousness.

When he recovered his senses, he was lying on a bed of yellow algae, on the edge of a pond as vast as a sea that has allowed itself to be imprisoned by the earth. Nearby were a cat, a motionless black mule and a peasant who was breakfasting on shellfish and white bread.

The sun had been up for several hours; its vigorous tints were animating the dying verdure of olive-trees and running like fire over the pond. To the right, a village emerged from the water, agitating the shrill bells of its three churches madly; to the left, the horizon was split by indecisive white lines that might have been mountains or the clouds of a spring morning.

Hummer was in that state which we sometimes attain by night when, in a light and troubled sleep, we dream that we are dreaming, and are awaiting our awakening impatiently. He interrogated the peasant, but the other relied in a dull, guttural and primitive language that was either above or below the intelligence of polyglots. Hummer understood, however, by the peasant's

---

[70] Méry could not anticipate that Les-Baux-de-Provence—which gave its name to the mineral bauxite—would one day be entirely dependent on the tourist trade, nowadays claiming to be one of the most picturesque villages in France.

expressive and manifold gestures, that he had been picked up unconscious in the deserted village of Les Baux and brought to the edge of the pond in order to be transported, after a brief halt, to the little village with the three bell-towers. Hummer thanked the peasant and offered him his purse, which was refused with proud disdain.

Hummer was taken to the town of Martigues, the Provençal Venice. He obtained a room at the Hotel du Cours, the residence of Monsieur Castellan, where one led an ichthyophagic existence that rapidly gave a salutary excitation to the most impoverished blood. Hummer recovered his strength there, in a sojourn of three months, and departed in perfect health for Munich, his ardor for antiquities a trifle cooled, in search of a new passion.

THE TOWER OF DESTINY:

A Story of Events That Did Not Happen

Foreword

One day, following the advice of one of our wittiest and most charming writers, Jules Lecomte[71] I shall publish a book entitled *My Feverish Nights*. Those nights have a special kind of dreams, a phantasmagoria of Chinese shadows, that other nights lack. The *aegri somnia* is more fantastic than the *bene valentis somnium*. Fever is the mother of imagination.

In the meantime, here is a succession of dreams that are the offspring of health. I ought to tell you that I have a privilege—perhaps I'm flattering myself but the word is written and I don't have time to erase it; my indefatigable publisher, Michel Lévy, is waiting. Perhaps everyone has my privilege, in which case it no longer exists. Judge for yourself.

When I begin an interesting dream, I continue it. If two nights are insufficient, I take four, five or ten. I divide it into chapters; I put bookmarks on my pillow. The next episode follows on. Those sorts of dreams have a reasonably physiognomy, and make me see things as they are; there is not that crazy incoherence that leads you to the altar with a young blonde and leaves you, in

---

[71] Jules Lecomte (1814-1864) had a career and interests very similar to Méry's, working as a journalist and travel-writer, with particular interests in French maritime history and antiquities. He quarrelled violently with Méry's friend Alexandre Dumas, but that does not seemed to have affected his friendship with Méry.

the nuptial chamber, with a white-haired old woman smiling at you. These dreams, in chapters, don't play you such nasty tricks; they have a relentless common sense; they begin methodically, at the beginning, and guide you, by way of logical deductions, to the end.

However, it is necessary not to abuse these sensible dreams too much; one might as well not go to sleep. One only dreams to continue wakefulness. The absurd has its charm, and one does not marry old women every night.

One day, I saw an artillery regiment filing along the Boulevard du Temple, which was returning to Vincennes with its cannon. The artillerymen were young, vigorous and well-equipped. The canon were shining in the sunlight like gold. I don't know why, but I made this remark to Monsieur Féraud: "If only Bonaparte had had those men and those cannon at Saint-Jean-d'Acre, eh?"[72]

Monsieur Féraud is an industrialist and an accredited national guardsman. He stared at me and said: "Well, what?"

I understood the error that I had committed, in communicating my reflection to a pacifist who did not care about Saint-Jean-d'Acre, and refused any explanation.

Fortunately, the omnibus that goes along the boulevard passed in front of us, not full, and Monsieur Féraud leapt aboard.

Left alone, I communicated to myself the explanation refused to Monsieur Féraud; if it had evaporated in

---

[72] The port of Acre, now in northern Israel, was renamed "St. John of Acre" when it was taken by the crusaders; the expanded name never caught on in English but was sternly retained in French. I have retained the French version because it seems more appropriate to the story.

the atmosphere of the boulevard, in the deaf ear of an excessively pacifist interlocutor, it would have lost the degree of concentration that excites the fibers of the brain and predisposes them to the vagabondage of the imagination. The process is obscure; if I had the time, I would make it clearer; but then it would seem less profound to serious men.

In 1799, I said to myself, Bonaparte launched sixty attacks on Saint-Jean-d'Acre and did not capture it. There was a tower there, nicknamed the Accursed—an infernal tower—that resisted everything. The French had poor Turkish cannon, captured at Jaffa; the English had captured ours. Those Turkish cannon made breaches, but they were sealed. A renegade French engineer was directing operations in the city. Sidney Smith, who subsequently became a philanthropist and invented a mechanical seed-drill, was in command of two vessels, *Tiger* and *Theseus*, and peppered the bank with an inexhaustible prodigality of musket-fire.[73] In brief, it was necessary

---

[73] Méry does not mention that the "renegade engineer" in question, Antoine Phélippeaux, had been at military school with Bonaparte, where the two conceived a mutual loathing that was almost settled by a duel. After the Revolution, when Phélippeaux emigrated to England, the personal enmity seems to have lingered. It was Phélippeaux who liberated Sidney Smith from prison in Paris, by means of an exploit worthy of the Scarlet Pimpernel, thus enabling the two of them to lend Djezzar Pasha much-needed support at Acre against Bonaparte. Bonaparte later said of Smith that "That man made me miss my destiny"—thus lending some encouragement to the central thesis of Méry's story—but he might equally well have said it of Phélippeaux, who paid with his life for the defense of Acre, dying there of the plague not long after Bonaparte's withdrawal. The comment about Smith's seed-drill is a trifle

to lift the siege after the sixtieth attack, and Bonaparte pronounced these words, which no one nearby understood: "The fate of the world is in that tower."

Bonaparte had despaired of the Occident, like Alexander of Macedon—and like him, too, he wanted to reawaken the civilization asleep in the fabulous realm of the great Indian domain that extends from the Himalayas to the cape of Ceylon, and which was, in the earliest ages, the cradle of the arts, the sciences and poetry, because it was the cradle of the sun. In 1799 a struggle was engaged between the sultans of India and England; Tippoo-Sahib appealed for help to Bonaparte, but Bonaparte, held at Saint-Jean-d'Acre, did not succeeded in reaching Bengal, and reluctantly let India's cry of distress expire in its deserts.

If Saint-Jean-d'Acre had been taken, another history would obviously have commenced, and nothing that we have read or seen would have happened. Bonaparte would have become Emperor of India, and Lord Cornwallis would not have invaded Mysore. History would not have recorded Marengo, nor Austerlitz, not Friedland. Moscow would not have burned. Waterloo would have retained its anonymity. St. Helena would not have made the acquaintance of the imperial Prometheus. The accursed tower of Saint-Jean-d'Acre was the tower of destiny, *Turris fatidica*.

Now, on that day, having entertained these thoughts without communicating them expansively to an interlocutor, I went home with a veritable despair in my heart.

There are professors of the humanities who exhale poignant regrets from their chairs at the idea that Hanni-

churlish; his philanthropic endeavors were mostly associated with his stern opposition to slavery.

bal did not march on Rome after the battle of Cannes. Those professors cannot console themselves; one might think that they would have gained something from that march by Hannibal, and that their university salaries would have been doubled. I resemble those professors somewhat myself; my regrets nevertheless seem to me to be more legitimate. I have never shed tears over the delights of Capua, but I am profoundly saddened by the check at Saint-Jean-d'Acre, the loss of India and the defeat of our heroic ally the Sultan of Mysore.

A touch of the Indian sun put me to sleep in the midst of those thoughts, and in a series of dreams enlightened by Bengal fire I saw a whole other French history, beginning with the sixty-first and victorious attack on Saint-Jean-d'Acre and ending with Bonaparte's triumphant entry into Tippoo Sahib's capital.[74] One consoles oneself with dreams, and the lies of one's nights often compensate us for the verities of our days.

---

[74] The story is actually anachronistic in more ways than one. Bonaparte's siege was not abandoned until May 20, by which time Tippoo Sahib was already dead (in our history), having been killed at Seringapatam on May 4. Méry must have known that, but presumably chose to overlook it, in the interests of the story. In a more general sense, France had effectively given up its last hope of building an empire in India in the treaty signed to end the third Carnatic War in 1763; from then on, the English were effectively mopping up (although they never did quite mop up Afghanistan, whose stubborn fighters put up infinitely more effective resistance than those imagined by Méry).

I

Sergeant Lamanon, a prisoner in Saint-Jean-d'Acre, had obtained permission to walk for an hour every day on the ramparts. The day after the sixtieth attack, Lamanon, despairing of deliverance, measured the height of the wall with his eyes. It was about seventy feet above the level of the ditch; there was little chance of finding his salvation in such a fall. Hesitation was permissible, as on the Baron des Adrets' platform.[75]

At the same moment, two Turkish sentinels advanced to the edge of the rampart in order to watch the maneuvers of the two English vessels *Tiger* and *Theseus*, commanded by Sidney Smith. A sudden idea occurred to the imprisoned sergeant, and he made a mental calculation of patriotic proportion. *There are two of them, and one of me; there is, therefore, a fifty per cent benefit to France*. Thinking thus, the sergeant vigorously grabbed hold of the two sentinels and dragged them with him in his fall. Three bodies fell together to the foot of the rampart. Two did not get up again; Lamanon got away with a slight sprain, and got back of Bonaparte's camp easily enough, under a hail of bullets that escorted him harmoniously but did not reach him.

The rumor of that escape, and the mathematical calculation that had prompted it, soon spread throughout the camp.

---

[75] The Baron des Adrets was a 16th century Huguenot leader famed for his cruelty in persecuting Catholics, who subsequently converted to Catholicism, presumably for political reasons, in the final phase of an extremely turbulent career.

The young Joachim Murat, deeply touched by the sergeant's heroic action, took him to the tent of the commander-in-chief, and there the brave Lamanon, while giving a simple account of his escape, gave many precious details about the condition of the besieged town. He affirmed that the engineer Phélippeaux had been wounded the day before; that Commodore Sidney Smith, by virtue of lavishing his vessels' ammunition on the shore, had only one round of cartridges left; that the garrison, weakened by its numerous daily losses, was only sustained by the terror inspired by the ferocious Djezzar Pasha; and, finally, that the Accursed Tower, pierced all the way through, ought to crumble under one last effort of the artillerymen.

Sergeant Lamanon received General Bonaparte's felicitations, and on leaving the tent he was surrounded by his comrades, eager to hear the same story and the same details.

At that moment, Kléber, Murat, Eugène Beauharnais and Lannes were at Bonaparte's side, and they made twenty mental conjectures regarding the meditative silence that the young general maintained after Lamanon had told his story.

Suddenly, Junot came in and said: "General the men of my advance guard are ready. When the first star rises this evening, we'll be on the road to Jaffa."

Bonaparte made an abrupt movement, and extended his right hand, as if he wanted to halt that advance guard. "Junot," he said, "You're not leaving."

A murmur of astonishment ran around the tent.

"That surprises you, my friends," Bonaparte added. "In war, one sometimes changes one's mind. We're not leaving."

Murat jumped for joy and cried: "Very good, Bonaparte! That's a superb idea! The other day, I almost took Saint-Jean-d'Acre by myself. We're fifteen thousand strong; we'll take it."

"I hope so," said Bonaparte, with a serious smile. "That's why we're not leaving." He point to the west. "Our business no longer lies in that direction. Destiny is driving us toward other lands. Our fleet has been annihilated at Aboukir. Mustapha Pasha has arrived from Constantinople with a fresh army, and will join up with Mourad Bey, whom Desaix cannot hold for long in Upper Egypt. The road to France is closed; Nelson holds the sea, and Commodore Sidney Smith will serve as his scout.

"Our boats are burned. Alexander the Great and Fernand Cortès burned their own. Thus, one was forced to defeat Porus and take Lahore; the other vanquished Montezuma and took Mexico. Fleets are an obstacle to great conquests; they chain you to a shore. Our feet are free. Like Themistocles' Athenians, 'we have only to find our salvation in wooden walls.' Let's take Saint-Jean-D'Acre, and then seek the footprints of Alexander; they're imprinted in the desert.

"As I said to you, in showing you the Accursed Tower, *the fate of the world is in that tower!* The Orient is appealing to the Occident; the sovereign of Mysore, Hyder Ali, the Mahrattes and the people of the Deccan have been appealing to France since the English took Pondicherry in 1761; Tippoo Sahib, the son of Hyder Ali, has continued his father's work and made the same vows. Let's go visit the cradle of the sun; we'll go back to France when the advocates of the Directoire are no longer talking."

An unprecedented enthusiasm burst forth among Bonaparte's young lieutenants; their heroic hands closed on the hilts of their sabers; their eyes darted flames toward the promised Orient.

Junot cried: "Now we need my dromedary squadron, which I tried out in the battle of Mont Tabor; there are riding dromedaries in the vicinity; I'll fill the empty spaces, and I request, General, to be maintained in my command."

Only the sage Berthier retained a cool attitude—which did not escape Bonaparte's penetrating eye.

"My dear Berthier," he said, with a charming softness, "I believe I know what you're thinking; you're making calculations. I can see the mathematical lines on your forehead. Well, don't worry. We have unity; we shall find the zeroes. Our army comprises fifteen thousand men. You think we can't go far with that number. Wrong! We can go anywhere. The zeroes await us. Mithridates, in his plan of campaign, counted on the Dacians, the Panonnians and the Germans. Hannibal had scarcely twenty thousand Africans at Sagonte; he had a quarter of a million men at Cannes. The Iberians, the Gauls, the Ligurians and the Etruscans had joined the Carthaginians. Fernand Cortès had only six hundred Spaniards and fifteen horses, but with his Uacalan auxiliaries he fought twenty-five thousand Mexicans at the battle of Ottumba, which opened the doors of Mexico to him.

Bertier nodded his head, smiling, and appeared to yield to these historical demonstrations..

"Eugène," said Bonaparte, "go give my orders to the engineers immediately; after sunset, it's necessary that they repair the Dufalga battery and the Rampon battery with the greatest urgency. The decisive blow will depart from there. You, my friends, steep yourselves in my thoughts and prepare the minds of the soldiers for the great things we shall accomplish."

The young hero, left alone and wanting to prepare for a long night, lay down on a heap of dry maize-leaves and soon went to sleep, in order to continue his beautiful dream of the Orient.

The next day, at dawn, two unmasked batteries commenced a terrible fire against the tower, which collapsed like a chess-piece, dragging part of the rampart down as it fell, and thus opened a vast breach, impossible to fill in. When the gusts of the south wind carried the smoke of the artillery out to sea, they saw the interior of the town and the parvis of the great mosque inundated with women and children. At the same moment, the drums and clarions sounded the charge. Murat, Kléber, Lannes, Junot and Eugène Beauharnais set themselves at the head of the assault columns.

The simoom seemed to carry our soldiers forward on its wings of flame. The floodgate was finally broken, and a living flood surged over a hill of rubble. It extinguished all the fires; it uprooted the obstacles; it swept away the weapons from the strongest hands. Thus, the town was finally invaded, in a matter of hours, and Bonaparte finally held the key to the Orient, so long disputed by a kind of infernal power.

Bonaparte installed himself in Djezzar's palace, whose terraces overlooked the harbor and the sea. From there one could see Sidney Smith's two vessels heading out to sea under full sail to avoid the fire of our artillery, already positioned in the fort's batteries.

Djezzar Pasha had been killed on the breach. Phélippeaux and four other renegades had disappeared. The inhabitants, reassured by a proclamation by Bonaparte, welcomed the victors hospitably. The Muslims, who expected, after such a long siege, to be subjected to all the horrors destined for towns taken by storm, blessed the young Christian general who ordered that the mosques and harems by respected, and protected their houses and wives. The rumor of that magnanimous generosity did not expire within the walls of Saint-Jean-d'Acre; it was to expand everywhere and prepare favorable results for the expedition.

Bonaparte had before his eyes at that moment the two venerable towers of a palace much more ancient than Djezzar's, and pointed them out to his lieutenants, saying:

"Louis IX has preceded us here; there's the palace in which the hero of Damiette and Mansourah resided some five hundred and fifty years ago. That's where he waited for a ship in order to return to France after his first captivity. What a glorious history ours is! Louis IX had also dreamed of the conquest of the Orient. From 1095, when the first crusade was preached at Clermont in the Auvergne by Pope Urbain VI, until 1270, the efforts of France were turned against the Orient six times. The time has come to collect the harvest sown by our ancestors and watered with their blood. Joinville relates that the Sultan granted Louis IX permission to make a pilgrimage from Saint-Jean-d'Acre to Jerusalem. We shall make ours too, and too bad for the children of Voltaire who will criticize us! A Bonaparte, my ancestor, fought courageously for Pope Clement VII during the siege of Rome; it shall not be said that his descendant passed through the Holy Land without visiting Jerusalem. We shall begin our voyage there; that will be our first stopping-point. Afterwards, the star of the Magi will be ours; it will guide us on the high road to the Orient. I believe in my star more than ever."[76]

Bonaparte's young lieutenants did not share profoundly in his vast oriental dream, but they would have followed him to the ends of the Earth without worrying about the goal, so great was their confidence in him. Bonaparte completed the excitement of their imagination by adding: "The day after the Battle of the Pyramids, remember, Murat, Eugène, Kléber, Junot, Lannes, Desaix and I left Cairo on horseback; the heat was excessive; your uniforms of thick cloth and your fur hats were a great inconvenience, for it was a matter of scaling the pyramid of Cheops to the summit. Half way up the monument, you adjusted your clothing—or, to put it more accurately, stripped down to your underclothes. It would have been impossible, you said, to climb any higher with your northern equipment. We called a halt."

Desaix took over, saying: "Alexander the Great, Parmenion, Ephestion and Clitus climbed that pyramid, like us, three hundred and thirty years before the Christian Era. Macedonian armor and helmets were even heavier than our uniforms, and I wondered whether they stripped off, as we did."

"Then I said to Desaix: 'Alexander climbed much higher in the Macedonian uniform; he reached the Indus.'

"'We shan't go as high as that,' Desaix said.

"'Why not?' I said to him.

---

[76] The author inserts a footnote: "V*idimus enim stellam ejus in oriente* (Gospel of the Epiphany)" The quotation is taken from the Vulgate Bible's version of the gospel according to St. Matthew; the English equivalent is "We have seen a star in the East."

"'Well, in that case,' he said, 'we'll wear the costume of the Indus.'

"'Certainly, we'll take it,' said Kléber. 'Alexander the Great was born in a hot country; if he'd been born in Strasbourg, like me, he wouldn't have reached the Indus in the golden helmet and breastplate he wore at the siege of Oxidraka...'

"Today, my friends," Bonaparte added, "I'm reminding you of that conversation on the pyramid to enjoin you to discuss between yourselves the reform of our costume and headgear. You'll adopt what seems to you to be appropriate for this long and ardent expedition. We shan't stop mid-way up the pyramid; let's go all the way to the summit."

From that moment on, there was a great activity of preparation in Saint-Jean-d'Acre. The soldiers, initiated into the secret of the new expedition, redoubled the ardor of their labor, each in the specialty of his primary profession, in order to hasten the moment of departure that would launch them on the road to the Indian unknown. They carefully reestablished the fortifications dismantled by the long siege, for not all of them were to follow Bonaparte; five hundred men, chosen from among the youngest and less nimble, were reserved to occupy Saint-Jean-d'Acre and defend it against any attack from land or sea.

The soldiers' new costumes bore no resemblance to the vestments of the Macedonians; they were reminiscent of the Albanian and Greek militias. Every man carried a light rolled-up cloak that would serve for crossing mountains and would often be useful during wet nights in hot climates.

Before leaving they waited for the arrival of Christian from the valley of Lebanon and the division that

Desaix had brought from Upper Egypt. Those two reinforcements were welcomed with equal joy. Denon accompanied Desaix and brought his treasure of Egyptian antiquities with him.

"My dear Denon," Bonaparte said to him, "your work is magnificent, but I'm going to take you into a country where you'll find better things than Tentyris and Luxor."

Only Desaix manifested a slight hesitation, or at least some scruple; he wanted to know whether the Directoire had approved the new expedition. Bonaparte took Desaix aside and said to him: "The Directoire is treating me as the senate of Carthage treated Hannibal. The Directoire won't send me a single soldier or ship. If Hannibal, instead of finding himself at Tarente, with Sicily or Greece ahead of him, had found himself at the gates of India, like me, he wouldn't have ended up dying stupidly in the home of Prusias, king of Bythinia, from whom he had requested hospitality as an exile. Europe is old; the oriental lands are still young; glory is everywhere. Let's give France the département of the sun. The Directoire will weave crowns for us when we've succeeded.

The austere Desaix made a sign of assent and said to Bonaparte: "You're the commander-in-chief; I obey you. I'm already converted."

The next day, the French army, twenty thousand strong and provisioned with every kind of munitions and food-supplies, set off to mach to Jerusalem. The fanfares sent the triumphal air of Grétry's *Caravane* to echo from the mountains of Garizim and Carmel.

They stopped for a while in Samaria, where the last crest of the Carmel expires, and at Emmaus, immortalized by all the immortal painters. Then they crossed the final summits that separate ancient Nicopolis from Jerusalem, and at sunrise, Bonaparte bowed in salute to the holy city, which appeared on the horizon. Immediately, the sons of the soldiers of Godefroy and Louis IX cried "Jerusalem!" as their ancestors had, and presented arms to the cupola of the Holy Sepulcher and the distant crest of Golgotha.

II

The expedition had been blessed in Jerusalem; Godefroy's holy spur had touched Bonaparte's horse. They left the vestiges of the crusades behind, following in the footsteps of Alexander, who had also bowed to Jerusalem.

Enriched by the immense treasures of Djezzar, Pasha of Saint-Jean-d'Acre, our soldiers, on arriving at Damascus, bought superb weapons, of which that city is the eternal arsenal. Murat and Junot experiences the joy of Achilles at Scyros, and added to their traveling panoplies the curved sabers that cut silk cushions and iron lances in two.

The inhabitants of Damascus, delighted by the generosity of an army that could have taken anything but bought everything, accompanied Bonaparte as far as the paved road that leads to Ephesus, under vaults of trees and flowers.

From Ephesus, where the army rested, Bonaparte set out, with Desaix, Denon and a few cavalrymen, to salute the noble cadaver of Palmyra. At the sight of the silent plain that was the noisy city of Zenobia, Bonaparte said to Desaix: "It's sad to think that there are people stifling in our European cities, where the people rise up to demand air and sunlight, while there are stones lying idle here with which to build a new Paris in a delightful land! We shall repopulate this void."

The army then crossed the Euphrates near Circesium and entered the land of Mesopotamia. Nineveh was soon revealed, with its hills of ruins and its solemn desolation. Every time they arrived on august terrain, Bonaparte dictated a page to Berthier, which, swiftly printed and distributed to the soldiers as a verse of their poem, told them of the things once accomplished in those places. Before Nineveh, the army was touched to read, at the foot of the order of the heroic day, the quotation of the prophecy of Jonah: *Within forty days, Nineveh will be destroyed!*

From Nineveh, they set out to march to Arbela, and there our soldiers saluted enthusiastically the battlefield of Alexander and Darius.

They descended into Assyria and followed the banks of the Euphrates as far as the ruins of Babylon. Since leaving Jerusalem they had only halted for one day and one night; they stayed for three days between the Tigris and the Euphrates in order to visit the ancient domain of Semiramis religiously. The bulletin dictated to Berthier had a verse of the Bible for its epithet: *Super flumina Babylonis sedimus...*[77]

That evening, Bonaparte, Murat, Junot, Desaix and Denon were sitting up late in the same tent, open to the breezes of the Euphrates, and Murat, in response to a sign from Junot, shook the beautiful leonine mane of his hair and said to Bonaparte: "General, we've been passing through lands for some time in which a great many battles have been fought, and we've found none for us.

---

[77] The opening words of Psalm 137: "By the waters of Babylon we sat down..."

Our army is a mere caravan; we're no longer soldiers but voyagers. What has become of the sons of those fathers who fought so well here?"

"Be patient, my dear Murat," Bonaparte said. "Your Damascene weapons will be useful to you. The voyagers will become soldiers again."

"It's just that it's cruel," said Junot, "to follow in the footsteps of Alexander and not to find the shadow of a Darius. When I was told that we were coming to Arbela, I put my hand on the hint of my sword, for it seemed impossible to pass through Arbela without at least a cavalry charge."

"My friends," said Bonaparte, "Since Damascus we've followed Alexander the Great, but we haven't arrived at his Pillars of Hercules."

"But he died in Babylon, at which we've arrived!" said Junot.

"Yes," Bonaparte replied, "he died in Babylon, but on the way back. We're following his campaign into the ancient kingdoms of Taxile and Porus."

"Those people," said Murat, "still seem to me not to have left any children, like Darius."

"Ask Denon," Bonaparte added. "Denon, you can tell us about Alexander."

"On the contrary," said Denon. "Taxile and Porus have left innumerable children; once they called themselves the Oxidrachians, the Ossadians, the Sibes, the Catheans and the Assacenians; today, there is Afghanistan, Kabul, Punjab and the Kingdom of Lahore. All these lands of Taxile and Porus are more populous than before; the men there are brave and strong."

"Ah!" said Junot. "So much the better!"

"And if we go as far as the limit known as the twelve altars of Alexander," Denon continued, "I believe that we'll have to fight, as under Taxile and Porus."

"Good!" said Junot. "Now, I'd like to know why Alexander stopped at his twelve altars."

"That was the young hero's great despair," Denon went on. "It appears that his soldiers refused to go any further. He was certainly not a man to stop voluntarily at the limits of his beautiful oriental dream; he was thirty-two years old, and he was ambitious; he divined Bengal and the islands of the Indian Ocean; his ardent imagination suspected the existence of a new world, of which he wanted to be the conqueror and the king. He looked with scorn upon the meager Italian peninsula, the narrow Peloponnese, the pale banks of the Euxine; he glimpsed Asia Major, and for one side of the globe he anticipated Christopher Columbus. What Alexander lacked was an army worthy of him. He didn't want to survive the extinction of his dream; he turned violent hands against himself, and died in Babylon like Sardanapalus, in the flames of orgies and feasting.

"We would have followed him," said Junot.

Bonaparte thanked Junot for such well-disguised flattery, shook his hand and said: "If Alexander had had the soldiers and generals of the Pyramids and Tabor, he would have changed the face of the world and left nothing great to do thereafter. His Macedonians were good enough soldiers against the effeminate Persians. With all due respect to Denon, Alexander did cast a glance one day toward Italy, in the time of the consulate of Papirius Cursor, but he soon changed his mind and understood that Darius would be easier to vanquish than the Roman consul."

Denon persisted in his opinion and added: "Judge him by yourself, General Bonaparte. You've fought a brilliant campaign in Italy, ennobling by your victories a few of the names of the vulgar geography of the bourgeois map; you've crossed the Lombard rivers that a hundred general, our compatriots, have crossed. Well, your Oriental glory already eclipses your Occidental radiance. The Nile, the Pyramids and Mont Tabor have given you the ancient and holy aureole that made a hero a demigod. Now look what awaits you on Indian soil! What are the streams of Italy compared with the Indus and the Ganges? What are Venice and the Adriatic compared with Calcutta and its Ocean? That's what Alexander had understood, what he had dreamed—that which you alone can accomplish!"

"Alone...with my army," said Bonaparte, smiling. "I agree with your opinion."

It is with those sorts of conversations that the leisure-time of halts was taken up. A host of soldiers and young officers surrounded the general's tent on those occasions; they listened religiously, and nothing thereafter could have made the army forget what Bonaparte and his lieutenants had said.

On the fourth day, before sunrise, the Catholic monks of Mont Liban celebrated mass in the ruins of the temple of Belus, and the army resumed its march, heading for Susa.

After leaving Susa, Alexander had followed the River Euleus as far as the lake of Chaldea. The King of Macedonia knew his roads; he knew how to take advantage of all the accidents of the terrain, in order not to exhaust his army, and by dint of intelligence, he always divined the favorable path when he came into unknown territory. Thus, Bonaparte, who knew Alexander's itinerary admirably, did not hesitate to take the River Euleus for his guide, which would take him to the Persian Gulf on the borders of ancient Chaldea. That journey pleased the soldiers, who thus savored without interruption the coolness of trees and water, and found delightful encampments. Denon did not fail to remark on the admirable clarity of the nights and the splendidly starry sky that had revealed astronomy to the first Chaldean shepherds.

Xenophon, in relating with so much charm the retreat of the Ten Thousand, speaks of the delirious joy that burst forth among the Greeks when, after having traversed so many barbaric lands, especially the formidable ravines of Chalybes, they finally discovered the sea from the height of the crest of Teches and the mountains of Colchis. In intelligent and far-ranging armies there are traditions of enthusiasm that the passage of centuries cannot interrupt. Thus, the sixth hussars—who had clapped their hands before the colossi of Memnon as the Romans of Mutius' tenth legion had under Diocletian—on finding themselves the advance guard on the road to India, greeted the Persian Gulf with a great cry of joy, as Xenophon' soldiers had on seeing the Euxine.

At that cry, Junot, with his squadron of Syrian dromedaries, and Murat, with his cavalry, climbed the last hill alongside the Euleus. The entire army followed, and twenty thousand voices saluted the splendid sheet of azure and gold that sparkled on the horizon like the mirror of the Indian skies.

Bonaparte, surrounded by his lieutenants, said to them with an entirely new emotion:

"My friends, there is the road to Malabar and Mysore; there, thirty years ago, cries of distress rose up toward France, but the noise of our civil discord drowned them out. Colonies and principles perished. To the left, we have the ancient kingdoms of Taxile and Porus. Opposite is the port to which Alexander gave his name. Overhead shines a sun that has given birth to the great civilizations of the Carnatic and Java, the ancestors of Egypt and Greece. There before you is the cradle of the wisdom of the world; France, which has opened the gates of the Orient six times in the last five centuries, has merited the conquest of those plains, those archipelagoes, those oceans and gulfs, where civilization is extinct, where the sun alone has conserved its light, where life will reappear everywhere in the wind arriving from the Occident."

The entire army understood then the great mission with which it was charged, and the meaning of the memorable words pronounced in before Saint-Jean-d'Acre—"The fate of the world is in that tower!"—was evident to everyone.

They resumed marching immediately, with an ardor that the proximity of an objective seemed to increase, and after further fatigues, heroically endured, they arrived one evening at the ancient part of Apostona, before Alexander's Isle.

The locale was almost deserted; a few sparse houses and huts attracted the gaze at first, but the soldiers of the advance guard, on examining the port, discovered with an unparalleled surprise a tricolor flag rising up in the midst of the masts of fishing-boats. That curious news was immediately relayed to Bonaparte, who did not manifest any astonishment, as he had expected some such encounter. In fact, there was nothing extraordinary about it. At that time, the Indian seas played host to many French corsairs, who always took their leaves far from enemy possessions. It was, therefore, a compatriot corsair sheltering in the deserted harbor of Apostona.

A few moments later, all doubts were clarified. Three young mariners, whose attitude expressed an unequaled amazement, came to meet the advance guard and greeted them in a language they all understood. They embraced one another, in expectation of introductions, and when the name of Bonaparte was pronounced, the three sailors uttered a cry of joy.

The one that seemed to be the leader exclaimed: "We were expecting him! We've all been expecting him, and for a long time. Personally, I was convinced that he'd come! Where is he? Take me to him; I have many things to tell him. We've come from over there." And he pointed at the horizon of Malabar.

The corsair was taken to Bonaparte, who gave him a very friendly welcome, and asked him for information regarding the situation in Bengal.

"Oh, General," said the mariner, "things are not going very well. Why didn't you come when the Bailiff of Suffren asked Versailles for help, in the name of Tippoo-Sahib? It's said that you were amusing yourselves making revolutions—it's here that revolutions needed to be made! Anyway, the harm is done; let's not talk about it anymore. In Bengal, we had the support of the Mahrattes; they've abandoned us. What can you expect? The Mahrattes are not at fault. People said to them: the French will come, the French will come—but the French never arrived. They were making revolutions. Then the Mahrattes didn't want to hear any more mention of us. We need allies in India, though—where can we get them? I think that the Sultan of Kabul or the King of the Sikhs might easily become our auxiliaries. They have good soldiers, and if we had them with us, we wouldn't miss the Mahrattes and our former allies in the Deccan."

Bonaparte thanked the corsair and said: "We'll have a great deal to ask you, but what you've just told me in interesting. Stay here."

Junot shook his head and said to Bonaparte: "If Taxile and Porus want to be our fiends, with who shall we fight?"

Bonaparte extended his right hand toward Junot, with a gesture that signified: *Wait!*

III

On arriving at Tarsus, Alexander the Great, breathless with sweat and fatigue, threw himself into the icy waters of the Cydnus—and that imprudence would have cost him his life without the restorative beverage that his physician Philip gave him. The King of Macedonia was not running the same danger before the Persian isle that bears the name of Alexander's Baths. The seas of beautiful zones do not wound heroes and soldiers with pleurisy like the waters of the Cydnus. On the contrary, they impart that bituminous vigor so favorable to long expeditions.

By warming the sea for travelers and soldiers, and lavishing warm baths around the continents and peninsulas of Asia, God has shown a predilection for the great Orient, and seems to be inviting humankind to the marvelous pilgrimages that ought to found or reconstruct civilizations in the lands of the sun. The peoples that have misunderstood that attention of Providence, and have stupidly built cities on the edges of polar seas or icy rivers, recognize their mistake sooner or later, and septentrional potentates experience dreams of sunlight and warm baths, tossing and turning on their snowy beds and seeking impossible pretexts for pestering the wise peoples of the South, whose have refused to put on snowshoes, dress in the fur of monsters and set icicles upon their heads.

Without having read the history of Alexander, Bonaparte's soldiers savored, on that first evening, the delights of the Macedonian baths, and thanked the Providence that had aligned Bengal between two hygienic Thermal springs ornamented by pearls and coral, gratuitously warmed by the sun. Diocletian, Titus and Antoninus Caracalla, those three illustrious bathers of the Roman people, with their magnificences of marble and mosaics, never equaled the Thermal baths of the Indian Neptune.

Bonaparte, who knew the history of Alexander by heart, naturally recalled the anecdote regarding Philip at the Macedonian baths, and summoned Desgenettes. "My dear doctor," he said, "try to reach agreement with Denon. It's a matter of an item of medical history. Our soldiers, at their first halt on the shore of the sea, are imitating Alexander's warriors. Is there any risk for that army of tritons?"

"None, General," said Desgenettes. "If Alexander the Great had only bathed in the Persian Gulf, he would not have contracted his famous fluxions of the breast, which all the historians mention."

"A hero with fluxions of the breast!" said Bonaparte. "That's humiliating."

"A hero," Desgenettes replied, "is a man who fears icy baths when he is covered in sweat. Jean Bart died of pleurisy."[78]

"Good!" said Denon. "There's a fact that brings us back to our original discussion with the general. Why,

---

[78] Jean Bart (1651-1702) was a Flemish privateer.

Doctor Desgenettes has science made so little progress? Jean Bart died on pleurisy, without being able to find a Philip, but, twenty centuries before Jean Bart, Philip, a Macedonian doctor, cured Alexander with a beverage! What was that beverage? Why has the recipe for that beverage, which brought an invalid to his feet, and suddenly, been lost?"

"Alas," said Desgenettes, "history has not given us the recipe for that medicament."

"History is greatly at fault," Denon went on. "All Alexander's victories are not worth as much as that beverage, which cured a fluxion of the breast in the blink of an eye. We know the recipe for making a Macedonian phalanx, but that's all; I'd much rather know the other. Physicians were guilty of a crime in not transmitting it from faculty to faculty by tradition."

"But Doctor Desgenettes," said Bonaparte, "Denon is not adding that he has himself discovered that famous remedy of the Macedonian faculty against fluxions of the breast."

"Ah! Indeed!" said the physician. "I'm ready to applaud you, colleague."

"I didn't want to confide it to a physician," Denon said, "but since the general commands, I obey. All powerful remedies come from India. The beverage that cured Alexander was an Indian remedy, an infusion of *ayapana*."

"He's right!" Desgenettes exclaimed. "It's *ayapana* that cured the King of Macedonia! *Dignus es intrare!* Now here we are in the land of *ayapana*![79] I must send a consignment to France. It's deplorable that there isn't a

---

[79] No they aren't; the supposedly-medicinal herb *ayapana* is American in origin.

single *ayapana* leaf in pharmaceutical herbarium in Paris!"

"If that's unanimously agreed," said Bonaparte, "We'll print at our own expense, in Lahore, an edition of Quintus Curtius with a new chapter on Philip's remedy. Denon can write it for us in good Latin."

"Let's get to Lahore first," said Denon.

"I'll prepare the road for you," said Bonaparte.

The day was ending, but the night, with its great constellations, seemed to want to continue daylight in the sun's absence. Bonaparte mounted his horse, escorted by Murat, Desaix and a few hussars of the sixth, in order to reconnoiter the terrain on the far shore of the Persian Gulf. They would resume their march the next day, it was said, three hours before dawn.

The evening of the bivouac was joyful; unlike the ancient Hebrews, the soldiers did not regret the land of Egypt; they were desirous of unknown lands, and were already building castles in India, all along the regimental line.

Among many of the groups where the conversation as most animated, a much greater number of listeners was noticeable; the talk was of contemporary history, and those who were listening were carefully retaining the tales in their memory, in order to transmit them to their comrades the following day.

Without being aware of it, the French corsair and Sergeant Lamanon were giving a curious history lesson to the soldiers on the edge of the Gulf, which is the first wave of the Indian Ocean.

"Personally," said the corsair, "I know the whole story better than anyone; I've been sailing the Indian Sea for fourteen years—I left Paris in 1785."

"Ah! You're Parisian!" said Lamanon.

"Obviously I'm Parisian," said the corsair, "since my name is Honoré Lefebvre."

"That's right!" said Lamanon. "Go on."

"So I'm telling you, Lamanon, that it will be your fault if the English come to take possession of India one day."

"My fault!"

"I mean the fault of Paris," the corsair went on. "Fortunately, Bonaparte has arrived just in time to repair all your stupidity, for if one thing is certain, it's this. Listen, Lamanon: if the English manage to get their hands on India, the Devil won't be able to get it away from them. Today, we can still fight them, although it's already a little late. Oh, if only our six ambassadors had succeeded!"

"You sent six ambassadors?" asked Lamanon.

"Get away!" the corsair replied. "It was Tippoo Sahib who sent them to Louis XVI, by three different routes, in 1787. Only one arrived; the others didn't make it."

"One was enough," said Lamanon. "What did he do?"

"He didn't do anything. How can one talk about colonies in Paris? There are always philosophers, advocates and poets—dreamers who invent hollow words and stifle good things! However, the poor ambassador, recommended by Monsieur Léger, our French Commissioner in India, was introduced to Louis XVI buy the minister Bertrand de Molleville. The king received Tippoo's ambassador very kindly, and spent four hours with him."

"And then?"

"Well, then you started a revolution, in order to leave the English a free hand in India. Reduced to our own resources, we supported Tippoo Sahib on our own. But think what we could have done of Paris had sent help! With twenty-five thousand Indians and a thousand Frenchmen, Tippoo Sahib would have had the advantage at Badmor and Bangalore against General Harris, Brigadier General Mathews and the Marquess of Wellesley.[80] If the Sultan of Mysore had had the twenty thousand men for which he asked Louis XVI, and which Bonaparte has now brought, perhaps India would be French today, in 1799."

"It will be," said Lamanon.

"It will be," the corsair repeated. "The present is surer than the future."

"But we haven't been wasting our time back there," said Lamanon.

"Where?" asked Honoré Lefebvre.

"In Europe."

"And what have you done in Europe?"

"We've beaten the Germans and the Russians."

"And what good has that done you?"

"Not to be defeated is a great deal," said Lamanon.

"It's nothing," the corsair said. "What's the point of beating the Russians? What do you want with Russia? I wouldn't take it as a gift. I was born in Paris in the Rue des Filles-Dieu. Do you know it, Lamanon?"

"The Rue des Filles-Dieu?" said Lamanon, looking up at the stars. "I never heard of it."

"It's a street," Lefebvre continued, "that begins at the Rue Saint-Denis, near the gate, and ends, I believe, at the Rue Bourbon-Villeneuve."

---

[80] Méry adds the name "Wellington" in brackets each time he cites this name, although it is hard to believe that his readers would not have recognized the name of the Duke-to-be.

"Ah! Got it!"

"So much the worse for you, if you had it!" Lefebvre went on. "It's a street as narrow as my hand; I've never once been able to pass along it unimpeded. There'd be a gutter there, if there were room for one; there'd be light there, if the sun could poke its nose in; there'd be air there, if the two sides of the streets weren't kissing one another. I left the Rue des Filles-Dieu to come and breathe in India. Well, if I were forced to make the choice, I'd rather be in the street of my birth than a palace in St. Petersburg. Look at the English, how well they're doing here; I believe that England , too, is nothing but a Rue des Filles-Dieu, devoid of light, life and sun—well, they aren't wasting their time beating the Russians; they're dreaming of creating a new England in the sun, as big as half the world! They want to have a London in Calcutta; they're tired of darkness, they want sunlight; they're sick of fox-hunting, they want to hunt tigers; they're weary of horses; they want to sit on elephant; they've been blinded by the fogs of the Thames, they want to open their eyes to the radiance of the Ganges; and if the ramparts of Mysore crumble, all their beautiful dreams will come true, and they'll leave Russia to languish with its polar bears, in the glaciers of the Neva."

"Unfortunately for the English," said Lamanon, "we've taken Saint-Jean-d'Acre."

"And fortunately for us," the corsair Honoré Lefebvre went on. "If you hadn't taken Saint-Jean-d'Acre, we'd be lost forever, in India."

"Did I tell you," said Lamanon, with comical pride, "that I was the one who took Saint-Jean-d'Acre?"

"That's true! That's true!" said the voices of several soldiers who were listening.

"What! It was you?" cried Lefebvre, raising his arms.

"General Bonaparte proved mathematically that it was me, and I didn't want to argue with him."

"And what rank did you have before the taking of Saint-Jean-d'Acre?"

"I was a sergeant."

"And you're not an officer? You haven't had a promotion, then?"

"Listen, Lefebvre," said Lamanon. "General Bonaparte asked me to choose my reward. Do you know that in our Lamanon family, in the Rue Perpignan, in Paris, we've all been professors of mathematics, father and son, for two hundred years. Now, I immediately made a calculation of proportion; if I've contributed something to the taking of Saint-Jean-d'Acre, I said to myself, as they all maintain, that merits a solid reward; it's worth more than an epaulette. A town is worth a town, and since we're leaving to take possession of India, if General Bonaparte happens to take some little town of inferior quality, I'll ask him for that as a reward. A town like Saint-Denis or Melun would be sufficient for me; I'd administer it in the capacity of Bailiff, and I'd teach the Indian citizens—the ones I'm administrating—mathematics. 'I'll think about a reward,' I said to General Bonaparte, and he said: 'I'll give you three months to think.' 'I'll take them,' I replied, and here I am—a sergeant."

"You'll make your way, I can see that," said the corsair. "I can see you as Governor of Colombo or Matura, or Nellorah Sattarah, or Trivanderum..."

"Are those towns like Saint-Denis or Melun?" asked Lamanon.

"Get away!" said Lefebvre, bursting into laughter. "in Melun, on fishes for eels; in Trivanderum, one fishes for coral and pearls, in a gulf the color of indigo."

"That's good—that'll suit me," said the sergeant. "I'll remember the name."

"And you'll give us good fishing-stations?" several soldiers called out.

"Yes, yes, comrades," shouted Lamanon, extending his arms toward the company. "Yes, I promise you good seamen pearls and coral."

"Long live the Bailiff of Trivanderum!" cried the soldiers.

The sergeant stood up and bowed. "Wait, comrades," he added, sitting down again. "Wait—we haven't finished yet. Now then, tell us frankly, Captain Honoré Lefebvre; we've heard much *en route* about the widows of Malabar. Have you seen these widows yourself?"

"I've seen a thousand of them."

"Who burn themselves alive?" added Lamanon.

"Who marry alive," Lefebvre said. "I've married one myself."

"You married her to laugh?"

"No, to weep, as one marries in London, Paris, Melun…everywhere. A superb Bengali, as tall as me, with black hair that never ends, and velvet almond-shaped eyes, who speaks to you in the universal language!"

"Then it's a fairy-tale," said Lamanon, "that story of windows burning themselves?"

"No, it's true—but there's always falsehood in the truth. So we fought a battle in Bangalore once; four hundred Indians, all married, were killed. You'll understand that it was impossible to burn four hundred widows, especially in Bangalore, where there isn't a stick of firewood. A few of them burned themselves badly, out of an excess of self-respect; the rest put on a show of looking for firewood, met Frenchmen and married themselves off at the first opportunity. I was in that batch myself; the children of mixed race are superb—I'm not just talking about mine, which are the most beautiful of all."

"Oh, you're a father?" said Lamanon.

"We're all fathers out here, and you will be too, after two or three of Bonaparte's victories. The future of India is there. It's necessary to cross the races to rejuvenate the world; it's necessary to marry the North to the South, the moon with the sun. If we continue to marry one another, between neighbors, we'll soon be a people of cretins; it's inevitable. Bonaparte's expedition to India is a marriage. When no one here is fighting any longer, everyone will marry."

"But all those Indian widows," the sergeant pointed out, "aren't of our religion."

"Bah!" said Lefebvre. "Women always embrace their husbands' religion. Mine worshiped Shiva, Indra, Brahma, Rama; she worshiped them all; now she no longer worships any. A missionary baptized her in Madras; she as devoted as a Spanish woman, and teaches the *Credo* to her children."

"Ah!" said Lamanon. "Bonaparte did well to bring the monks of Mont Liban to India! There's an idea!"

"Bonaparte always knows what he's doing," Lefebvre said. "Let's trust him. He wants to found a French and Christian idea. We'll all help him."

A drum-roll suspended the nocturnal conversations. They were about to resume marching, taking advantage of the cool night full of stars. On returning from his excursion, Bonaparte had decided that the army would rest in the oases during the hottest period of the day and would march half the night."

The corsair Honoré Lefebvre was summoned to general quarters.

"Farewell," he said to Lamanon. "I left the command of my felucca in the hands of my first mate; I'm disembarking—I've had enough sea voyages."

"I'll look out for you in Tri...what did you call that city?" said Lamanon, shaking Lefebvre's hand.

"Trivanderum," the ex-corsair relied. "There'll be a great many widows when we arrive with Bonaparte at that point in Malabar, and not one of the widows will burn herself."

IV

Before recounting the facts of an expedition that was continuing and completing Alexander the Great's plan after twenty centuries, we first wanted to give an idea of the progress of our soldiers from Saint-Jean-d'Acre to the first of Alexander's ports in the Persian Gulf. Now we shall allow the army to follow its route from the port to which the King of Macedon had given his name on arriving at the frontier of Indo-Scythia, on the ancient Erythrean Sea. We shall catch up with Bonaparte and his soldiers on ground where the great things dreamed of since Saint-Jean-d'Acre are to be accomplished, but our liberty as a historian permits us to leave the battlefield momentarily, on the brink of being set alight by the fire of our artillery, and transport ourselves to the center of Paris in 1799.

The Théâtre du Grand-Opéra is in celebration. Méhul's *Adrien* is being performed; the success is sky-high; all the connoisseurs and critics agree that *Adrien* is the masterpiece of grand operas, and that it will traverse the centuries, sung forever, from age to age, by the counter-tenors of posterity.[81] *Adrien* is being staged with unprecedented luxury and the collaboration of all the dramatic talents of the day. Lainez, the great Lainez, quavers the role of Adrien with admirable energy; Dufresne plays the consul Flaminius; Moreau plays Rutile, the military tribune. Laforêt plays Cosroës, King of the Parthians. The celebrated Maillard sings the role of Sabine. In the ballet in the third act, Vestris, the god of dance, performs a *pas de deux* with citizeness Gardel. Citizenesses Clotilde, Saulnier, Chevigny, Chameroy and Pérignon complete the *corps de ballet*. In an entr'acte, one must applaud Rode and Garat.

In the artistes' foyer, Mallet-Dupan, citizen of Geneva, the poet Saint-Ange, who has translated Ovid, Ducray-Duminil, the most illustrious of well-known

---

[81] The première of Étienne Méhul's opera *Adrien* took place on June 4, 1799, but that was belated; a première planned in 1792 had had to be abandoned by virtue of political controversy. The librettist, François-Benoît Hoffman, was extremely reluctant to make the changes demanded to make it acceptable to the Revolutionary government, but eventually consented to demote Hadrian from emperor to a mere general. Alas, that only caused further trouble when the play was taken by some critics to be a veiled reference to Bonaparte (with whom Méhul was on friendly terms) and it was taken off again, in spite of its enormous success, after only a handful of performances—although Bonaparte, not surprisingly, lifted the ban again when he became First Consul in 1800. Perhaps ironically, the libretto was actually a standard exercise in Classical drama, lifted wholesale from Metastasio's *Adriano in Siria*, and had only been given to Méhul after the composer for who it was written had turned it down.

novelists, and Clairval, a singer at the Théâtre-Italien, surround Hoffman, the author of *Adrien*'s libretto.

"Are you quite sure that Hadrian went to war against the Parthians, my dear Hoffman?" asked the poet Saint-Ange.

"As sure as if I had witnessed it," said Hoffman, with a prolonged stammer. "Hadrian waged war everywhere."

"Except against Cosroës, the King of the Parthians," said Saint-Ange.

"Well," said Hoffman, "what's it got to do with you. You've translated Ovid. You've skinned Pyramus and Thisbe, along with their lion; your verses are as harsh as claws. There's only one that made me laugh—this one: 'Speech passes, but it doesn't matter.'"

This dispute, a fruit of the mores of the epoch, was suddenly interrupted by the entrance of Mademoiselle Saulnier. She was a superb blonde dancer, in the transparent costume of a Parthian slave; she briskly cut a path, with her ivory elbows and the span of her gauze, through the sacred battalion of poets, writers and journalists, and, taking hold of the choreographic bar, she said:

"Forgive me, citizens; I've got to do two hundred *battements* before the third act; let me get to work."

"You've got a superb audience this evening," said Mallet-Dupan, citizen of Geneva, offering the young Parthian a praline."

"And another!" said the dancer, launching the tip of her foot into the journalist's face. "And another! The Théâtre des Amis-des-Arts has taken at least four hundred écus from us with its play this evening."

"What play?" asked Saint-Ange.

"Oh, I know, said the Genevan. "It's a five-act drama in verse, *L'Auberge allemande ou le Traître
démasqué*."[82]

"There's a title!" said the dancer. "If I weren't at
work, I wouldn't have missed that German inn. In the
theater, there are only two things I love, inns and traitors. If they don't whistle me this evening, I'll go see the
tomorrow with my ex-Duc. This evening, we're honored
by the presence of the president of the executive
Directoire. I shall dedicate this pirouette to him, to Citizen Sieyès."[83]

"Ah!" said Saint-Ange. "Sieyès is in the theater?"

"He always is," said Hoffman.

"Hoffman," said the dancer, "you'll get yourself
fructidorized."[84]

"Saint-Ange," Hoffman added, "you ought to profit
from Sieyès' presence to offer him a copy of your
Métamorphoses d'Ovide."

"'Good! Add that!' as Racine said in *Les
Plaideurs*," exclaimed Saint-Ange.

"He picked a good day to launch his malign darts at
Sieyès," said the dancer. "Rumor has it that he's in a

---

[82] This five act comedy by Hyacinthe Dorvo and Chazel père
actually premièred at the Théâtre Molière in January 1799. It
is unclear whether the anachronism is deliberate or not, or
what it signifies if it is.

[83] In our history, the renegade priest and leading light of the
Directoire Emanuel Joseph Sieyès (whose name is misrendered, perhaps deliberately, by Méry as "Siéyes") was the
instigator of the coup that brought Bonaparte to power in No-
vember 1799.

[84] Fructidor was the month of the harvest in the Revolutionary
calendar.

frightful mood. If he doesn't applaud me, I'll grant all my sweetest smiles to the third-estate stalls."

"What's up with him, then—the president of the executive?" asked Mallet-Dupan.

"Well!" said the dancer. "A journalist who doesn't know the day's big news."

"But I'm only a journalist four times a month!" said Mallet-Dupan.

"I heard the news at five o'clock," the dancer relied. "My *ci-devant* told me when I got up."

"Well, let's have it! Tell us the news!" sang all the writers in the foyer, in chorus.

"Ha! Do you take me for a *Mercure*?" the dancer said. "Here, go to the source. There are two executives, citizens Lagarde and Moulin. With all your chitchat you've cost me eighty-four *battements*. Let me work."

The artistes' foyer was, in that era, frequented by serious men, deep thinkers and political orators; they came in search of a little distraction after the cares of the day, and, as they said themselves, in the mythological style of the Directoire, they came to beg Terpsichore to help them forget Minerva until the morrow.

The following day, all those serious men went back to Minerva, and the wheels of the Directoire turned very smoothly.

Thus, on seeing Lagarde and Moulin come in, the literary men of the foyer crowded around them to ask whether Suvarov, the victor of Massena, had entered France by way of the Swiss frontier, after a return match with Zurich.

"Oh, it's more serious than that!" said Moulin.

"Much more serious," said Lagarde.

And they bowed to Mademoiselle Saulnier, who replied with an arabesque.

"What!" said Saint-Ange. "More serious than a defeat! What's happened, then?"

"A very stormy session," said Lagarde.

"Oh, we've been used to stormy sessions for ten years," Mallet-Dupan remarked. "You've had lots of them."

"This was stormier than the rest," said Lagarde. "We were read a dispatch that announced…guess what? Which announced that General Bonaparte is going to take possession of India."

"Well, so much the better," said the frivolous men of letters.

"Cashmere will sell for the same price as calico," said the dancer. "Suits me."

"Oh, you're taking it like that," said Moulin. "Can't you see the consequences, then? Principles are perishing!"

"But colonies doesn't perish," said Saint-Ange.

"Can one comprehend such an excess of audacity?" Moulin went on. "A general who takes it into his head to take India without being authorized in advance by the Directoire!"

"Good!" said Malet-Dupan. "Moulin's not talking seriously."

"You're right," said Moulin. "We supported General Bonaparte, Lagarde and I. We've been called reactionaries. The most furious of all was Gohier."

"Ah! Tell us about Gohier," said the writers' chorus.

"Gohier made a superb speech!" added Moulin.

"Supreme being!" cried Mallet, comically. "So people are still making speeches?"

"Yes, it's an English fashion that the emissaries of Pitt and Coburg have naturalized in France. In London, speeches are innocent; the people pay no attention to them. In Paris, they pay too much."

"And what did Gohier say in his speech?" asked Mallet.

"He proved that General Bonaparte doesn't have the right to take India; that General Bonaparte didn't have the right to say that the fate of the world is in the tower of Saint-Jean-d'Acre, the fate of the world being exclusively in the hands of the executive Directoire and not elsewhere—loud applause. We applauded ourselves. Gohier then tried to prove that India was a prejudice, that there was no such place as India; that nothing existed on Earth but the frontiers of the Rhine—prolonged applause. Finally, it was necessary to conclude..."

"Oh yes, let's have it! What was concluded?" demanded the chorus.

"Nothing was concluded," Moulin continued. "A proposal was made; it's a matter of sending two commissioners to Madras, Lahore, Calcutta and Bombay to stop General Bonaparte."

"I wouldn't want to be those two commissioners," Saint-Ange remarked.

"Personally," Moulin went on, "I proposed that Gohier himself should appoint himself as a commissioner, and go to stop Bonaparte in Ceylon. It's so easy!"

"And what did Sieyès say?" asked Mallet.

"He's waiting."

"Oh, he always waits."

"Sieyès," Moulin continued, "is stunned. A tile from a pagoda has fallen on his head. Sieyès has taken on a distracted air; he often opens his handkerchief and his snuff-box, in a symmetrical fashion. He seems to be preoccupied with a cold that he doesn't have. 'Bonaparte in India!' he says, in a monologue. 'Has he any chance of success? If I were sure of his success, I'd celebrate the enterprise today, but there's considerable doubt; let's abstain, and have a cold.'"

"Oh, he's a great politician, Sieyès!" said Mallet. "Everyone knows his method; no one's fooled, and yet he still succeeds, the great politician..."

The King of the Parthians, Cosroës, came into the foyer humming: "*I defy your power, temeritous enemy.*"

"Ten minutes, Citizen Laforêt," the prompter said to him.

"Good," said the King of Parthia. "*I defy your power, temer...*Citizen Hoffman, a scholar told me this morning that my costume isn't Parthian."

"The scholar is an imbecile," said Hoffman. "No one has ever resembled a Parthian more than you."

"Have you see Parthians yourself?" asked the dancer.

"There are two in the Jardin des Plantes, stuffed and represented at the very moment when they're launching a mortal arrow as they flee."

"I can't get my mouth around this line," said Laforêt. "*I defy your power...*Citizen Hoffman, wouldn't you rather have me say, as in Venceslas. '*You defy my power...*' That's not as difficult.

"My stand is taken," replied the librettist.

"Anyway," the King of the Parthians added, "it's all the same to me tonight. They're making an infernal racket in the front of house. No one's listening; they're opening and closing the doors of all the boxes, without controlling the latches; députés are going in to Sieyès' box all the time, raising their arms to the heavens. It reminds me of the thirteenth of Vendemiaire; I was playing Polynice."

A quavering voice resounded outside and Lainez appeared, intoning: "*Who, then, is the enemy who defies my power?*"

"They all defy everyone in operas," remarked the dancer, in *à parte*.

"Citizen Hoffman," said Lainez, "did the Emperor Hadrian wear a helmet in his bedroom?"

"Always, my dear Lainez. A Roman without a helmet is not a Roman."

"That may be, but it's very inconvenient when one isn't a Roman," said the great artiste. "When I play Adrien in Madras, I'll play him bare-headed."

"In Madras!" cried the lettered chorus. "You're going to Madras?"

"I've just signed my contract..."

"Me too," said Vestris, entering on the point of a pirouette.

"And me," said Citizeness Gardel, in an attitude of Renown.

"My fare's paid," said Lainez, "and I'm getting ten thousand piastres a year, guaranteed, twenty piastres per performance, and three months leave to take advantage of the suburbs of India."

"I've got a superb contract too!" said the other artistes.

"And you're all going to sign?" asked Hoffman.

"All, at present," said Vestris. "It's Citizen Sabatier de Cavaillon who's just appointed himself agent for the theaters of India and is hiring all the actors. He's paying the compensation."

"But he's forgotten me!" said the dancer, Saulnier. "Where is this Citizen Sabatier de Cavaillon? Where's he perched at present?"

"You'll find him at home tomorrow, 69 Rue Saint-Anne," said Vestris. "There's no time to lose. The whole *Italien* troupe is already hired. We're going to give General Bonaparte's a surprise. It's an excellent idea, Sabatier de Cavaillon says."

"Nothing truer," said the celebrated Italian singer Clairval, who came back into the foyer at that moment; I was the first to sign; we leave in a week. Troupe complete. We make our debut in Madras with *I Zingari in Fiera*."

"But is there a theater in Madras?" asked Mallet.

"There's ground," said Clairval. "That suffices, in hot countries. One can play *I Zingari* under a tent, with coconut trees for wings. They're Bohemians."

"My word!" said Lainez. "I shan't be sorry to put some distance between myself and the speeches in the Directoire."

"It's superb!" cried Clairval, enthusiastically. "We're the missionaries of art; we're going to naturalize great music among the barbarians; we're going to civilize them all with cavatinas! And it's just the beginning of a long story; we're just the advance guard; Bonaparte knows that! Everything that sings, declaims and dances is taking flight for India; it's the land of pearls, coral and diamonds—three things invented for artistes. Let's go."

The foyer resounded with a long cheer of enthusiasm; the voice of the stage-manager tried to restore silence; that tumult of joy imported a disturbance into the performance of *Adrien*.

Almost at the same moment, a multicolored army descended from the Suleiman Mountains, from Khordan, from Gundava and the southern frontiers of the Punjab, to the aid of the threatened religions, bristling like a barrier of bronze before Bonaparte's soldiers. An unprecedented battle was about to be joined, compared with which the old battles of the North, with their cold sites, their measured strategies, their absurd uniforms, their terrains of snow or ripe rye, were ferocious children's games in which the absence of poetry left nothing but the dull horror of the scene.

V

In those lands, the great news followed the courses of rivers and the lines of valleys, traversing immense spaces from echo to echo with a mysterious rapidity.

The peoples became excited on learning that an Occidental army, small in numbers and very audacious, was advancing on India to destroy and conquer it. Holy war was preached from Mount Immaus to the Gulf of Canthy, throughout the mountain chains that are the roots of the Bengal peninsula. Defenders arrived from everywhere; they came from the banks of the Indus, from the Kabul, from the Lora, from the Ravi, from the Seledy, from the Helmand, from all the rivers where Alexander's soldiers had slake their thirst in the century of Taxile and Porus: those warrior peoples, always divided, but united this time by common interests, comprising the strangest and most formidable of armies.

Almost all those warriors had conserved the bow and arrow, as in the battles of Noor-Jehan and Jehangir, and those weapons were terrible in their hands.[85] They

---

[85] The author inserts a footnote: "One may read about the wars in the Punjab and Afghanistan in the curious volume by Hugh Murray, *A Historical Account of British India*." The book in question appeared in 1843.

were seen descending like torrents of fluid bronze from the mountain-tops, through the valleys and over the plains, with the evident intention of cutting the French Army off on the roads to Hyderabad and driving them back to the sea. The chiefs, mounted on elephants, regulated the disorder of the multitude by waving red pennants from the top of the animals.

Behind the first lines, the bulk of the army, doubtless faithful to ancient instructions of war, formed into a Macedonian phalanx, resembling from afar and immense pyramid of bronze, inverted under the impact of the elephants, which held it immobile beneath their feet, rounded like towers.

The landscape of that wilderness has retained the savage and sublime character of the earliest days of creation. The mountains, the hills, the plans, the torrents and the rivers are confused in the infinite perspectives, gigantic clumps of centuries-old trees bursting forth everywhere, or flat ground enameling itself with a dazzling carpet of unknown flowers or euphorbias, cacti, aloes, nopals, reeds and a host of vigorous plants dried out by the sun by day and delivered to the following day by the dew of the night with a inexhaustible prodigality, to embellish a desert.

A large torrent falling from the summits of the Nehul stagnates in the plain and forms a vast peninsula whose rocky terrain overlooks steeps banks on three sides, and three natural moats filled with deep water. It is there that Bonaparte has retrenched his soldiers, as in a fortified location. The tongue of land that links the peninsula to open country is defended by a battery entirely covered with aloe leaves. Murat is at the head of the cavalry; Junot commands his dromedary squadron; Kléber and Desaix have to direct the movements of the infantrymen. Eugène and Berthier are riding alongside Bonaparte.

The Indian sun rises and reveals to the Occidental soldiers all the marvels of that powerful nature, which will become, after the victory, their adoptive mother.

"Soldiers," says Bonaparte, "at the news of our expedition, our friend the King of Mysore has hope in us, and his enemies are marching through Bengal to fight and stop us. First, it is necessary to vanquish that barbarian horde, and in a few days, we shall be in Hyderabad, on the rich territory of Golconda. That day will see the battle of barbarism against civilization; our cannon will blast down the bronze gates of India; they resisted Alexander's lance, but they will fall before you. Before your gaze, God will then display a splendid specimen of the wealth of the new world that he has destined for you. Soldiers, once again perform a task worthy of the sun is gazing down on you, and the Orient will be yours!"

And summoning Eugène, Bonaparte said to him: "Give my orders to the troop-commanders everywhere. These Indians are defending their land. They have a right to do so. We are also in ours, and we are defending it. Let them attack us. Let's not be the first to fire."

Eugène left, and Murat rode up at a gallop, to say to Bonaparte: "I'll wait for your orders to sound the charge; it won't take long. These Indians are in the infancy of the art..."

"Joachim," Bonaparte said to him, "there is always strength in numbers. There are more than a hundred thousand of them, all brave and fanatical. A hundred thousand men ready to be killed for their country and their religion are always dangerous. If we want to defeat them, let's not despise them. Wait for my orders, Joachim."

Murat bowed to that wise speech and raced to resume his position in the battle-line. As he passed before Kléber he said to him: "Bonaparte is definitely greater than us."

"I've told you that already," Kléber replied. "His battle plan is formed. An ordinary general would allow himself to be surrounded, but he always knows his terrain, even in countries that he does not know. One might think that he had had this peninsula constructed last night by engineers."

"What a fine battlefield!" said Murat. "One might say that it too had been constructed. Look at the enemies, superb to see—semi-naked monsters with all the shades of bronze; it seems that we're about to do battle with the forces of Hell! Good! That's new! I was bored with the grotesque uniforms of our northern enemies; with their absurd clothing, a battle scene is an epic caricature turned to blood. We have a young painter with us who said to me just now: 'Finally, I'm liberated from cartridge-cases, shakoes, harnesses, flints and gaiters. Those atrocious names are as harsh in the mouth as on the brush. What barbarians invented them? He was neither a painter nor a poet, that's for sure! He must have been a scholar.'"

A tempest of cries reminiscent of the roaring of all the tigers in Bengal put an end to the frivolous conversation between Murat and Kléber. It was the prelude to the attack.

The mass of Indians was immediately seen to rush toward the edges of the peninsula, and the air, silent until that moment, was ripped by arrows and rifle bullets. The French army remained immobile and made no response. The soldiers were protected by a massive rampart of tropical oaks, baobabs and palm trees; no order having arrived from the leader, the artillerymen held up their lance, the cavalrymen kept their sabers sheathed and the infantrymen held on to their weapons. Arrows and bullets were still whistling, in the midst of a hurricane of wild cries and strident abuse, which, extending from echo to echo, died away in profound valleys, waking up the monsters of India that had been asleep since sunrise.

The silence of our army still replied to the racket of Asia Major hurling itself against the Occident, and the soldiers were not giving any sign of impatience, although the battle seemed strange to them in all its dispositions. They had faith in their leader; that was sufficient; victory lay ahead.

Never, moreover, had Bonaparte ever shown his men a face more serene and calm. The young hero was finally beginning the realization of his great Oriental dream. Born in the radiance of the south, like Alexander, Hannibal and Caesar, he was living in his atmosphere, surrounded by his landscapes, breathing the air of his life—for it was not for the pale and cold battles of the North that the eaglet had launched himself forth from the warm natal valley of Ajaccio; he would soon have exhausted his military strength in marches through the snow, in vigils on damp nights, in the cold dawns of bivouacs, in rainy reviews, in all the prosaic scourges that give warfare a stupid physiognomy, extinguishing its aureoles and causing its heroes to catch colds. What the young Bonaparte really needed was that blue sky of India, that sun of life, those shadows of vast wildernesses, those rivers filled with sparks, those splendid oceans, that powerful nature, which surrounds humans in a luminous vestment and infuses him with a little of the generous sap that flows in the stems of palm trees and the veins of lions.

The circle of living bronze contracted around the peninsula on which Bonaparte's army was entrenched as if in a citadel. The Indian leaders advanced to the banks and their elephants were giving signs of anxiety, refusing to swim across the deep water, which hid traps and protected an enemy that was redoubtable because it was unknown to their instincts and their family traditions.

The sun, almost arrived at its zenith, was setting fire to the plain and changing the hollows of the valleys into ardent furnaces. The barbarian army exhausted its strength in futile attacks on an invisible enemy, and sought, on a terrain bathed by its sweat, for some breach or issue that the deep water did not defend. An immense cry of joy finally announced that discovery; the secret of the peninsula was betrayed; a massive phalanx headed toward the tongue of land, and the soil trembled beneath the regular tread of so many men, preceded by a legion of elephants, which opened a passage with their tusks and trunks, plowing through the inextricable masses of vegetation with which the desert bristled.

Soon, the only road to the peninsula was invaded, and disappeared beneath a rising tide of animated bronze; a superb confidence drew the Indians toward that irritating mystery, covered by tall trees and still redoubtable by virtue of its silence. The first elephants were already reaching out with their trunks over the first retrenchment, which veiled a dark mass of aloe stems and foliage. The cries had ceased. A deafening noise was audible, like the undulation of an earthquake and the song of a multitude of birds, the only inhabitants of these deserts since the day of creation.

Suddenly, the artillery burst forth like Occidental thunder and informed the echoes of the wilderness with an unknown din. The first elephants responded with muted trumpetings, and, seized with panic terror, they folded up on the Indian phalanx and rolled like boulders, crushing everything in their passage and sowing disorder in the ranks.

The clarions sounded the charge. Murat stood up to his full height on his horse, whirled his Damascus blade, caused a thousand sparks to gleam in the sun, precipitated himself toward the breaches opened up by the elephants, and drew his cavalrymen with him like a flight of hippogriffs. The drums beat; the fanfares played the tune of the *Caravane*. The army cried: "Vive la France!" on the frontiers of India. The artillerymen carried the cannon away at a gallop. Junot launched forth with his Syrian squadron, as at Mont Tabor. Kléber and Desaix shook up the battalions of the infantry. Bonaparte shone forth everywhere, indicating with the point of his sword the two greatest things in Asia, the sun and Bengal, as if to say to everyone: "Your guide is up there, and your conquest is here!"

There was undoubtedly—and Bonaparte had foreseen it—something supernatural in that peninsula asleep beneath its shade and its silence, and which, suddenly revealed, vomited forth on to the road to India those battalions, those cavalrymen and those artillerymen, who overturned the elephants on the corners of the phalanges and covered with cadavers that wilderness where human blood had never been shed.

One might have thought that the Occidental army had the power to borrow from the heavens the secret of storms, hiding within a bleak and somber cloud for hours, and then ripping it apart with lightning in order to let loose thunderbolts and death. The Indians fled in disorder toward the mountains, and their leaders, carried away by their elephants toward the forests of the horizon, could not give their orders or hoist their signals. The light artillery followed in its flight all the furrows of the uniform terrain, and filled the desert with its outbursts and its terror.

Murat and Junot, launched in pursuit of the Indians, would had crossed the limits of the ancient kingdoms of Porus if the drums had not recalled them to the banks of the peninsula at the moment when Bonaparte said to his generals: "We don't demand a complete victory, but a free passage. It's necessary to spread terror lavishly and spare blood. We shan't see those enemies again. The road to Bengal is clear. Forward, soldiers! We'll rest in Hyderabad!"

The formidable army had disappeared behind the crests, in to the depths of woods and the hollows of valleys; in reed-beds holed by the artillery a few loose elephants could still be seen, which seemed to be reflecting determinedly and appeared disposed to change masters. Over the tops of the trees, flocks of multicolored birds were seen flying, seeking shelter for the first time from an unknown danger.

As nightfall approached, raucous murmurs were heard in the jungles, as if the feline races were protesting against the invaders from the Occident. New masters were arriving in the domain of the wild beasts; the wilderness as about to be populated; the fecund earth was about to open itself up to cultivation; the sun promised its smiles to the crops.

A tricolor flag floated over the top of the tallest palm tree, as if on the tower of a citadel, announcing that France was taking possession of Asia, and that Bonaparte, by virtue of a victory obtained without shedding a drop of Christian blood, had come to found the Empire of the Sun.

They did not pause on that battlefield; they resumed their march that same day, once the obstacle had been overcome. Our soldiers soon found before them one of those ancient Indian roads paved with bricks, the work of an unknown civilization. They marched with a resolute step beneath vaults of baobabs, alongside a nameless river, glad and proud to have passed through Alexander's zone and to be conquering a world coveted by the most intrepid and most intelligent of kings.

Thanks to the conversations of Bonaparte and his generals—conversations always avidly relayed by his soldiers—even the most ignorant were aware of the grandeur of the enterprise and knew the ancient histories that were associated with great conquests and illustrious names.

Alexander, they said, had merited the title of the Great, not by virtue of what he had done but by virtue of what he had attempted to do, and the example he left behind. Hannibal had nobly undertaken a war of vengeance; Caesar had fought for the people against the aristocracy; only Alexander had not formulated a human dream but the dream of a demigod. Hannibal and Caesar had heroic, but human, proportions; they were the first among the vulgar greats. One had only seen Italy, the other only Gaul; they had destroyed much, but built nothing. Alexander had created thirty cities; he had excavated harbors; he had tamed the Nile and submitted it to irrigation; he had given himself, in the oasis of Ammon, the aureole of the son of Jupiter in order to raise himself above other men, and to merit the supernatural confidence that was so necessary to him in the accomplishment of his divine labors. Stopped on the banks of the Indus, he had left at the gate of India more than a victory; he had left an idea: a fecund idea, the hope of the Occident.

And twenty centuries later, Bonaparte picked up that idea, after the taking of Saint-Jean-d'Acre, and treating the empty globe of Charlemagne as a child's toy, he preferred the disk of the sun blossoming in radiance over the cities of the great Orient.

VI

The army continued its march into Bengal without any obstacle, hoping to arrive in Mysore before the fall of Tippoo Sahib.

Bad news was coming from the south; it was said that Lord Cornwallis, with his new auxiliaries the Mahrattes, had laid siege to Seringapatnam, and that artillery landed by ships was smashing the ramparts of the capital of Mysore. It was, therefore, necessary to hurry to defend the son of Hyder Ali, the noble ally of France, the friend of Louis XVI, the valiant Tippoo Sahib. The principal goal of the expedition depended on that. Mysore saved would subsequently give all India to France.

As usual, the news transmitted by word of mouth was not entirely true. Lord Cornwallis, seconded by a young colonel of whom much as hoped, the Marquess of Wellesley, having learned that the army of Saint-Jean-d'Acre was marching on India, had abandoned the siege of the capital of Mysore in order to prevent Bonaparte from crossing the river Godavery in the Deccan.

Tippoo Sahib thus found himself suddenly freed, on the eve of a siege, merely by the resonance of the name of Bonaparte, which seemed to be descending from the mountains of Poona. There was something stirring and supernatural about that great name, which frightened the imagination. Bonaparte had not revealed himself as some vulgar conqueror disembarked on the coast of Malabar or Coromandel; he was like a providential genius emerged from the confines of the world, escaping the English fleets, crushing the cavalries of Egypt between the pyramids and Tabor, the human mountain and the mountains of God, and, always driven by the divine breath, arriving across immense solitudes on Indian soil to accomplish there a mysterious work of civilization, which would be the renaissance of the Indian Orient.

The ancient friends of the French and of the heroic Dupleix[86] came running, therefore, to see Bonaparte pass by and to salute him as the messiah of the Orient; pilgrims were arriving in flocks from Delhi, Agra, Jesulmir, Jadpoor, Oojein and Indoor, and, demanding weapons and a flag, made themselves into the auxiliaries of France, with the same fanaticism that that burst forth among the mamelukes of Egypt when they sang the glory of Sultan Kebir.

At the same time, the King of Mysore raised in our favor the peoples of Belgaum, Balhary, Nellore, Salem, Tanjore, and even the islanders of Ceylon, asleep since the ancient battles celebrated in the *Ramayana* by the Indian Homer.

Bonaparte had good reason to count on the enthusiasm of the children of Bengal, and he was too fair-

---

[86] Joseph François Dupleix (1697-1763) was appointed governor-general of French interests in India, but could not protect them against the English, and was unjustly held responsible for his failure. As Méry notes, he spent his entire fortune on his Indian adventures; when he was recalled to France he was refused state aid, and died destitute.

minded to claim all the honor for himself. When the young hero arrived on the terrain where Dupleix had founded the city that the Indians named Dupleix-Fateabad—the city of Dupleix's victory—a proclamation revealed to the army the recent glory of that valiant precursor who had prepared the way so well for the expedition to India. Glory has singular destinies; very few men in that French army knew the name of Dupleix and the services he had rendered, but all Bengal remembered them.

In Paris, Dupleix had no statue, no painting, no bust, no bas-relief; his name was not inscribed at the corner of any street, but his name honored a city in Asia, and barbarians taught it to their children. Never was a nobler life employed in greater deeds. Dupleix had fought for thirty years on the soil of Bengal; he had named Soubabs like a king of India; he had given mortal displeasures to our enemies of that time; he had reigned over two hundred leagues in all directions; he had rallied the people of the Deccan to the French cause, and the generous Mouzaferzingue, the most powerful of the Mahratte sovereigns; he had spent, for the sake that immense work, fourteen million—his own fortune and those of his friends—and he died in France, indigent, steeped in scorn and forgotten, like Cortès and Columbus, like all those who, by rendering services too great, excite in royal courts the vengeful jealousy of those who have never rendered any!

Today, in the presence of the spectacle of English power in India, a gigantic and indestructible work, accomplished by the relentlessness of insular patriotism, one remains confounded with admiration by the genius of Dupleix, who dreamed for France what England has realized; Dupleix, who created a French India Company;

who understood before anyone else the true question of the Orient; who wanted to save the imperiled monarchy and distract minds patriotically by the exciting diversion of the conquest of Bengal.

That admiration for Dupleix, unfortunately, is mingled with a profound sentiment of retrospective sadness, when one thinks about the obstacles, the injustices and the jealousies that the great man encountered in his path, from the day when he entered Madras triumphantly, like the King of Coromandel. That conquest, which shook Bengal and caused consternation among those who were then our enemies, scarcely gazed the ears of the Statesmen of Paris; they had so many other things to do! They were reading *Candide*, and learning by heart the twenty-four verses of the anti-national poem that stigmatized the Maid of Orléans, victorious over the English,[87] and the philosophical Titans were building the folio foundations of the *Encyclopedia* in order to climb up to heaven and dethrone God! As for the French India Company, it tormented Dupleix at every opportunity; it bound his hands, covered him with slanders, and forced him to leave India in order to come to defend himself in Paris Finally, it killed itself in order generously to remove all competition from its nascent rival, the English Company, which was ready to found the London of India in Calcutta, to channel the Thames in the Ganges, to found the England of the Sun, from the summits of the Himalayas to Ceylon, from the Australian land of Carpentaria to Diemen's Isle.

---

[87] Voltaire's satirical mock-epic poem *La Pucelle d'Orléans* [The Maid of Orléans], begun in 1730, was never finished, having been banned on the strength of excerpts.

In confrontation with Saint-Jean-d'Acre, Bonaparte thought of all these things, and his ambition was to repair so many faults committed, and to continue the work of Dupleix with a powerful army, the only true French India Company. The young hero understood the question of the Orient in that fashion, extending himself on the ladders of the world. Like Dupleix, he saw the future clearly, and held in his hands a sword that ripped all the protocols of diplomacy to shreds, sibylline leaves carried away by the wind.

Bonaparte has arrived like a legitimate heir to claim Dupleix's legacy; he shows his soldiers a young Indian city, with its streets of gardens, bristling with palm trees, its public squares inhabited by colossal flowers, its solitary avenues in which lively springs imitate the voices of an absent people. It is the city of Dupleix's victory; at waits in the desert for traveling France, and its ruins, displayed in the sun since the departure of its founder, seem to rejoice in the shadow of the Occidental flag.

They set to work; they shift those idle stones; they dig channels to those springs; they covered the cracked walls with roofs; they chase away the wild beasts, usurping tenants. In less time than it takes to set up a camp, a city is built: a great French hostelry in Bengal, at the sign of Dupleix.

During that halt, one of the Indian couriers who traverse Bengal, abandoning themselves to the flow of the rivers, arrived in Fateabad and handed Bonaparte a letter from Tippoo Sahib, which read as follows:

Valiant Christian Saïd.

It is already fourteen years since I wrote a letter to Louis XVI; I told that powerful monarch, my friend, that my empire in Mysore would be in danger if his soldiers, always promised, did not arrive. My friend the Bailiff of Suffren replied to me that France could not help me against England, because philosophers, poets and advocates were denying the existence of India and demanding the convocation of estates general. I did not understand that letter from my friend Suffren very well, and continued waiting. God gave me patience, and I rejoice that France now believes in the existence of India, and the estates general have finally heard my voice. Is it true that my friend, the powerful King Louis XVI, has died on the scaffold? A king who sent me Lapeyrouse and Suffren, a king who wanted to found so many French colonies in India? That's impossible. I have never believed it. Distance is always a liar. Come, valiant Christian Saïd. My glorious father Hyder Ali died without having seen the awakening of Bengal; I shall be more fortunate than my father. The destiny of a country is at stake. If you had delayed for one more month, all would have been lost. Don't send a reply; march, and be blessed!

The French army resumed its march and arrived at the bank of the Godavery that evening. There was no sign as yet of the presence of Lord Cornwallis, the Marquess of Wellesley and the Anglo-Mahratte army. The river flowed in solitude and silence between two hedges of centuries-old trees, whose branches concealed the stems and floated on the water.

The crossing-point had been well-chosen; a verdant island divided the river into two narrow streams there, which were spanned by two bridges formed by giant tree-trunks. The Indian auxiliaries were marching as an advance guard; they knew the territory and the lie of the land, and were thus rendering to us the same services that their fathers had rendered to Dupleix's soldiers. Nothing had been lost, for France, of fine Indian traditions. Bengal seemed to be resuscitating our old friends in the Deccan.

Subsequently, there was a hill to climb, which is a kind of spur of the high mountains of Golconda, and a nocturnal encampment was established on a plateau overlooking the vast and fertile plains of Kurnool.

At sunrise, Bonaparte, greater than Hannibal displaying Italy from the Alpine heights, showed the French the magnificent domains spread out on the tip of the peninsula.

"We're between two seas," he told them. "To our left, the Gulf of Bengal; to our right, the Arabic Sea. Here, Mazulipatnam and Madras; there, Surat and Goa; facing us Mysore; at our feet, mines of precious stones; around us, reservoirs of coral and pearls; everywhere, the sun."

And the French army, more fortunate than the Carthaginian army, saluted that Italy of India, whose peoples were already its friends, with shouts and fanfares. One did not see at that moment, the cold enthusiasm that bursts forth in vulgar conquests, on the edge of the icy sands of the Rhine or the Muscovite steppes or the flat shores of the Danube; our soldiers were breathing a powerful air, the air of a new world; they could hear the voices of two seas, bathing with caresses the lips of Malabar and Coromandel; they could see surging forth amid the trees and flowers the cupolas of temples, the towers of pagodas, sculpted mountains, the monuments of a superb civilization buried in verdant abysses, with its gods of granite, its gates of bronze, its poems of marble and the stirring sculptures of its mysteries and its ten incarnations.

There are conquests worthy of humankind! Before those marvels of nature and art, the sword leaps from its sheath of its own accord; the soldier feels proud of his profession; the conqueror places an aureole upon his forehead; a battle is a work sanctified by the God of armies; life is a recompense from heaven; death is the glorious martyrdom of civilization!

Bonaparte had said; "If my calculations are correct, we'll encounter the Anglo-Mahratte army an hour after sunrise." The calculations were correct. From the height of the hill where they had camped for a few hours by night, the French army saw the gleam of weapons in the clearings of the woods of Kisnash, and all of Lord Cornwallis' forces were soon revealed on the horizon.

That anticipated obstacle blocked the road to Mysore; it was necessary to overcome it in order to save Tippoo Sahib. The English, at that time, were making an attempt to conquer India, but, although their mariners were excellent and intrepid, one cannot take the heart of a continent with mariners. Lord Cornwallis had scarcely brought together two thousand national soldiers under his Indian flags; the land army has always been neglected in London. It is true that a ship is nearly always worth more than a regiment, especially for England. Fifteen thousand Mahratte sepoys formed the bulk of the army of Mysore, and, as the artillery destined for the siege of Seringapatnam could not enter into the campaign, Lord Cornwallis had no cannon. A few months later, he would have had no lack of mobile batteries. In war, it is necessary to choose one's moment, and Bonaparte had chosen his well. Victory is a question of timing. What is won in the morning would have been lost in the evening. Another twenty days spent at Saint-Jean-d'Acre, and Lord Cornwallis would have stopped us at Hyderabad.

The Anglo-Mahratte army took up battle formation at the edge of the woods. At the center, the nationals organized themselves into two lines; the Mahrattes extended themselves on the two flanks, under the command of young Colonel Harris and the Marquess of Wellesley.

VII

Among our national prejudices, all of which are honorable, we have one that is very curious: we affirm that the French are beloved in every country in the world, for their intelligence, their grace, their gaiety, their brilliant qualities, and especially their brilliant faults.

That ubiquity of seduction by privilege is doubtless very contestable; there have often been revolts against us among peoples to whom we have brought songs and fraternity, from the Sicilian Vespers to the recent insurrections in Rome, Ronciglione and other cities of north Italy.[88] The flowers that peoples have strewn for us on our arrival have not always been renewed a month later, and the pavements have been hard after the flowers, Here and there, in our passage we have encountered invincible antipathies, stubbornly-engraved characters that did not want to adapt to our buoyant mores and in not laughing at our gaieties.

---

[88] The word "recent" gives no clue as to the story's composition, as the revolt in question was in the context of the short-lived Roman republic of 1798-99; the narrative voice appears to be adopting a viewpoint closely allied to the events of the story at this point. Ronciglione is the village later cited, rather coyly, as lying between Viterbe and Baccano.

Thus, for example, if we had roamed the world militarily in the time of Pericles and Sesostris, we would have been very well received in Athens and very badly in Memphis. Our vaudevilles would have been applauded by the cheerful Greeks and hissed by the austere Egyptians. Temperaments vary with climate, mores and latitude, and not all peoples are equally able to comprehend the French.

Nevertheless, we are able to say that historical compensations are to our advantage, at the moment when, as a little Italian village situated between Viterbe and Baccano rose up against a regiment of Republican France, all India declared itself in our favor. We excited the most passionate sympathies among the sons of Aureng Zeb and the worshipers of Brahma. The French were loved enthusiastically from the mouths of the Ganges to Ceylon, and, in spite of the geographical distance between them and the difference of religion, the two peoples seem to have been born to live together in perfect accord. Dupleix's soldiers and or brave corsairs founded that harmony. The Indians understood everything that was charming and serious in the frivolity of the people of France, who made Bengal tremble on a day of battle, gliding while laughing over the foam of their gulfs, playing with tigers in the jungles, and holding a ball the day after a combat or on the eve of an attack.

That appreciation of the character of the two peoples explains our success in India under Dupleix, and demonstrates all the rewards that a skilful conqueror can extract from an alliance with people who wish to befriend us.

The Mahrattes who had joined forces with Lord Cornwallis after having lost all hope of receiving help from the French, suddenly reverted to their first affections when they found themselves in the presence of their former Occidental friends and their Indian brothers who had rallied to Bonaparte's cause. Combat became impossible because the peoples of the Deccan enrolled in the two armies came together fraternally as soon as they recognized one another on the battlefield.

Two thousand Englishmen isolated on the plain, after that defection, were no longer a serious obstacle; they retreated in an orderly manner in the direction of Nellore; following the banks of the Pennar as far as the river's mouth and going along the coast, they reached Madras and their ships anchored in that port.

The French army continued its march to the banks of the Palaur without interruption; there it stayed for one night, to prepare for its triumphal entry into the capital of Mysore. There was then seen in Bengal, but on a much larger scale, what had been seen thirty years earlier, when the entire population of Madras emerged to receive Dupleix and strew in his passage all the flowers and palms of Coromandel.

To enter as a victor into a European capital is to humiliate a people and to prepare reprisals; it is to make oneself a future debtor; that was not at all what was seen on those two great days, thirty years apart, in Madras and Seringapatnam. Tippoo Sahib, his family, his court and his nabobs, mounted on superb elephants, emerged from the capital of Mysore to receive the French at the bridge over the river Palaur. An immense population formed the king's procession or lined up on the ramparts, the roofs, the pagodas and the trees, making the air resound with the music or the noise of the thousand instruments of the Indian orchestra. The sun, the eternal guest at all the celebrations of Asia, covered the great landscapes of Mysore with its radiance, and infinite vaults of trees, creepers and garlands offered a soft shade to the Occidental soldiers advancing toward the city, waving the flags of the Pyramids and Mont Tabor.

That prodigious military voyage, unparalleled since Alexander, had not slowed the pace of our soldiers; they all marched with the joyous step that had been admired at the other end of the world on the day when they emerged from the Val d'Ollioules to embark on the quay at Toulon. The band struck up a march and introduced Mysore to the triumphal marches of Grétry and Méhul, and the Indians were vibrant with enthusiasm as they listened to those striking symphonies of a new world, those sweet or ardent tunes that seemed to be sowing the seeds of concord and civilization all around.

The French band was a worthy advance guard, and its powerful voice, a universal tongue understood by all hearts, announced to the old Bengal artiste the arrival of a people who had no need of weapons to seduce and conquer. At that unprecedented spectacle, the Indians seemed to wake up after a long sleep, and rediscovered in themselves the fecund seeds of art, poetry and enthusiasm that had made their ancestors so great when they materialized in the granite of Golconda, Java, Delhi and Ceylon all the gigantic dreams of their sublime imagination, and when they wrote the history of divine amours under the dictation of the sun on the ridges of the mountains and in the subterranean caves of Ellora.

The army continued to advance, justifiably proud of the conquest of a world that was being granted to them without being reddened by a drop of blood. For the first time since the creation of the world, military virtue triumphed and did not open a tomb; that last campaign of our soldiers began in peace, and two unknown peoples embraced on recognizing one another on a battlefield of flowers. Soon, the illustrious city revealed itself on the horizon, with its pointed towers, its golden domes, its massive pagodas, its plumes of palm trees—with the stirring Indian physiognomy that gives a material creation the ideal character of a petrified dream.

At that sight, the Occident uttered a cry of enthusiasm heard by the two neighboring seas; the Orient replied with a religious hymn in that harmonious language composed of golden notes, the sound of pearls, the melody of waves, the murmurs of palms, and sunlight. All the ranks soon became confused: people and soldiers, conquerors and conquered, mingled their hands, their weapons, their banners, their flags; there was neither a victory, nor victors. Everyone entered thus into the capital as dusk fell, and daylight was immediately reilluminated by thousands of fireworks, which permitted an entire people to continue to contemplate the young French heroes, as if in the aureole of an apotheosis, on the horizon of the Indian sky.

We are now at the end of that expedition. The result of the conquest is easy to deduce. All of the Bengal peninsula has been acquired by France; the peoples of the Carnatic and the Deccan are our allies; we shall have no lack of fleets; we are about to set to work in all the neighboring construction-yards, in Coromandel, in Malabar, and Matura. Peninsular peoples are all born mariners; sailors will be as abundant as ships. Bengal is a ship anchored in the Indian Ocean; its poop is the Himalayas, its prow Cap Comorin.

We shall descend from its height to extend the domain of France further, and increase its glorious Empire of the Sun.

The peaceful army of the arts, that companion of conquering France, will also make its triumphant entrance into all those dead cities, once so great in the arts; we shall do more and better than colonize that old Asia; we shall give it back its civilization. Why should it not become again what it once was? Its sun has not cooled, its Ocean still has its bed of pearls; its earth is still fecund; its sky is still blue; its rivers still broad. What, then, is lacking in that land, the cradle of the world's wisdom and poetry? It lacks the intelligent breath that awakens. France retains that breath on her lips; she will exhale it everywhere.

It will ultimately be necessary to exhume from its darkness that luminous Java, which has so many mysteries to relate to us and which has been obstinately silent since ages unknown; that Indian Sicily, with its volcano of Mara-Api, must recount the idylls of its Theocritus, reveal its buried cities to us, explain the origins of its temples and tell us the names of the powerful architects and sculptors who built and chiseled its marvelous monuments in a epoch when Greece had not found its name. That generous island, the cradle of all great things, is not destined eternally to remain a counter for colonial commodities; it has too noble a past to merit so vulgar a future; what Sicily was once to great Greece, Java was once to vast Asia, and when the massive abysms of verdure that extend around its extinct craters have been excavated, we shall see unknown Herculaneums emerging therefrom, full of surprises and stimulating revelations.[89]

---

[89] It is not obvious where Méry got the (mistaken) idea that Java had been host to very ancient civilizations ancestral to many others; it was not from Sir Stamford Raffles' then-standard *History of Java* (1830), nor was it a common compo-

The conquests of peace and the arts will extend more distantly still.

It will also be necessary to fecundate Borneo, that immense miserly jewelry-box, which guards so much gold and fallow ground; Sumatra, which the line of the equator cuts into two sections, like a steel blade floating on the Ocean; the embalmed archipelago of the Moluccas and the Philippines, a terrestrial constellation, a Milky Way of islands which ask nothing but to shine in the sunlight; and all those oceanic regions plowed by Lapeyrouse's ship and the genius of the great Louis XVI; the peninsula of Segalin, Bengal in miniature, full of woods and grassy slopes; Segalin, where Lapeyrouse had founded the future of France between the Tarrakai Sea and the Sea of Japan; the isles of Jesso and Nippon, which excited the national covetousness of Louis XVI while a scaffold was being prepared for him; and, in the opposite zone, the entire Japanese empire, conquered by the cross of François-Xavier; the entire empire of Siam, which received Louis XVI's ambassadors; and the infinite lands that extend from the mouth of the Ganges to the extreme limits of the Punjab, which see Almora and Benares rising to their left on the banks of the holy river, and to their right the mountains of Assam, Bhotam and Nepal.

It is the awakening of a whole world; it is the renaissance of the primal world; it is the creation of the globe, after God's creation; it is the second endeavor of Shem, Ham and Japhet after the deluge of barbarism; an immense and noble endeavor confided to France, which Bonaparte alone had understood, when he pronounced,

---

nent of contemporary ethnological scholarly fantasies regarding the migrations of ancient humans.

before Saint-Jean-d'Acre, those memorable words: "The fate of the world is in that tower!"

AN AERIAL VOYAGE

The scholarly world knows Belzoni,[90] the illustrious voyager who discovered the second pyramid and published a book on Egypt and the course of the Nile from the Takase to the sea, nevertheless forgetting the peninsula of Meroë, which, according to Herodotus, was the cradle of the Gymnosophists and which has the privilege of having conserved, living beneath the crowns of its nopals, the sacred scarab dear to the priests of Isis.

Don't be alarmed by the gravity of my opening. Tedium is the child of seriousness, and always recoils before a parricide who renders books amusing, if that is the case. What tedium dare not do, out of filial piety, let us do this evening.

Before embracing the honorable profession of scholarship, Belzoni was a tightrope walker, and when Mehmet Ali, absorbed by the cares of the heritage of the Pharaohs and deprived to the good advice of Joseph, let his head full of pyramidal cares fall on to his beard, he

---

[90] The Venetian adventurer Giovanni Battista Belzoni (1778-1823) arrived in Egypt in 1815 hoping to market a hydraulic device of his own invention, having previously been something of a jack-of-all-trades, teaming up for some time with his English wife to make money as a circus performer. Having failed to find a market for his machine he became an explorer and dealer in artifacts, investigating Karnak and Abu Simbel as well as being the first person in modern times to get inside the second pyramid at Giza. He eventually perished in the Kingdom of Benin, probably murdered.

summoned Belzoni, who was not yet a scholar, and asked him to dance on a rope suspended between two palm trees. That exercise is very difficult in Egypt, and the tightrope walker's sweat, running on to the taut hemp, renders it slippery. Belzoni fell several times and handed in his resignation. Mr. Hogges, of the Royal Society of London, advised him to become a scholar, and he took the advice.

In Egypt, it is rather difficult to acquire knowledge since Omar the Great rendered humankind the immortal service of burning the library of Alexandria, which consoles present-day librarians, already so narrowly lodged. Belzoni, however, had the good fortune to acquire a high reputation in science by smoking a great many pipes before the inscription on Pompey's column, and explaining a few hieroglyphs to Mr. Hogges as rebuses of the day of the year and enigmas in the style of *Le Charivari*.[91]

One day, Mr. Hogges read in an English newspaper a translation of an article in the *Débats*, in which our celebrated composer Hector Berlioz, who is also a man of refined intelligence and style, suggested a new means of traversing sandy deserts without being exposed to the old inconveniences of such a journey. It was a matter of suspending oneself in mid-air in an aerostat harnessed to a dromedary, harnessed in turn to a fellah. The plan was probably an ingenious joke on the part of the witty writer, but Mr. Hogges took it seriously and communicated it to Belzoni. The Italian scholar, who remembered the horizontal rope, smiled at the idea of the vertical rope, and asked Mr. Hogges for a thousand pounds in order to

---

[91] *Le Charivari* was a humorous paper launched in Paris in 1832.

have the honor of accompanying him in his aerial voyage.

Mr. Hogges said to him: "Like all Englishmen, I don't have a thousand pounds on me; here's a money-order drawn on M. Jules Pastré in Alexandria. The expenses of our voyage will be so considerable that the sum will disappear in the whole. First, it's necessary that the viceroy give us firmans, and sends Arabs to the Mountains of the Moon, the presumed source of the Nile, to establish deposits of zinc and all sorts of provisions there in sound huts. I'll pay for the zinc, the provisions and the Arabs. We'll need all the balloon-fabric in Alexandria to construct an immense aerostat. Finally, we need to have a team of dromedaries to draw it along, replacing one another as necessary."

Then Belzoni said: "Mr. Hogges, what you've just said encourages me to ask you for a further thousand pounds, in order to be even more worthy of the honor of accompanying you. Such an opportunity doesn't come up more than once, and I want to seize it. I have a very dear wife and three children in Venice."

A tear moistened Belzoni's eye, and Mr. Hogges, moved to compassion, agreed to everything. "Now," he said, "this is the serious objective of the voyage—every voyage needs a serious objective. We don't want to make an excursion in mid-air to amuse the ostriches, crocodiles and ibises. Europe is watching us, as is its custom. We're going to complete the difficult work already begun by Mungo Park, Pritchi, Bruce, Rossignol and many others; we're going to discover the sources of the Nile, without being inconvenienced, as our predecessors were, by heat, insects, dust, sand and the humps of dromedaries. It will be our prerogative to discover the sources—unless the Nile has no sources, which would be contrary to the habits of the rivers of all lands. Since the reign of George III, the Treasury has spent seventy million on finding the cradle of the Nile; with that sum, the workers could have been given beer and sherry to drink until England's end, if England is to have an end someday, which I don't believe. Today it's at my expense that we're making this expedition, but the Lord of the Treasury will probably reimburse the money."

"That," said Belzoni, "authorizes me to ask you for another thousand pounds, because I'm the only scholar attached to the expedition."

"Agreed," said the generous Hogges.

It took three months to organize the construction of the aerostat. Belzoni employed that time in digging a few more shafts in the second pyramid, and discovered two mines of virgin mummies, of the same species as those which Mr. White, the chemist of King William Street in London, steams in order to produce remedies for laryngitis.

When everything was ready, Mr. and Mrs. Hogges—a young Alexandrian woman thirty years old—embarked on the Nile and sailed up as far as the brown rocks of Phil. Mr. Hogges had taken lessons in aerostatics from a pupil of Garnerin who had become a muslim in Cairo in order to espouse a seraglio out of hatred for marriage. Belzoni, with his natural intelligence, soon figured out the entire mechanism and its operation. Between Akhmounain and Aswan, they carried out a general rehearsal with the accessories, which was a complete success.

They were about to launch themselves into the azure under favorable auspices, and respire the aerial freshness that Mont Blanc retains on its summit in Egypt. To travel thus is to construct beneath one's feet an infinite succession of mountain crests, while econo-mizing on bases, according to the Italian scholar. The bare and waterless desert extended before them. Mrs. Hogges threatened her husband that she would hurl her-self down between two crocodiles asleep in a reed-bed if she was not accepted as a companion on the beautiful voyage. Mr. Hogges, much more fearful of seraglio-suppliers than crocodiles, offered his hand to his coura-geous spouse and helped her into the vast gondola.

They unrolled an endless rope braided in the vice-roy's rope-factory and connected it by means of an enormous iron hook to a leather strap circling a drome-dary between its two humps.[92] An Arab guided the ani-mal. The balloon rose majestically into the air.

Belzoni and Mr. and Mrs. Hogges experienced fris-sons of joy as they rose up above the level of the heat. From high in the air, the vast plain had a dazzling white-ness, and, by contrast with the balloonists of Mont Blanc, the ground seemed to them to be covered with snow, which made them feel even cooler. Mrs. Hogges put on her shawl, and the two voyagers—who, like Jo-seph, had left their cloaks in Egypt—started a card game. The aerostat, pulled by the trotting dromedary—more agile than a horse—left the heavy wind behind; they were traveling at twelve miles an hour.

At midday, Mr. Hogges left the game in order to correct a geographical error by Bruce, who had forgotten to devote a black dot on his maps to the peninsula of Meroë. From the gondola of the aerostat they discov-ered, in a torrid zone to the left, the four pyramids that Herodotus the Veridical had counted on his ten fingers.

---

[92] Dromedaries only have one hump, as Méry must have known.

When night fell, the aerostat descended into the bony valley formed by the dromedary's humps. The travelers had already reached the oasis of Belk-Alzir, which serves, so to speak, as a vegetal peristyle to the profound valley in which Cambyses' army was asphyxiated by the Kamsin while returning from his expedition against the august noses of the gods of Egypt and the sphinx.

At dawn the next day, the balloon resumed its flight; thirty Arabs sent to the oasis in advance had made the preparations for the second ascent. That was the second stage. On departure, the Fahrenheit thermometer already marked 33 degrees 8° '5and when the aerostat ran out of rope the mercury descended to 4 degrees 9° 3'.[93] The appearance of the landscape became frightful. Toward the north ran bare mountains that might have been a deviation of the dorsal spine of the Mokatan strayed into the desert. Abyssinia appeared between four horizons with its pale horrors; at enormous intervals, a few oases were revealed, like black dots on a white map. Ostriches resembled swallows skimming the ground. A stronger gust of wind having pulled the cards out of Hogges' hand just as he was about to play them, the trio of voyagers was relieved of all distractions, except that

---

[93] This makes no sense, not merely because 33 degrees is only just above zero on the Fahrenheit scale (he must surely be thinking of the Réaumur scale, as cited in "The Explorations of Victor Hummer") but because the symbol ° means degrees and the symbol ′ means minutes, as used with it in connection with degrees of arc, as in measuring latitudes and longitudes. It would be slightly less absurd if the second and third figures signified minutes and seconds (of arc), but minimal absurdity does not seem to be the effect for which Méry is striving.

Belzoni leaned over at intervals to try to catch an eagle on the wing.

When the immense obelisk of Nen-Assoun marked midday like a solar needle on a sundial, Mr. Hogges curled up to take a siesta on a bundle of ropes, and his wife did likewise. Belzoni, abandoned by his companions and not knowing what to do, fell in love with Mrs. Hogges and composed an Italian sonnet, which he wrote in pencil, with the intention of offering it to her at an opportune moment. It is always necessary for an Italian to compose sonnets.

Mrs. Hogges woke up before her husband and Belzoni, with a gracious smile, presented his declaration of love to her. The sonnet began: *Nel cielo tua bellezza.* Madame Hogges read the sonnet and apologized for being unable to understand it. The audacious Belzoni took the hand of the young voyager and squeezed it hard. Revolted by this impertinence, she uttered a scream, and Mr. Hogges leapt up from his pillow.

He was a very jealous and suspicious husband; on awakening he saw a considerable disturbance on Belzoni's face and a blush of modest anger on his wife's bronzed cheeks. The sonnet soon clarified the situation; it was on his wife's knees, and the wind had neglected to carry it away. Mr. Hogges took possession of that item of evidence and translated it into English, darting a glance of indignation at the infamous airborne seducer at every line.

Belzoni lowered his eyes like a guilty man. The husband, cruelly outraged, meditated a duel at twenty paces. His wife extended her arms toward the ground, as if to implore the sky to save her honor and her husband. The moment was solemn, the silence frightful, the altitude immeasurable. A few eagles, the only witnesses to the incident, grazed the gondola.

A violent shock, imparted by the rope to the balloon, turned their minds away from the jealous scene. Something terrible was doubtless threatening the voyagers. Mr. Hogges stuffed the sonnet into his wallet and opened the five tubes of his telescope in order to examine the situation on the ground. What he saw chilled him with fear. The Arab camel-driver had disappeared and the dromedary was fleeing at the end of its rope with two superb lushly-maned lions on its heels.

"We're doomed!" cried Mr. Hogges. He ceded the telescope to his wife, who looked through it and went pale beneath the brown layers of her Alexandrine face. Belzoni, absorbed by his infatuation, which had already taken profound root—passions develop swiftly in an aerostat, which is the railway of love—and as sentimental as Petrarch, composed another sonnet on the joy of dying with Mrs. Hogges and being buried in the same tomb, the belly of a lion: *Nella stessa tomba, colla mia Laura*.

The two lions caught up with the dromedary, and the balloon suddenly came to a standstill in the sky, like Joshua's sun. The emotion of Mr. and Mrs. Hogges was at its peak, and they were passing the telescope back and forth like two people sitting next to one another in a theater in order to watch a hundred-thousand-franc tenor declaim when not singing. Belzoni abandoned himself internally to the delirium of his love, and his pose was as calm as that of Daniel in the lions' den.

Meanwhile, according to the infallible report of his telescope, the lions were not wasting any time; one might have thought that they had been subjected to a long fast in the desert since the great feast of Cambyses' army. One of the two, presumably the female, detached a quarter of dromedary and carried it away, probably to her young family, domiciled in the caves of the Abyssinian Mokatan. The remaining lion crouched like a nonchalant sphinx over the other three-quarters of the camel, like a Neapolitan beggar over a dish of pasta, and began devouring the aerostat's tug piece by piece.

"My God!" cried Mr. Hogges, embracing his wife. "What will become of us?" The insolence of that conjugal affection irritated Belzoni, and he experienced a horrible desire to hurl the fortunate husband over the side of the gondola into the lions' den, by way of dessert after the meal of the dromedary.

"There's a lion," said Hogges, as if to explain the crisis clearly, "that will devour its prey to the last slice, to the last bone. It will doubtless require several days to finish off a dromedary; it will depart frequently and come back frequently, when it's hungry, as if to a restaurant. Then, when everything is devoured, what will happen to us? We'll run out of food. The balloon will remain stuck here like a ship at anchor, and if we drag the anchor, God knows where the wind will take us. The four cardinal points are four gulfs, four reefs, four towers of Hugolin[94]—no hope anywhere! Yet again, the sources

---

[94] This reference and two subsequent ones are to Hugolin della Gherardesca, a 13th century tyrant who ruled Pisa, after seizing power by treachery. Finally falling victim to a conspiracy organized by the city's archbishop, he and four of his male children were imprisoned in a tower where they were not given enough to eat and starved to death. Legend has it that Hugolin kept himself alive after the children perished by cannibalistic means, although this is probably a misinterpretation of a line in Dante, who placed Hugolin in the ninth circle of the Inferno, reserved for traitors.

of the Nile will keep their mysteries. O heavens, our helpful neighbor, come to our aid!"

Mr. Hogges had reasoned accurately. Appetite is not eternal, even in a lion's stomach. The beast, after having eaten two humps and drunk several liters of fresh blood, withdrew at a buoyant pace, shaking its mane, teasing the crowns of the nopals with its tail and occasionally uttering unctuous roars, like a gastronome humming a tune after a god meal.

"What do you say to that, Signor Belzoni?" cried Hogges, putting his hand over his eyes. "Your tranquility is offensive to us. Come on, what should we do? Give us your opinion..."

"Oh," said Belzoni, with a mysterious sigh, "life is odious to me, and it doesn't matter to me whether I'm buried in the clouds or elsewhere. Your happiness revolts me, and I'd like nothing better than to see you expire in my arms."

"Then take pity on this poor woman who is weeping and trembling, Signor Belzoni!"

"Do you realize, Mr. Hogges, that I'm losing the three thousand pounds of our contract? Sixty-five thousand francs in French money! Take pity on me!"

In the course of this conversation, dusk fell, and it was necessary to resign themselves to spending the night in the same shelter. Wild beasts could be heard roaring down below, as one hears frogs croaking in a marsh from a bed in an inn. At times, the balloon-fabric hostelry experienced an abrupt shock; that was doubtless some carnivorous animal tearing a cutlet from the dromedary and having a nocturnal snack as it passed by.

Belzoni quietly hummed an octave from Tasso, like a Venetian gondolier at anchor beside St. Mark's Square. Hogges, armed with a pole, was trying to chase away eagles, which, mistaking the aerostat for a mountain asleep on a cloud, were threatening to rip the envelope of the balloon with a thrust of a beak and let out the gas.

The night was long, but Mrs. Hogges managed to get a few hours of sleep.

At dawn the next day, the telescope permitted them to discern the mess that the guests had made on the white tablecloth of the feast. A few dromedary crumbs still remained; the skeleton was displayed in its bloody nudity, and if extreme hunger did not drive some starving animal or lover of fleshless bones in that direction, it was necessary to expect a permanent station in the region of the clouds. The aerostat had acquired the status of a fixed planet, serving Abyssinian astronomers as a half-moon.

The powerful carcass of the dromedary still retained the aerostat's rope by its iron hook, and the aerial navigators could not land beside the skeleton because the wild beasts of the neighborhood would have been bound to come running to devour the travelers who had descended with the aid of their emergency rope. The status quo was as desperate as any other maneuver.

Unfortunately, discord reigned among the population of the aerostat. The strongest passions were at odds. Two men comprised that population, rocked by the wind over a crater full of lions, and the two camps had drawn up battle lines to murder one another. If there had been two printing-presses in the gondola's luggage, two newspapers would have been born, and the woman would have opened a reading-room. Behold humankind! Are you astonished now by the violent disputes of the Greeks when Mohammed II was at the gates of Constantinople, threatening the cross with the two horns of the Turkish crescent?

Belzoni, in a praiseworthy desire for peace, made Mr. Hogges a rather odd proposal. "Sir," he said to him, "English law and your religion authorize divorce, do they not?"

"Yes, Signor," said Hogges.

"I'll consent to help you in this peril, if you sign this document that I drafted by moonlight last night."

"Are you asking me for another thousand pounds?" Hogges asked.

"Less than that; I'm asking you to divorce your wife."

"Heavens!" cried Hogges, as if appealing to a neighbor for help.

"If you hesitate, I'll cut the rope, and all three of us will take a trip to the moon. Your life is hanging by a thread; here is an open knife. I'm your Parca;[95] I'll cut it!"

Hogges grabbed Belzoni's arm.

"What about the sources of the Nile, Signor Belzoni? The sources of the Nile!"

"I scorn the sources of the Nile as a glass of water. I love your wife, and if you don't promise me to have the divorce pronounced by an English court when we get down to the ground, I'll burst our balloon."

"He'll do as he says!" cried Mrs. Hogges, wiping her eyes with a cloud. "Sacrifice yourself for your children, dear Hogges, and forget me..."

---

[95] The Parcae were the Roman equivalents of Greek Moirai [Fates], although there was originally only one, who performed the three tasks of spinning the thread of individual destiny, measuring it and then cutting it; the third task eventually devolved to Morta, the equivalent of the Greek Atropos.

"You see," said Belzoni, "that your wife agrees to the divorce."

"My God!" cried the female traveler. "In our situation, who wouldn't agree to it? We're four thousand meters above human laws and the social code!"

Hogges veiled his forehead with a cloud and demanded a quarter of an hour to think about it. Belzoni took out his watch and made a gesture of acquiescence.

When the quarter-hour has elapsed, Mr. Hogges reopened the conversation and said: "Do you realize, Signor Belzoni, that what you're asking of me is horrible?"

"So that, Mr. Hogges," said Signor Belzoni, taking hold of his knife again, "is what a quarter of an hour's reflection has produced! I repeat to you, sir, that I love your wife. I love her with a love that is four thousand meters above sea level; I love her as one must love in the vestibule of paradise. It's an inexorable passion, so don't try to stand in its way. Besides, you have no rights over your wife."

"Oh, that's too much!" cried Mr. Hogges. "I have no rights over my wife! And who has taken these rights away from me?"

"Our new situation, sir. Your ties are broken. What you contracted on the ground no longer has any value in a cloud. Think about it—your life is only hanging by a thread."

"Signor Belzoni, be just..."

"I'm in love!"

"So am I, Signor Belzoni. I'm in love with my wife."

"Insolence!" cried Belzoni. "Moderate your expressions, or fear my despair. How can you have the audacity to talk to me about your love?"

"But it seems to me that I have every right to do so!" said Mr. Hogges, with dignity. "Am I not my wife's legal spouse?"

"Wretch!" cried Belzoni, getting to his feet with a violent movement that almost caused them to capsize in the wavers of the atmosphere. "Wretch! The divorce that you refuse me, I shall take! The cutting edge of this steel blade will launch us into space; we'll rise up so high that it will take us five years to come down again. At the beginning of that voyage, I shall hurl you into space, as Mentor did with Telemachus,[96] and we'll remain alone, your wife and I, in a floating palace, as free as the air, glad to live without witnesses, acknowledging no laws but our own, free of the despotic yoke, eating eagles and drinking rainwater at our meals, humiliating the earth from the height of our gondola, mocking the cadis of Egypt and the constables of London, founding a new world like Adam and Eve and raising our sons in ideas of grandeur and liberty that the London mud would never give them!

"One day, we shall descend to some hospitable zone in the heart of Africa, near a lake crowned with shade; our young family, born in the sky, will bring to earth the virtues that are lacking there, and the city we shall build, we and our children, will be a virgin city, purified of all the inveterate evils that your inhabitants and citizens of Europe transmit to their descendants from generation to generation. That's my plan: consider it in all its profundity, and if you're not the least of men, you'll give it your support and you'll throw yourself

---

[96] Mentor, who encouraged Telemachus to go in search of his father Odysseus in Greek myth, was actually the goddess Athene in disguise.

overboard in order not to hinder my noble designs, and slip away, fleeing the spectacle of our happiness."

"Signor Belzoni," said Hogges, stirred by this speech, "You're asking me to do something beyond human strength. Permit me to remind you of the idea of honor. There's a fable that begins: 'Two cocks were living...'"[97]

"Damn your fables, Mr. Hogges!" said Belzoni. "I don't like them. The English never have anything in their beaks but tales of cocks. We're men, you and I, and your wife isn't a...respect her, or I'll make sure that she's respected here!"

"Well, I'd like nothing more," said Hogges, whose mildness of character was exhausted. "This has to end, and the fate of arms will decide it. Choose your seconds, the time and the place."

At these words, Mrs. Hogges, who had listened to this tempestuous quarrel with her head veiled by a cloud, emerged from her vaporous shelter and, uttering a lamentable scream, threw herself between the combatants, like Hersilia between Tatius and Romanus in David's painting.[98]

"What are you going to do, madmen!" she cried. "You haven't a meter of ground beneath your feet and you're thinking of fighting a duel? What about me? What will become of me in this atmospheric region that I don't know? What will become of me if you're both

---

[97] Jean de La Fontaine's fable in verse tells how two cocks are driven to fight over a hen; when the victor, which acquires a harem in consequence, crows triumphantly from a rooftop, he is seized by a hawk, leaving the defeated cock to collect the spoils.
[98] *The Sabine Women.*

struck dead? Famine will certainly oblige me, reluctantly, to nourish myself on your corpses, but when those meager provisions are exhausted, to what celestial inn should I go? What market is open to me in the midst of these clouds? In the name of heaven, our neighbor, take pity on a poor lone woman whom your crazed fury might deprive of a lover and a husband at a single stroke!"

Then, throwing herself at Mr. Hogges' knees, she added, in her softest and most tender voice: "Hogges, do you still love me?"

"Of course I love you!" replied the husband, with two tears that the clouds swiftly soaked up.

"Do you love me as much as you did in that sweet honeymoon we spent at the Star and Garter Hotel in Richmond, that isle of Cythera for newlyweds in the county of Middlesex?"

"Yes, my adorable wife, I love you as much as I did the day when I traversed Charing Cross to marry you at St. Martin's."

"Well, prove your love for me one last time."

"Speak; I shall obey."

"Hogges, we're in a dire situation..."

"My God! I can see that!"

"You can't see enough, my adorable Hogges. There are three of us in a stationary gondola, and three of us are too many. One of us must sacrifice himself in favor of the other two, and you're the one I've chosen."

"Me!" cried Hogges—and would gladly have taken a step backwards if he had had sufficient space behind him.

"You," his wife continued. "Signor Belzoni won't give way; his love has put down profound roots, and he won't renounce it to oblige you."

"Oh my God!" cried Hogges. "What strange things you're saying to me, Madame!"

"Calm down, Hogges. Pull yourself together. You can see that I'm tranquil, and I'm only a feeble woman, isolated between two deserts. Just now, Signor Belzoni was kind enough to submit an admirable plan to us, much finer and saner than that of discovering the sources of the Nile, which probably has no sources. Signor Belzoni's plan is providential; he and I, his unworthy collaborator, are probably destined to found a model colony in the strangest of lands. Attempting to oppose the realization of such a beautiful plan is to try to raise a sacrilegious obstacle to the future destiny of humankind. Remember, Hogges, that in London you're the president of the Philanthropic Society, and that your duty is to immolate yourself, for the two of us in particular and for the world in general."

"Yes," said Hogges, "I'm the president of the Philanthropic Society, but I'm a misanthrope, like all the philanthropists in London. You know that as well as I do, Madam. You know that the goal of our charitable organization is to ameliorate the conditions of the savages who live in the vicinity of Cape Horn and in Van Diemen's Land, and that we make a hundred speeches about those cannibals every month—but you also know that we close our eyes to the twenty-five thousand women in London who wander around London Bridge and Kensington Gardens night and day without shoes or virtue. So, no more bad jokes, Mrs. Hogges; you know that I'm in no mood to render a service to the human race."

"So much the worse for you, sir!" his wife replied, dryly. "Yes. I've always known you to be an egotist on earth, and you aren't any better in the heavens."

"But after all," Hogges exclaimed, "what you're proposing is unthinkable!"

"Unthinkable for cowards, sir!"

"Put yourself in my place, Madam!"

"I'm staying where I am, sir."

"Would you quit your position, Madam, to attempt a vertical drop from the height of Mont Blanc?"

"Yes, sir."

"Well, attempt away—I'll give it to you in triplicate."

"Oh! You're mocking me, sir! Is that how you remember the precepts of French gallantry that you learned at Birmingham Grammar School? Good God, where are we? What kind of world are we living in? A man, an English knight, dares to propose to a woman to measure Mont Blanc from top to bottom like an avalanche! You're a felon, sir!"

"Good!" said Hogges, calmly disguising his alarm.

"You're going to attempt the drop, then?" said the wife, pointing into the abyss.

"Well. well—she means it!" said Hogges. "Madam, if you continue to exert against me this attempted homicide by precipitation, I shall have you up in court."

"Have away, sir—you're free."

"You know, Madam, how I detest domestic quarrels."

"If you really detested them, you would already have jumped over the side of the gondola, and we'd now be tranquil."

"And I'd be dead in the desert down there, covered with sand!"

"So what, sir, if that noble devotion had worked to the general advantage of the population of this aerostat?"

"But I'm part of that population myself!"

"You're the minority, sir."

"I'm a third of the population."

"Oh, please, spare us these shameful statistical calculations, sir! The noble Curtius didn't waste so many idle words when he precipitated himself into a gulf to save the people of Rome."

"Bah! That's a fable! Curtius!"

"Don't insult heroes, coward!"

"I'd like to see what this Curtius would do in my place!"

"In your place, he would have jumped at the first request, along with his horse."

Silence reigned for a few moments.

If anarchy had not reigned in that little aerial colony, composed of a trio devoid of social harmony, the unhappy people would have enjoyed a truly superb spectacle, for the daylight, weakening rapidly, permitted the sight of a succession of mirages, infinitely perpetuated. The eye of a calm spectator would have followed, in its fantastic exhumation, a long street constituted by two thousand colossal cities, of which the Nile was the gutter, from Elephanine to the province of roses, the gracious and Arsinoe that our barbaric modern geographers call, flatly, Faioun.

Herodotus saw that marvelous street, which was nothing other than old Egypt; today it has been hacked into pieces on the banks of its ever-young river, but the magic virtue of the mirage recomposes it from time to time, by means of secrets of the prism unknown to physicists, and when that prodigy occurs, one might even believe that one is witnessing the complete resurrection of that empire, as if the thousand catacombs were rendering to the cities of the Nile a world of mummies more numerous the grains of sand of Suez and Ophir.

One sees the interminable processions of Isis and Osiris filing along the avenue of Sphinxes under the colonnades of the temple of Luxor; one follows with one's gaze the living flood of the crowd beneath the arches of the hundred gates of Thebes; one admires the sacrifices to Anubis in the gold and azure sanctuary of the temple of Hermes, and the Pleiades of astronomers descending into the crypt of Tentyris.

But the most marvelous of all the pompous ancient scenes thus exhumed by the decomposition of solar rays, is the one that presents the labyrinth of Lake Moeris. It is even easy to distinguish, at the limits of the horizon, the two pyramids a hundred and eighty-five meters in height, surmounted by two statues of gilded bronze, which the veridical Herodotus saw as I see you, and which were swallowed up, according to Strabo, by the deep waters of the lake.

Those marvels escaped our three voyagers, two of whom were scholars.

Hogges resembled an aerolith; he was petrified; he thought he had fallen from the moon and had stopped half way.

"Mrs. Hogges sees things from on high," said Belzoni, with a calm dignity, and I give my entire approval to her words. "The wisdom of her speech has imparted a new violence to my passion; I sense now, more than ever, that nothing will be able to disunite our two hearts; we have inscribed the pact of our love in the heavens."

"Really!" said Hogges, in the voice of a melting statue. "I've never been so astonished, or so embarrassed. I'm falling from the clouds."

"Fall, fall!" said Mrs. Hogges. "Follow that good inspiration and leave the field open for us. We promise to go every day to weep over your grave, if you can find one down there with the protection of Mehmet Ali..."

"What perplexity!" murmured Hogges.

"Go on then," said his wife, persuasively. "Go on, my dear Hogges; it's only the first step that's difficult, you see then how easy it is to continue...you're still hesitating, imprudent spouse! Do you want me to crush you with one last and victorious argument? Well, Hogges, here it is: have you forgotten up in the air, ingrate father, that you've left two little children in Cairo, at the Coulomb Inn?"

"Oh no, I haven't forgotten!" said Hogges, with great feeling.

"What will become of those children?" cried his wife.

"If I die?"

"No, if you're cowardly enough to live. Oh, wretch, those poor children will be orphans, engaged as drummer-boys in the viceroy's army. Signor Belzoni, swear to take them under your protection."

"I so swear," said Belzoni.

"Well," the wife continued, "you're still hesitating, after that example of devotion that Signor Belzoni has just given you. Don't you know that there are many fathers in history who have sacrificed themselves for their children: Brutus, Abraham, Icarus, Hugolin?[99] Add one more name to that paternal list; remember that forty cen-

---

[99] All these references are, of course, ironic. The first is not to Caesar's assassin but to Lucius Junius Brutus, the founder of the Roman Republic, who acquire a reputation for stoicism by allegedly watching the execution of his two sons without turning a hair.

turies are contemplating you, from the depths below! Come on, my dear Hogges, make a gesture!"

"She calls that a gesture!" murmured the unhappy spouse, in a melancholy tone. "A gesture that will procure me a four-thousand-meter fall! Oh, if I could only, like Hugolin sacrifice myself for my sons by eating them for dinner, and thus conserve their father's life for them, to save them from the misfortune of being orphans!"

So saying, he picked up one of his feet with his hands and put it over the edge of the gondola.

Mrs. Hogges clapped her hands and cried: Finally, he's decided! My children will live, and so shall we."

Belzoni stopped the second foot just as it was about to lift itself to follow the other. "That's all right," he said. "I'm content with you, Mr. Hogges; you don't need to do as much, since you're prepared to do more. I'll be content with the divorce. Will you sign?"

"But why rob Mr. Hogges of the advantage of choosing the manner of his devotion for himself?" said the wife. "One can divorce in all sorts of ways, and if my adored husband leans toward a four-thousand-meter fall, that will eliminate any ulterior difficulty, and provide much more assurance for the future of our African colony and the wellbeing of our children."

"That's true," said Belzoni. "One can't argue with matters of taste. Mr. Hogges is free to choose."

"I'd rather sign," said Hogges, after a moment's thought.

"Think harder," said his wife. "Perhaps one day, on the ground, you'll regret this opportunity to obtain another kind of divorce, which would have reconciled all domestic interests and guaranteed you tranquility in the clouds of the future."

"No," said Hogges. "On due reflection, I'll gladly risk exposure to those regrets."

"Take care, husband, take care! When you're down there, a witness to our happiness, you'll say to yourself: 'Oh, if only I were up there again, with one foot outside the gondola, so well placed to sacrifice myself for the happiness of my sons!'"

"Well, I'll resign myself to making that exclamation. I'd rather sign..."

"Imprudent!" murmured Mr. Hogges. "Let's see, Signor Belzoni; you have common sense, what would you do in my husband's place?"

"Oh, I'd throw myself over without further ado."

"Because you love me, Signor Belzoni—but him...him...that ingrate, he's never loved me!"

"At any rate," said Belzoni, "it's necessary to content ourselves with a vulgar divorce; our happiness ought not to be too demanding..."

A further incident, drawn from the utmost depths of the situation, distracted the voyagers from the question of divorce. The food supplies had run out, and hunger had been crying out, sounding the dinner gong in the voyagers' entrails since the previous day. Alas, as the poet says, hunger is a bad counselor. Belzoni, who ate like a tightrope-walker, suddenly complained about his condition and muttered muted threats reminiscent of the raft of the shipwreck-victims of the *Medusa*.

"Sir," he said to Hogges, "the question of divorce is becoming secondary; before anything else, it's necessary to eat. Our sojourn here might be prolonged, and there's no inn or market in the vicinity. I'm the stronger, so you're the weaker, and if this goes on for one more day I'll be obliged to become a cannibal in the interests of survival. It's also necessary that the lady lives, and the law orders you to nourish her. Tomorrow, if we haven't been rescued, I'll be obliged to sacrifice one traveler in order to give the other two something to eat. You see, Mr. Hogges, that divorce is inevitable in either case."

Mr. Hogges bowed his head, like savage imprisoned on Robinson Crusoe's island.

At that moment, a lion passed by on the ground, and its roar suspended the conversation. The telescope was aimed at the last remains of the dromedary.

Tarde venientibus ossa![100] Such was the reflection that the king of beasts seemed to make before the last fragments of the skeleton. There was, however, one sufficiently delicate morsel, and that was the ox-leather strap to which the iron hook was attached. La Fontaine has remarked that wolves at gluttonously—what would he have said about lions? This one, lured by the odor, precipitated itself upon the ox-leather strap and swallowed it gluttonously.

A sharp shock shook the aerostat. The animal had swallowed the iron hook, and its furious bounds attested to pain beyond leonine endurance. The balloon, stationary for such a long time, was agitated convulsively, but without any definite direction. It floated at hazard, according o the caprice of its strangled conductor.

"Sign the paper," said Belzoni to Hogges, and I'll save you..."

"Sign, then!" said the wife. "It a matter of necessity."

Hogges uttered a sigh and signed.

Belzoni took hold of the rope and shook it forcefully, like a fisherman who senses that a fish has taken the

---

[100] Whoever comes to the table last will find nothing but bones.

bait. The lion uttered roars of agony and struggled with the final efforts of its vigor. A death-rattle resounded in the solitude, and the monster fell on to the sand, a dead weight, communicating an abrupt downward motion to the balloon.

"And now," said Belzoni, "help me, both of you; six hands on the rope and all together!"

The hope of salvation doubled the voyagers' strength. Belzoni, as strong as a tightrope-walker and accustomed to rolling up ropes, took the place of two carthorses. The lion rose up majestically at each effort of the six combined hands, and when it arrived level with the gondola, Belzoni cut off its four paws and a few succulent fillets. Then, abandoning the rest to the vultures, he said to Mr. Hogges:

"The wind's blowing toward Elephantine; we're going to dine on our catch, and this evening, we'll be sleeping in the huts of Aswan."

The balloon, no longer captive, cleaved through the air with the speed of an arrow, while the three diners set about preparing their feast as a family. Belzoni, who was the strongest, abused his strength again and took the lion's share, but he was gallant enough to serve the most delicate morsels to Mrs. Hogges.

As Belzoni had foreseen, the aerostat came down in the oasis of Syene or Aswan shortly before sunset. They were in a inhabited land.

"Mr. Hogges," said Belzoni, offering him his hand, "I'm tearing up the paper you signed up there, and returning our wife to you!"

Mrs. Hogges made a slight movement of chagrin.

"Forgive me," Belzoni went on. "It was a joke; I was bored up there, and wanted to invent a game to kill time. After playing cards, we played divorce. Take back your wife, as a consolation prize."

The next day, they embarked on the Nile, and slept all the way to the pyramids of Giza.

BERTRAM'S BROTHER

A Midnight Story

The theater in Mansfeld was staging the first performance of Meyerbeer's masterpiece.[101] I managed to
get a seat, with considerable difficulty, beside a fashionable young Parisian, a traveler like me, who generously

---

[101] Giacomo Meyerbeer's *Robert le Diable*, often regarded as
the first grand opera, premièred in Paris in 1831. Initially
planned as a three-act comic opera by its librettists, Eugène
Scribe and Casimir Delavigne, Meyerbeer persuaded them to
work in larger dimensions. It was a monumental success.
Nicolas Levasseur played Bertram, a supposed friend of
Robert, Duke of Burgundy, who wins all his money in a game
of dice, and subsequently reveals that he has promised to deliver Robert to the Devil by midnight, although Robert might
be able to redeem himself by means of a magic branch that
can make him invisible. The branch is hidden in a ruined con-
vent, the setting in Act Three for a startling ballet danced by
the phantoms of debauched nuns. There are also romantic
complications, involving Robert's fiancée Isabelle, his rival
the Prince of Grenada and his half-sister Alice, which are all
resolved in Act Five, when Robert is saved and Bertram, having revealed that he is Robert's father, descends into Hell. The
opera's title had become totally inappropriate by the time that
Scribe and Delavigne had finished adapting the Medieval
legend that has stigmatized Robert the Magnificent of Nor-
mandy—the father of William the Conqueror—with the nickname in question. It might be relevant that the performance
featured in the story takes place in Martin Luther's home
town.

offered to let me share his stall. A typical French impatience burst forth from the boxes in the form of stamping feet.

The curtain went up; everyone collected themselves, settled down, folded their arms and assured themselves of all the advantages of audition. Bertram advanced to sing his first line; he stood there open-mouthed, and did not sing. The choir stopped. Robert asked anxiously whether Bertram had forgotten the first note of his role. Bertram uttered an A sharp and sat down convulsively, making signs that said: *I can't sing.*

"He can't sing!" cried fifty barons simultaneously. "What does that mean? We've come twenty leagues to see *Robert* and we're going to see it!"

Bertram got up and made further efforts; nothing could be heard but the orchestra; nothing emerged from the actor's throat.

The conductor of the orchestra turned round and said: "He's lost his voice."

"No one loses his voice!" cried the barons, brandishing their canes.

A young man leaned over the edge of a box and said: "Someone fetch a doctor! Is there a doctor in the house?"

General silence.

"Someone fetch Doctor Sterm."

At that moment, Dr. Sterm was hosting a philosophical dinner party. He emptied his Bohemian glass perfumed with Johannisberg and ran to the theater's wings. He felt Bertram's pulse, palpated his throat and said, gravely: "Stage fright has paralyzed the nerves in his throat. He needs rest and sea-baths."

And Dr. Stern disappeared.

"What, sea-baths!" cried the barons. "There's no sea in Mansfeld! And even if there was one, the remedy wouldn't give us *Robert le Diable* this evening. We need *Robert*!"

The stage-manager advanced, radiantly, and bowed three times; the entire auditorium was hanging on the lips of the scenic orator. "Gentlemen," he said, "a traveling artiste, who was in the audience, and who knows the role of Bertram, has offered to play it; it's a stroke of luck that..."

Two thousand applauding hands interrupted the stage-manager. He withdrew. The new Bertram excited a storm of acclamations on his entrance to the stage.

"Why, I know him," said my neighbor, the young Parisian. "I saw his debut at the Feydeau in *Zampa*.[102] His name's Florival, or Florval, or Blinval...he's not very talented, but he'll render a service today."

In the first act, the new Bertram enjoyed a minor success of esteem and gratitude. At every note the Parisian exclaimed: "Oh, that's not as good as Levasseur, not as good as Levasseur. What a man, Levasseur! Have you heard him sing the passage *Console yourself; do as I do...*? This Florival, or Florval, isn't getting into the spirit of his role—he's no demon. Where the devil did he get that costume? You have to see how Levasseur..."

A grave German interrupted curtly. "Monsieur," he said, "you're deafening us with your Levasseur. Let us listen to the music, or get out."

In the third act, after the comic duo, just as Bertram was singing *King of the fallen angels*, there was a fearful

---

[102] Louis Hérold's comic opera *Zampa* is almost exactly contemporary with Robert le Diable; it too features a character who is dragged down to Hell.

silence. Bertram smiled as he let the melancholy notes fall. The infernal choir emerged from the wings like a hurricane of subterranean voices. It seemed as if a supernatural orchestra was accompanying the scrapings of the visible orchestra, and that the voices of giants were rumbling in the copper megaphone. From time to time the conductor turned round palely to seize the torrent of mysterious notes emerging from unknown instruments in passing.

Above it all floated the Tartarean voice of Bertram: that voice flowing between two orchestras with a metallic and harmonious fluidity; that portentous voice, which said to Alice: *Come closer, then*; that mocking voice which made the skin crawl, mingling with the strident and corrosive laughter of the violoncello; which cried *Henceforth you belong to me*, while tearing the nerves like the intolerable sound that follows the flight of a shell.

Alice had replied, like the dove beneath the vulture; she had forgotten that it was all merely a game; Bertram's breath had fallen upon her lips like an eddy of sulfurous air. She uttered three screams—not three stage-screams but real ones, such as nature scores them for the mother who sees her child crushed beneath a wheel.

Alice had fainted.

Ladies rose to their feet in the stalls with pale faces and crazed eyes, throwing their arms around the barons' necks with loud laughter, tears and epileptic frissons. Voices shouted: "Lower the curtain!"

The curtain came down.

"That's odd!" said my young Parisian. "See how impressionable those ladies are. What would they do if they heard Levass…?"

He stopped, for a silence had fallen around us that was alarming, and which no one dared interrupt. No one dared to communicate to his neighbor the sentiment of stupor and admiration that dominated the auditorium.

The scene with the nuns was awaited with impatience and terror. Personally, I did not know how to categorize my impressions.

The curtain went up, and revealed the nuns' tombs. Oh, I shall remember that scene for a thousand years. My quill bristles as I write it, and every letter seems to me to shine like a phosphoric diamond. Bertram reappeared. He had definitely grown by a foot during the entr'acte, illusion apart.

The entire auditorium was as black as night; there is no chandelier in the Mansfeld theater. A feeble light shone palely on the stage. In that dark atmosphere, Bertram's eyes could be distinguished, like two forgotten stars in a stormy sky. Already, the trombones were bursting forth with an unprecedented din, with a verve so supernatural that it nailed the conductor's baton in mid-air. He sought in vain to divide up that superabundance of notes improvised by the instruments, and which were nevertheless in harmony with the written notes; then, astonishment paralyzed the fingers and lips of the musicians; the accompaniment ceased.

Bertram seemed to be accompanying himself in singing the evocation; two quite distinct sounds were emerging from his throat: the song—and what a song! it corroded the nerves like a succession of tom-tom beats—and, with the song, an infernal echo of the breast that rumbled in time with the words, and which reached our ears like the repercussion of a hammer on a bell, or a subterranean minting-machine producing false coins.

When the nuns gathered around Bertrand they were pale beneath their make-up; they believed that they really had been dead for an hour. The mother superior fell face down on the boards, wounding herself in the breast with the cross suspended around her neck. Dying, she was replaced on the tomb where she had been playing dead a little while before. The weak women, frightened by seeing her covered with the shroud, were instantly seized by an epidemic of panic.

The entire auditorium was invaded by a recrudescence of mad terror. That darkness streaked with phosphoric gleams; that monstrous two-part voice with which Bertram was bruising the listeners; the twin embers of his eyes; the screams of the nuns; the incomprehensible silence of the orchestra; that double row of tombs; that desolate décor; and finally, a mysterious terror running through the theater like an evil perfume—all of that caused chaos in the assembly. Ladies were seen fleeing through the doors of the boxes; other were carried out, unconscious; children were stabbing us with their exceedingly shrill screams. A few women were saying, in phantasmal voices:

"Oh my God! It's a nightmare!"

"We're dreaming!"

"Wake me up!"

"Wake me up, for God's sake!"

In that tumult, the curtain fell with the noise of a large oak branch on twenty drums, and the auditorium shook. There was a stampede through all the exits, with the fury that is produced in a theater by a cry of "Fire!"

"Air! Air! Give us air!" people cried, in chorus.

A few voices backed by strong minds were staying: "Sit down, sit down! There are still two acts to go."

The crowd replied, *en masse*: "It's over, finished—to Hell with *Robert le Diable!* We've been murdered!"

In two minutes, the auditorium was empty. My young Parisian, calm and intrepid, watched the irresistible panic of the crowd regretfully.

"I've got an idea!" he said. "I'm going to invite this Florival or Florval to drink a glass of punch with us. He's come on a lot, the rogue, since his debut at the Feydeau. These Germans are crazy; Kant and Goethe have ruined them. The Germans see Mephistopheles and black dogs everywhere. Let's go invite Florival, or Florval..."

We climbed up to the wings; they were deserted. My young scatterbrain shouted: "Florival! Florival! Come out and receive my compliments. He's probably getting changed in his dressing-room. Let's go up to his dressing-room. Where is it? You, Monsieur the Prince of Grenada, where is it?"

The Prince of Grenada stared at us, and said: "Are you looking for the actor who plated Bertram?"

"Yes, Prince."

"He disappeared after the act."

"What do you mean, disappeared? Costumed as the Devil?"

"Yes, Monsieur. We looked for him for some time, but couldn't find him. It's over. Oh, what an evening!"

And the Prince of Grenada retreated, raising his arms to the celestial friezes.

"That was a strange adventure," said the Parisian. "Best go to bed."

The following day, we were at Baron von Halstein's schloss, situated a pipe and a half from Mansfeld on the Erfurt road. It's a feudal residence that meets all the conditions of the genre: pine-forests, lakes veiled with dead leaves, abandoned summer-houses, smallholdings devoid of livestock; ponds devoid of fish; fountains devoid of water; heaths devoid of game; melancholy everywhere.

I had introduced my young friend of the previous evening, Wilfrid de V , to Baron von Halstein. The Baron had a delightful daughter; Goethe had been her godfather in Weimar, for the Baroness was taken by surprise there, while traveling, by the pangs of childbirth. Goethe had named his goddaughter Marguerite, according to his custom. The Baron's daughter was seventeen, blonde, smooth-skinned and dazzling. She was afraid of ghosts and her illustrious godfather's books.

After lunch, Wilfrid signaled to me to follow him. We went into the pine-wood.

"Once could be bored to death," he said, "in this nest of phantoms. The little blonde's quite nice, but I don't like blondes. Then again, she puts on the airs of one of Auguste Lafontaine's heroines, looking at me with eyes of tormented virtue.[103] There's nothing here for me, therefore. I'm going back to Mansfeld, and bidding Germany adieu. One dies of boredom here when one isn't a philosopher. Is there anything I can do for you in Paris?"

"Yes," I said "Are you complaining about the solitude? Here come two riders along the high road; I believe they're coming to the schloss."

---

[103] Auguste Lafontaine (1758-1831) was a prolific German novelist who used several pseudonyms and far outstripped the popularity of Goethe; he was famous for the moralism and sentimentality of his plots.

"Oh, I see them. They're two travelers gone astray, or two equestrian phenomena. Why do they build roads in this country? First, one ought to have travelers. But they're good horsemen—very good. Let's go a little further forward; I need to see some human faces...oh my God! No, I'm not mistaken...it's him! Him, Florival, with a *groom*! What an eccentric!"

He dragged me toward the high road, and the two riders paused as they divined our intention to accost them.

"Ah! I've finally found you, Monsieur Florival. Without indiscretion, might we interrupt your little excursion briefly, in order to chat as artistes?"

The man that Wilfrid called Florival smiled in a singular fashion.

Wilfrid continued, pointing to me as he said: "My friend here, who is staying at the Schloss von Halstein—the charming schloss that you can see over there in the trees—invites you, in the Baron's name, to pause briefly in this domain. We need to have a chat about yesterday's performance."

"I'd like that," Florival replied, "if it would oblige you."

"Oh, that's charming—too good of you. Follow us; we'll show you the way. Finally, we'll shake off boredom. It'll be a charming evening; I'm crazy about artistes."

Florival, the previous evening's Bertram, was a young man of about thirty; he had a face of graciously beautiful ugliness, ebony-black hair, eyes of stormy azure and a fine moustache shaped like a typographical brace. His costume consisted of a blue coat with shiny metal buttons, a white double-breasted waistcoat, iron-gray trousers and Hungarian riding-gloves, all as lustrous as Staub brackets.[104] The trousers had a hole on the left knee, though. Wilfrid could not stop looking at that knee.

They were about to take their places at table at the Schloss when we came in with the stranger. Wilfrid, with the audacious politeness of high society, introduced Florival to the company. "We thought," he said, "that we would be doing Madame la Baronne a favor by asking Monsieur Florival to spend a few hours at the Schloss von Halstein. As yesterday's singular performance has been an inexhaustible subject of conversation for you, Mesdames, we thought that Monsieur Florival might give us explanations that..."

"Explanations of what?" Florival interjected, in a voice with the timbre of brass. "Nothing happened at the theater yesterday that was not perfectly natural. Imaginations are too excitable here. The ladies are as highly-strung as horses; they have violin-strings in their nerves, and my voice passed over them like a bow, that's all."

"That's very strange, what this gentleman is saying," murmured the ladies, in low voices. Marguerite went pale.

"Why did you leave abruptly after the third act?" asked Wilfrid.

"The audience frightened me," Florival replied, coolly.

"Oh! That's odd! Have you seen Levasseur play Bertram, Monsieur Florival?"

"Levasseur? Yes, I've seen him. He imitates me. He's my plagiarist."

---

[104] Staub is a brand of cast iron cookware popular in France; for that reason I have translated *potences* as "brackets," although the more usual meaning would be "gibbets."

"Well then, why didn't you make your debut in the Rue Lepeletier?"

"Because there's a church in the Rue Laffitte."

"Oh!"

The announcement was made that dinner was served. The table had been laid in a vast hall with monochrome tapestries. In the four corners there were four full-length portraits of ancestors of the Baron von Halstein. A chandelier with five branches was suspended over the table. A colossal piano was stationed between two windows.

Florival sat down opposite Marguerite, and looked at one of the family portraits with singular attention.

"That's my great-grandfather," said the Baron.

"I thought I recognized him," said Florival.

"That's difficult to believe; he died in 1743. The local people gave him a singular nickname."

"What?"

"Halstein the Damned."

"Don't say that, Father!" cried Marguerite. "It frightens me."

There was a heavy silence. The guests were eating.

Marguerite wasn't eating. She was leaning all of her upper body forwards, mingling her gaze with the fixed gaze of Florival, as if she were yielding to some irresistible attraction of fascination; her beautiful eyes were become smaller, distilling pearly tears; her bosom was as breathless as a bride's at the stroke of midnight at the wedding ball.

She raised a crystal goblet to her lips in order to distract herself, to give the lie to an impression that was not yet felt, but replaced it on the table without having drunk, and ran her little white fingernails, pure and delicate, over its uneven surface. There was something strange about her, some mysterious sensation that women do not admit, even those who talk about everything.

I attempted to distract Marguerite with an idle question; she reacted against my indiscretion with kind of dull cooing sound, and long and musical sigh that did not articulate any speech. Then a shiny pallor covered her face, like a wax mask; her long eyelashes bristled, her eyes opened to supernatural dimensions; she extended her arms across the table contorting them; she stiffened, threw her head back, struck the floor violently with her heels and fainted, crying: "Halstein the Damned!"

At that moment, a gust of wind caused the orchestra of pine-tress to moan, and its harmonious roulades broke over the battlements of the manor; it was engulfed in the heavy curtains of the hall's windows, giving them phantasmal forms; it began to laugh behind the billowing tapestries and behind the loosely-hung painting of Halstein the Damned; it caused the flames of the chandelier to palpitate like the tresses of the Eumenides; it stirred the strings of the colossal piano, exhuming therefrom a brief and funereal melody like the accompaniment of a "Here lies..."

All the guests were gripped by such a stupor that no one thought of bringing help to poor Marguerite. The intrepid Wilfrid ran to her, and talked to her in a soft voice, taking her hands with touching delicacy. From time to time, Wilfrid said, as a kind of aside: "Yesterday's scenes are recommencing..."

"It's nothing, nothing," said Florival, coldly. "This will bring her round."

"Oh!" exclaimed the Baron. "It's reading her godfather's books that's killing her! I'll burn them all tomorrow; I'll subject her to a regime of Gessner's idylls."[105]

A neighbor, one of the guests, got up and beckoned to his wife to follow him.

"Are you leaving, Baron?" Halstein said to him.

"Yes, the evening's ill-omened," the neighbor replied, shaking his head in a melancholy fashion.

"Marguerite had recovered consciousness. "What!" she said, in an emotional voice. "It's me who's putting you to flight! Stay, I beg you. Don't let my accident alarm you. It's very warm in here. Have the windows opened—the air will revive me."

"Open the windows," said Wilfrid. "The wind's died down; the air is calm."

Through the open windows, a nightmare landscape was revealed. It was as if the countryside were being eaten away by the tints of an artificial moon. On the edge of the pond, a clump of tall thin pines was distinguishable, reminiscent of conspiratorial specters. The forest extended distressed forms around the hill; there were plaintive bird-calls in the air, and the whinnying of delirious horses.

"Cramrr is up to his old tricks in the stables," said Florival.

"What do you call your horse?" asked Wilfrid, laughing.

"Cramrr."

---

[105] Salomon Gessner's pastoral *Idyllen*, two volumes of which were published in 1756 and 1772, were renowned for their melodic mildness. Though very popular, they were stigmatized by critics for alleged sickliness.

"A pretty name! I'd like to give it to my Arab mare. Cramrr! How do you write it?"

"I never write it."

The whinnying of the horses in the Baron's stables increased.

Wilfrid got up, saying: "I'll go settle Cramrr down. I think he's biting your horses, Baron."

"Stay," said Florival, in an unusual tone—and Wilfrid sat down heavily, as if an iron hand had shoved him back into his chair.

He was not a man to sit still for long, though. He suddenly became excited with that joyful intoxication that dessert wines impart. "Come on," he said. "Cheer up! Cheer up! Let's sing. In Paris, we sing during dessert. Let's sing!"

"Yes, yes, let's sing," aid the ladies, with sad and distressed faces.

Wilfrid went on: "let's sing the great trio from Robert; I know my own part... *Have pity on me...look to the heavens! Have pity on me...which await you...* Oh, we need an Alice! Well, we need to go in search of Mademoiselle Zoe Briton, who played her at the Mansfeld theater. It'll only take an hour in a berlin. Baron, you have German aristocratic scruples. Oh horror! An actress in your schloss. Bah! All these prejudices are melting away. I'm from a family as good as yours, and when I entertain in my town house I invite Dorus, Damoreau, Grisi[106]...come on, which of you will go?"

---

[106] Julie Dorus played Alice in the première of *Robert le Diable*. Laure Cinti-Damoreau played Isabelle. The reference to the dancer Carlotta Grisi seems slightly out of place, as she did not make her debut until 1836 and had her greatest success in *Giselle* (1841), the libretto for which was co-written by

"Wait," said Florival. "I'll send my servant. Listen, Furcger—mount up, go to Mansfeld and bring Zoe Briton back *en croupe*. She lives at number thirteen, What Time Is It? Street.

Furcger left.

"Who'll play the piano?" asked Wilfrid.

"Furcger," Florival replied.

"Oh! Your servant is a pianist?"

"He's given lessons to Field and Thalberg."

"Damn! What a servant!"

"Gentlemen," said Marguerite, in a charming voice, "my piano isn't tuned; it's a family heirloom; it also lacks three octaves."

"I shall tune it, Mademoiselle," said Florival.

He got up and ran his long fingers over the keyboard with a marvelous agility. While he was tuning the piano, the diners finished dessert.

The clock chimed eleven.

"Eleven o'clock!" Florival exclaimed. "It's very late. Today's Friday, I believe. I have a rendezvous at..."

"At?" Wilfried promoted.

"Nowhere. Here's Furcger and Zoe."

They were, indeed, just coming into the room. The actress had an effrontery that terrified the Baron. She made a series of strange jerky bows, like one of Vaucanson's automata. She visited all the corners of the room in pirouettes, and laughed like a madwoman in front of the portrait of Halstein the Damned.

Théophile Gautier, who was infatuated with her. Méry's story appeared in book form in 1841, and this reference might be a clue to the date of its composition.

Furcger sat down at the piano. Florival, Wilfrid and Zoe came together at the back of the hall, each with the part to be sung in hand.

It was not two men and a woman who sang the trio; it was the trio of Heaven, Hell and the Earth: Hell, which sang with its groans, its wails and its roars; Heaven with all its melodies of love, elation and endless sensuality; the Earth with its painful anguishes, its atheistic blasphemies and its savage cries of despair—and all those harmonies unfolded in unison with a monstrous joy; and the infernal or divine power that caused the triple cataract of devouring sounds to fall upon our ears also gave a marvelous strength to our nerves, in order that we would not perish of emotion, while the schloss itself seemed to shiver between its eight towers.

Plunged in our armchairs, we closed our eyes, for fear that some distraction might rob us of a single note of that gigantic music. We opened them at the conclusion of the trio.

Wilfrid was slumped on the sofa, as if exhausted, worn out by the prodigious efforts that a superhuman power had imposed upon him. Furcger and Zoe had disappeared. The abandoned piano was still bellowing, like the sea after a tempest.

"Where's Florival, then?" I asked Wilfrid.

He pointed to the panel of the woodwork on which the enlarged face of Halstein the Damned had been painted. In its place, another painted and improvised image was laughing sardonically: Florival's face.

A woman's voice cried: "But who was that man, then?"

And the piano replied with the lugubrious refrain from Raimbaut's ballad[107]: *He's a demon!*

This story was told by Meyerbeer at a ball held by Mademoiselle Taglioni.[108] The illustrious maestro smiled and said to me: "It's a tale that's very difficult to believe, but anything is believable at a midnight ball."

---

[107] The ballad sung by the minstrel Raimbaut is the lever that starts the plot of *Robert le Diable* in motion.

[108] Marie Taglioni was the ballet dancer who played the Abbess Helena in the première of *Robert le Diable*, leading the voluptuous dance—appropriately enough, as she caused something of a scandal when she was the first ballerina to dance in a short skirt (in order to show off her *pointe* work). Méry once accompanied her on a tour of England.

SF & FANTASY

Henri Allorge. *The Great Cataclysm*
Guy d'Armen. *Doc Ardan: The City of Gold and Lepers*
G.-J. Arnaud. *The Ice Company*
Charles Asselineau. *The Double Life*
Cyprien Bérard. *The Vampire Lord Ruthwen*
Aloysius Bertrand. *Gaspard de la Nuit*
Richard Bessière. *The Gardens of the Apocalypse*
Albert Bleunard. *Ever Smaller*
Félix Bodin. *The Novel of the Future*
Alphonse Brown. *City of Glass*
André Caroff. *The Terror of Madame Atomos; Miss Atomos;*
The Return of Madame Atomos; The Mistake of Madame
Atomos; The Monsters of Madame Atomos
Félicien Champsaur. *The Human Arrow*
Didier de Chousy. *Ignis*
Captain Danrit. *Undersea Odyssey*
C. I. Defontenay. *Star (Psi Cassiopeia)*
Charles Derennes. *The People of the Pole*
Georges Dodds (anthologist). *The Missing Link*
Harry Dickson. *The Heir of Dracula*
Jules Dornay. *Lord Ruthven Begins*
Alfred Driou. *The Adventures of a Parisian Aeronaut*
Sâr Dubnotal *vs. Jack the Ripper*
Alexandre Dumas. *The Return of Lord Ruthven*
Renée Dunan. *Baal*
J.-C. Dunyach. *The Night Orchid; The Thieves of Silence*
Henri Duvernois. *The Man Who Found Himself*
Achille Eyraud. *Voyage to Venus*
Henri Falk. *The Age of Lead*
Paul Féval. *Anne of the Isles; Knightshade; Revenants; Vam-*
pire City; The Vampire Countess; The Wandering Jew's
Daughter
Paul Féval, *fils. Felifax, the Tiger-Man*
Charles de Fieux. *Lamékis*

Arnould Galopin. *Doctor Omega; Doctor Omega & The Shadowmen*

G.L. Gick. *Harry Dickson and the Werewolf of Rutherford Grange*

Edmond Haraucourt. *Illusions of Immortality*

Nathalie Henneberg. *The Green Gods*

V. Hugo, P. Foucher & P. Meurice. *The Hunchback of Notre-Dame*

Michel Jeury. *Chronolysis*

Gustave Kahn. *The Tale of Gold and Silence*

Gérard Klein. *The Mote in Time's Eye*

Jean de La Hire. *Enter the Nyctalope; The Nyctalope on Mars; The Nyctalope vs. Lucifer; The Nyctalope Steps In; Night of the Nyctalope*

Etienne-Léon de Lamothe-Langon. *The Virgin Vampire*

André Laurie. *Spiridon*

Gabriel de Lautrec. *The Vengeance of the Oval Portrait*

Georges Le Faure & Henri de Graffigny. *The Extraordinary Adventures of a Russian Scientist Across the Solar System* (2 vols.)

Gustave Le Rouge. *The Vampires of Mars The Dominion of the World* (w/Gustave Guitton) (4 vols.)

Jules Lermina. *Mysteryville; Panic in Paris; To-Ho and the Gold Destroyers; The Secret of Zippelius*

Jean-Marc & Randy Lofficier. *Edgar Allan Poe on Mars; The Katrina Protocol; Pacifica; Robonocchio; Tales of the Shadowmen 1-8*

Xavier Mauméjean. *The League of Heroes*

Joseph Méry. *The Tower of Destiny*

Hippolyte Mettais. *The Year 5865*

José Moselli. *Illa's End*

John-Antoine Nau. *Enemy Force*

Marie Nizet. *Captain Vampire*

C. Nodier, A. Beraud & Toussaint-Merle. *Frankenstein*

Henri de Parville. *An Inhabitant of the Planet Mars*

Gaston de Pawlowski. *Journey to the Land of the 4th Dimension*

Georges Pellerin. *The World in 2000 Years*

J. Polidori, C. Nodier, E. Scribe. *Lord Ruthven the Vampire*

P.-A. Ponson du Terrail. *The Vampire and the Devil's Son*

Henri de Régnier. *A Surfeit of Mirrors*

Maurice Renard. *The Blue Peril; Doctor Lerne; The Doctored Man; A Man Among the Microbes; The Master of Light*

Jean Richepin. *The Wing*

Albert Robida. *The Adventures of Saturnin Farandoul; The Clock of the Centuries; Chalet in the Sky*

J.-H. Rosny Aîné. *Helgvor of the Blue River; The Givreuse Enigma; The Mysterious Force; The Navigators of Space; Vamireh; The World of the Variants; The Young Vampire*

Marcel Rouff. *Journey to the Inverted World*

Han Ryner. *The Superhumans*

Brian Stableford. *The New Faust at the Tragicomique; The Empire of the Necromancers (The Shadow of Frankenstein; Frankenstein and the Vampire Countess; Frankenstein in London); Sherlock Holmes & The Vampires of Eternity; The Stones of Camelot; The Wayward Muse.* (anthologist) *The Germans on Venus; News from the Moon; The Supreme Progress; The World Above the World; Nemoville*

Jacques Spitz. *The Eye of Purgatory*

Kurt Steiner. *Ortog*

Eugène Thébault. *Radio-Terror*

C.-F. Tiphaigne de La Roche. *Amilec*

Théo Varlet. *The Xenobiotic Invasion; Timeslip Troopers* (w/André Blandin); *The Martian Epic* (w/Octave Joncquel)

Paul Vibert. *The Mysterious Fluid*

Villiers de l'Isle-Adam. *The Scaffold; The Vampire Soul*

Philippe Ward. *Artahe*

Philippe Ward & Sylvie Miller. *The Song of Montségur*

MYSTERIES & THRILLERS

M. Allain & P. Souvestre. *The Daughter of Fantômas*

A. Anicet-Bourgeois, Lucien Dabril. *Rocambole*

A. Bernède & L. Feuillade. *Judex*

A. Bisson & G. Livet. *Nick Carter vs. Fantômas*
V. Darlay & H. de Gorsse. *Lupin vs. Holmes: The Stage Play*
Paul Féval. *Gentlemen of the Night; John Devil; The Black Coats ('Salem Street; The Invisible Weapon; The Parisian Jungle; The Companions of the Treasure; Heart of Steel; The Cadet Gang; The Sword-Swallower)*
Emile Gaboriau. *Monsieur Lecoq*
Steve Leadley. *Sherlock Holmes: The Circle of Blood*
Maurice Leblanc. *Arsène Lupin vs. Countess Cagliostro; Lupin vs. Holmes (The Blonde Phantom; The Hollow Needle); The Many Faces of Arsène Lupin*
Gaston Leroux. *Chéri-Bibi; The Phantom of the Opera; Rouletabille & the Mystery of the Yellow Room*
Richard Marsh. *The Complete Adventures of Judith Lee*
William Patrick Maynard. *The Terror of Fu Manchu; The Destiny of Fu Manchu*
Frank J. Morlock. *Sherlock Holmes: The Grand Horizontals; Sherlock Holmes vs Jack the Ripper*
P. de Wattyne & Y. Walter. *Sherlock Holmes vs. Fantômas*
David White. *Fantômas in America*

SCREENPLAYS

Mike Baron. *The Iron Triangle*
Emma Bull & Will Shetterly. *Nightspeeder; War for the Oaks*
Gerry Conway & Roy Thomas. *Doc Dynamo*
Steve Englehart. *Majorca*
James Hudnall. *The Devastator*
Jean-Marc & Randy Lofficier. *Royal Flush*
J.-M. & R. Lofficier & Marc Agapit. *Despair*
J.-M. & R. Lofficier & Joël Houssin. *City*
Andrew Paquette. *Peripheral Vision*
R. Thomas, J. Hendler & L. Sprague de Camp. *Rivers of Time*

NON-FICTION

Stephen R. Bissette. *Blur 1-5. Green Mountain Cinema 1; Teen Angels*
Win Scott Eckert. *Crossovers* (2 vols.)
Jean-Marc & Randy Lofficier. *Shadowmen* (2 vols.)
Randy Lofficier. *Over Here*

HEXAGON COMICS

Franco Frescura & Luciano Bernasconi. *Wampus*
Franco Frescura & Giorgio Trevisan. *CLASH*
L. Bernasconi, J.-M. Lofficier & Juan Roncagliolo Berger. *Phenix*
Claude Legrand, J.-M. Lofficier & L. Bernasconi. *Kabur*
Franco Oneta. *Zembla*
L. Buffolente, Lofficier & J.-J. Dzialowski. *Strangers: Homicron*
Danilo Grossi. *Strangers: Jaydee*
Claude Legrand & Luciano Bernasconi. *Strangers: Starlock*

ART BOOKS

Jean-Pierre Normand. *Science Fiction Illustrations*
Raven Okeefe. *Raven's L'il Critters*
Randy Lofficier & Raven OKeefe. *If Your Possum Go Daylight...*
Daniele Serra. *Illusions*

www.ingramcontent.com/pod-product-compliance
Lightning Source LLC
Chambersburg PA
CBHW030356020726
47493CB00003B/837